Reckless
Revelation

Nina LekKa

Queen of Hearts
Publisher

"You didn't act like a virgin."

Zachary raised his eyebrows, and gave her a skeptical look. "I got the impression that you knew what you were about."

"Well—I've had experience, but technically—I'm still a virgin."

"In other words, you've done everything but have sex." He shook his head. "I see I'm not the only poor fool you've tempted beyond reason." He stood and stared at her. "You must leave a lot of frustrated men behind."

"I don't mean to." She sat forward, and gave him an appraising glance. "But I do want you."

"You want me, your body wants me." He scanned her from head to toe. "I can see that."

The Reluctant Virgin Series

Book one:

Reckless Revelation

By Nina LekKa

Copyright ©2015 by Nina LekKa

ISBN-13:978-0692575154
ISBN-10: 0692575154
Ninalekka.com

Cover design by L. Tesseris
Cover Photo: Mytilene, Greece taken by
D.C Andrianis
Queen of Hearts Publisher

This is a work of fiction. Names, places, characters or
incidents are a product of the authors imagination or
used fictitiously. Any resemblance to actual events, lo-
cals or persons, living or dead, is coincidental. Novel
is intended for adults only. Must be 18 years or older.

Acknowledgement

I would like to express my gratitude to all those who helped in the creation of this book especially the members of the Cornwall Writers Circle. Their valuable advice caused me to constantly reexamine my work and make much needed corrections.

Special thanks to Tessa Sullivan who helped me get back into writing, and to my family for encouraging and supporting me.

"The most important thing in a work of art is that it should have a kind of focus; that is, there should be some place where all the rays meet or from which they issue."

Leo Tolstoy

Chapter 1

Drowning. She was drowning. Water rushed her, surrounded her. The current's force pulled and pounded her. She gulped, coughing and gasping, struggling to keep above the waves.

Caved roofs encircled her. Toppled walls, crumbled roads surrounded her. Furniture floated, buffeted by wind and water. She grabbed at a bobbing table, held on, determined to keep from sinking. Rain blown hard by the wind bit into her skin with the sting of bullets. She froze with fear. The current sucked her under. Death neared.

Alethea Karras woke, panting. Not again—no freaking way. Her palms sweating, her heart racing, she took several deep breaths and closed her eyes. Why can't I be normal?

She slid out of bed and headed toward the tiny kitchen, at the back of her historic New York City apartment. She drank water and put the kettle on.

Her icy hands warmed clutched around the tea mug and her breath steadied, soothed by the chamomile scent. Moistening her dry mouth, she tried to recall her dream.

She sensed its importance, but couldn't decipher its meaning. Despair and hopelessness were taking their toll. Water swelled, land flooded—chaos and calamity ensued.

Damn these dreams.

She listened to the tick-tock of the clock—the sound shocking in the silence of the night.

Too upset to go back to sleep, Alethea picked up her deck of playing cards and shuffled them.

Grateful for their calming effect, she spread them before her. The two of spades fell—this meant trouble. The ace of spades and the three of clubs together showed a long trip with misfortune before it.

Just to be sure, she laid them again. The ace of spades with the four of spades, indicated a torrid love affair—a love that would change her life.

Hmm. She shuffled again. Cards appeared—danger, but with the two of clubs, prevented danger.

Still, trouble ahead, and death. How awful! She felt her skin prickle. Damn the cards. They've twisted my stomach into knots. "Enough of this," she muttered and went to dress for work.

She opened the outside door, and bumped into a police officer who stood on the stoop with his hand raised as if to knock.

"What the …."

"Are you Alethea Karras?"

She nodded.

"I'm arresting you for non-payment of parking tickets." He read her the Miranda, shifted his feet and held up the handcuffs. "We can do this nice or we can do this nasty, it's up to you."

"Wait…how can you? I haven't done anything wrong." She raised her eyebrows in question.

"You've received notices in the mail from the city, haven't you?"

"Well—yes."

"You shouldn't have ignored them. You've got a pack of tickets that you haven't paid, so yes, I can arrest you." He watched, a blank look on his face, while she stood at the entrance.

"For parking tickets?" She put her hands on her hips. "That's absurd."

"It's the law. So why don't you come with me." He took her arm and started down the stairs, where he was joined by a woman cop.

Alethea blinked rapidly to keep from crying, then chewed her lip. She looked out at the passing pedestrians. One was hailing a taxi, another was hurrying down the subway steps nearby. Some youngsters boarding a school bus, turned, calling out greetings to the officer, while he waited for her to comply.

Just an ordinary city day. The smell of garbage from the nearby cans overwhelmed her senses, she heard the cooing of pigeons and sighted a fire truck streaking past. She tightened her trembling hands into fists.

Resigned, she stopped at the bottom of the stairs. She eyed the humiliating handcuffs, then obliging, turned her back. Ignoring everyone's stares, she stooped into the squad car.

Damn her psychic talents—they had certainly deserted her this day.

Alethea called her boss from the station, determined to get this done as quickly as possible. He assured her, after an annoying lecture, he would send his lawyer to bail her out.

Satisfied, she settled in to wait, watching blue uniforms coming and going.

Her scalp started to prickle and chills ran up and down her spine. She looked around, but noticed nothing unusual—just broad, muscular shoulders, a deep resonant voice with sun-streaked brown hair talking to one of the officers.

She couldn't see his face, but she stared at his back, wondering at the strange emotions he stirred.

A plain-clothed man, came out of his office to join him. She heard, "Hey Zachary.

You're Mitch's brother-in-law, Zachary Artemidis, aren't you? He mentioned you would stop by when he called."

She didn't see Zach turn and glance at her. "Yes, Carlos, he suggested I come."

Carlos Ramirez, head of New York City's homeland security, followed Zachary's gaze.

"She's a looker. An officer just brought her in." He raised his eyebrows.

"I don't know why she's here? She could start a crime wave with those amethyst eyes alone." He took a last glimpse at Alethea, then closed his door.

"Well that was interesting. Nothing like being talked about," Alethea mumbled. "And I didn't even see his face."

She was distracted by a knot of reporters, who hurried by, shouting out questions.

They were in pursuit of a well-dressed individual escorted by two detectives. The reporters swarmed around the man bombarding him with questions. Jeez, they remind me of vultures circling, waiting for the dying to draw their last breaths. She spotted her nemesis, Karl Hendrickson, in the group. Handsome as sin, tall, with finely chiseled features, he might have been every woman's dream, but her personal nightmare.

She slouched in her seat and hoped he wouldn't see her.

Karl Hendrickson cornered the man. "Doctor, how will these charges of unethical behavior affect your practice and your home life? Isn't it a well- known fact your wife's a socialite with all the right connections?"

"If you print a word of that gibberish I'll sue you and your paper. Now go away." The man stiffened his back and joined the officers.

"Last thing I need is another lawsuit on my head." Mumbling, he stared after the doctor.

She observed the tableau unfolding before her. The reporters had dispersed probably in search of a better story. Sighting a woman officer nearby, Karl put on his most persuasive smile. *Damn, he's probably trying to pry facts from her.* The officer ignored him.

Karl shrugged his shoulders, glanced around, and caught her eye.

She turned her head away. She didn't need to deal with him right now. He had humiliated her enough in the past. She could just hear his mouth if he found out about her arrest. He would laugh himself sick making fun of her and her psychic talents.

"Well, well, what have we here, Alethea Karras. You must be here investigating something, hmm?

Had one of your intuitions, did you?" He studied her face, searching it as he sidled over. "Trouble always seems to follow you. So what's going on?"

"Really." She eyed him. "After what you did to me, you have a nerve. Nothing is going on. Stay out of my life, 'Don Juan,' I mean it."

She stood, spotted her lawyer and hurried across the room.

"Mark, I'm glad you came. Can you believe it? They arrested me."

He peered at her from under prominently winged eyebrows. "This is no small town, it's the big city. If you break the law, you'll be punished. You should've paid the tickets."

He set his briefcase down, and went through his papers one more time. "I'm relieved it's just parking tickets. We'll pay the fine and finish before your court date." He fixed his glasses more firmly on his nose and smoothed back his graying hair

She followed him as he presented the bond papers to the clerk for her release.

"I don't use my car. I keep it in a garage. I got those tickets three years ago, when I first moved here and I— forgot about them.

"That might be true, but your inattention has cost you."

They went out into the busy street. Mark helped her into a yellow cab. "I'll drop you off, it's right on my way."

They sat in comfortable silence until he signaled the driver to stop at 59th street between Madison and Park Ave.

"Thank you for your help." Alethea answered. "I appreciate it."

What else could possibly happen today? She thought as she hurried to her office building just up the bloc.

Chapter 2

Alethea entered the ultra-modern structure and waved at the security guard.

"What a morning." Alethea muttered aloud as she stepped into the stainless steel cage. Her stomach lurched, as it sped to the seventeenth floor. "Must be the evil eye. Damn—these dreams…why are they taking over my life? Then handcuffed and arrested for traffic tickets…unbelievable. And that man at the police station…his back *so* attracted me. What am I nuts? I mean, really, *his back*."

Glad to be back on schedule, she stopped at the last door. *Anthony S. Petros - Private Investigator* was stenciled in large, gold letters. She pushed it open.

A light skinned woman seated behind an onyx reception desk looked up from a note she was reading. Outlined by the yellow curtains covering the windows, she made a stunning picture with her chocolate eyes and short afro.

"Hi Lucretia, what's happening?"

"Hey girlfriend, nothing special," she said. "But I hear you had an interesting morning." She winked her eye. "Meet anybody exciting in the slammer?"

"Now that you mention it, I did notice one or two fascinating types. Too bad I had to leave," she grinned, "before I could make their acquaintance."

"How was your date?" Alethea asked, distracting her from asking more questions. "You know the one you met at Charley's Club."

"Did I tell you we went out?" Lucretia knitted her brows. "I don't remember. Anyway you were in great shape that night. Your blond hair flowing around you - perfect. The black mini dress with the halter top - awesome. You had the men drooling. You certainly are a tease."

"I like the power it gives me. When they're attracted, they'll do anything to please me."

"Hon, that's dangerous," Lucretia grimaced. "You're playing with fire."

"Maybe I like playing with fire."

"Just don't get burnt," her friend cautioned.

Lucretia folded her arms across her chest and narrowed her eyes. "Girlfriend, you'd better pick lambs to play with, because if you pick a lion, he'll gulp you down for sure."

"But isn't that an interesting way to go, devoured by a lion." Alethea sat on Lucretia's desk and crossed her legs. "I entice them, excite them, ignite them, push them to their limit, and then tell them I've changed my mind." She arched her eyebrow. "They're frustrated, curse under their breaths, but they stop. Of course," she rubbed her chin," they never call again.

Lucretia gasped. "And that makes you happy? That sounds downright sadistic."

"Happy." Pursing her lips together, she turned her head to the side. "No it doesn't make me happy. But I'm not a sadist, I don't do it on purpose. It just happens." She shrugged. "I want to be interested, but I'm not, so rather than make a mistake, I stop."

"You're confusing me," Lucretia shook her head. "You just told me the opposite."

"No, not really," Alethea folded her arms one over the other. "I entice, hoping I'll be attracted enough to lose control, to find my lion."

"So you haven't found Mr. Right," Lucretia asked. "The one who will make you wild?"

"Exactly." Alethea got off the desk. "Restraint has ruled my life. And I'm tired of it. I want to lose control. I provoke hoping he'll be the one, but all I've done is leave angry, unsatisfied men who curse me." She started to walk away. "You didn't tell me about your date."

"How did you know about it?" Lucretia asked.

"Oh I have my ways." Alethea relished the expression on her friend's face.

Alethea enjoyed bantering with her. Lucretia Toya Johnson was twenty-two years old, a night student at City College working toward a law degree. She had worked in this office a year.

"All kidding aside," Lucretia remarked in a low voice, nodding toward the executive office.

"He's holding a staff meeting and giving out assignments. You'd better hurry." As an afterthought, she added. "Oh, before I forget, you think you could read my cards? I want to know if this guy's interested in me."

"Remind me at lunch time, we'll take a few minutes." Giving her a backward glance, she proceeded to the inside rooms.

She hurried through the reception area, where yellow table lamps accented the room, the paintings on the walls color-coordinated to match the décor.

A magazine article on an onyx coffee table caught her eye. Leafing through it, she continued over plush carpeting, through a Plexiglas divider into the area beyond.

Walking a long hall flanked by offices, she paused before two adjoining doors.

Composing herself, she pushed open the oak door on the right.

Around a teak conference table, her boss, Anthony S. Petros, his secretary, Sandra Wilson, and two of his investigators sat in plush chairs. She slipped into a vacant seat.

"Alethea, you're just in time. I've been giving out the new job assignments. You wrapped up your last case successfully. I'm not sure how you guessed he was faking, or how you managed to get photographs of him walking and lifting heavy objects, but it was the proof we needed—his back wasn't injured. Good work."

The other agents rifled through their folders as he described their assignments, outlining the most important points.

A former F.B.I agent, Anthony Petros had retired at age forty-five, and started this upscale agency, taking advantage of the influential contacts he'd made while in the bureau.

As a private investigator, he worked with some of the larger insurance firms, the police, CEOs of large corporations and wealthy private clients. A few of his cases had even involved Interpol.

He liked his comforts and the good life—had pepper grey hair, wore expensive silk shirts, and always kept his nails manicured. Never married, his playboy lifestyle made him well known about town. He claimed he socialized to help his business, and tried to play down his flamboyant image. Good at his job, he employed many top-notch investigators. And, due to his capable secretary, things ran smoothly.

Sandra was a computer whiz, in her late thirties. Anthony had hired her as a charitable gesture, after her spouse died on a mission for the agency. But she soon became indispensable to him. She dealt well with clients, organized his office and his employees so all ran smoothly. Her forceful character made sure no one dominated her, especially her boss.

After the meeting's conclusion Anthony nodded to Alethea. "I'd like to see you in private."

In his office, Alethea sat in one of the two comfortable chairs facing his large teak desk. She rubbed her sweaty hands on her jeans and waited for him to speak.

"Why didn't you pay those tickets?"

"I'm sorry Anthony. I made a mistake. So shoot me. My goodness! You'd think I committed a major crime."

"Never mind that. What about that little incident last month? You just missed getting arrested by a hair. Lucky for you the police chief owed me a favor."

He leaned back in his chair and set his lips in a thin line. "Instead of going to the authorities with your hunch, you took pictures of a supposedly dead man. Damn it! If he had caught you, you'd be minced meat. He was conniving to collect on a million dollar double indemnity claim with his wife as the beneficiary."

Anthony leaned over his desk. "You take too many chances. When I sent you on the case, I didn't tell you to risk your life. It's a good thing I called the police, as soon as I got your prints.

I saved your ass. You would be dead or in jail otherwise." He pointed his pen at her. "Sometimes I think you have a death wish. This isn't the first time you've endangered yourself."

"I couldn't go to the police, not until I had proof. Nobody believes in hunches or psychic talent or the sixth sense. They need tangible proof."

"I know, but you scare me. You're too confident, too determined to be right, and damn the consequences. You're not afraid of anything." He threw the pen down, muttering, "I can't let you risk your life again."

Aghast at his comment, she put her hand to her head. "Damn, Anthony, I left home for just that reason. I was an only child, a late overprotected child. They never left me alone. I felt like the whole town was watching me. I had to get away." She crossed her legs and folded her hands.

"All the women in my family have this special ability, to one degree or another. But in my case, it proved to be more powerful." She shook her head. "I'd end up in these *weird* situations. That made them even more protective, even more afraid."

Sitting forward in his chair, he pierced her with a look. "I've seen things as an F.B.I. agent, things that couldn't be explained by normal means. So I can understand this talent, but most people can't."

"I can swear to that. In my home town, people knew and it didn't cause a problem. My mother often advised the Chief of Police. A subtle warning, nothing conspicuous, and they often avoided trouble."

"Yes, I called him. Captain Arnold Duffy, I believe he vouched for you. He never came out and said you had special powers, but he inferred it." He cocked his head. "About this new assignment, it's a strange one but one suited to your talents. In fact, they asked for you." He loosened his raw silk tie, glanced down at his trimmed nails and avoided her eyes.

"Someone stole a valuable painting from a private collection. It's very hush, hush. Though heavily insured, they'd rather get the painting back then collect on an insurance claim."

She raised an eyebrow. "Why would they ask for *me*?"

He tented his hands and stared at her unblinking. "It's that article the Hendrickson fellow wrote a few years ago, which showcased your abilities. They must have read it because they asked if it was true."

"That stupid article—a complete breach of trust. I thought Karl was a decent sort when I dated him. I soon found out otherwise." She looked over at him.

"A young girl had disappeared, I had a vision and helped the police find her. He asked how I did it, I confided in him and swore him to secrecy." She grimaced in disgust. "He made it into a major story, *Does she or doesn't she?* He described my psychic abilities, and humiliated me. People called and called trying to get my help, or to out and out mock me."

Alethea shuddered at the memory, then turned and glared. "I won't do it—no way. Tell your client I'm not interested."

"Too late—I already committed you." He held up his hand to stop her protest. "I didn't think you'd mind.

They only want the painting back." He looked at her. "It's simple. A millionaire mogul, on an island in Greece, is thought to have it."

"So, what am I supposed to do?" She gave him a questioning glance, then held out her hands in a help-less gesture. "Steal it back, or what?"

"They want you to use your gifts to find it. They'll do the rest." He knitted his brows. "I'm just as confused as you, but they're paying me *very* good money so I can't just ignore them."

"I don't like to openly use my talents." She bit her lip. "Just last month, the Los Angeles police arrested a woman. She had shown them where the body of a miss-ing person could be found. She had seen her murdered in a vision, the body tossed in a ditch."

Alethea grimaced. "They jailed her for *three days.* And released her, only after they found the murderer. It's sickening." She glowered at him.

"I'll not be subjected to that type of suspicion."

"Be reasonable. You rely on your talents in most of your cases. Why not on this one?" He baited her.

"And you get to go to Greece, the home of your an-cestors, all expenses paid." He sighed. "The clear skies, the aquamarine sea, the ancient temples. I envy you this trip. Why, it's almost a vacation."

Not fooled by his cajoling tone she shot him a sharp look. "Be my guest, then you can go in my place. I'm sure it would be as easy for you to find the painting as it is for me."

"Alethea, I know you speak Greek. This is an easy assignment for you." He nodded, adjusted his sleeve, and took on a brisk tone.

"It's settled, then. I'll have Sandra make the arrangements.

She wondered why this assignment bothered her so much. Did it have something to do with this morning's dream? She had seen a long trip in the cards accompanied by danger. Now it seemed silly to protest.

She would love to go to Greece. "It doesn't seem I have much choice, but you owe me."

"Good." He stood and beamed at her. "You'll have a hefty expense account. I want you to enjoy yourself.

After all, the client is paying for it." He extended his hand.

Alethea shook it, and gave him a questioning look. "Why are you anxious to get rid of me?" Still holding his hand, she tried to read his thoughts.

Wait she could sense suspicion, but also greed. She could feel his nervousness. But the money—it tempted him. He didn't want to turn it down. But why was he uneasy? She tightened her lips.

There was more to this assignment then he had told her? She could sense this and it intrigued her.

Back in the reception area, Alethea and Lucretia, found a quiet spot. Her grandmother had taught her the cards at a young age. She'd used them ever since as a tool to help her focus, to decipher what her sixth sense was trying to say. They also helped her to channel her psychic powers.

They sat on a small couch with a coffee table in front. Alethea handed the cards to Lucretia. "Shuffle them and concentrate. Think about what you want to know while you do this."

Lucretia lifted an eyebrow. "These aren't Tarot cards. Just part of a regular pack. Can you teach me how to tell fortunes?"

"It's not hard. I'll write out the meaning of each card and the procedure for you." She paused a moment. "Do you know anything about this new assignment? I'm going to be on a Greek island investigating a theft. Sounds strange, doesn't it?"

Lucretia stared at her a moment. "Come to think of it, I got a call this morning. The man talked with a heavy accent. He wanted Anthony, so I connected him right through, but I overheard part of the conversation. They were adamant that *you* should be the one on the case." She gave her an apologetic look. "Sorry I couldn't be more help."

Alethea shook her head and laid the cards out on the table. "It's more than I had. This case is getting more and more puzzling. Why should they want a psychic?"

Chapter 3

Alethea watched the seagulls while she waited for her friends in the Hudson River café.

Blossom White lived and worked near Poughkeepsie, so it wasn't a problem to see her. But Camila Melo rarely came home. Thanks to the holidays, she could see them both.

She leaned back in her chair and spotted a display of three tiered trays—one of cinnamon rolls and cakes, one of soft butternut scones with whipped cream, and the third with an assortment of mouth-watering chocolate sweets.

She savored the aromas, decided the cinnamon rolls smelled too divine to pass up.

She gazed around the quaint store, admired paintings framed in wood paneling hanging on felt patterned wall paper. Filled bookcases helped create atmosphere; simulated gas lamps gave off a soft glow in private corners where people could eat and talk without being noticed.

Lost in thought, comfortable in the red tufted chair, she stared out the window.

The wharf was covered with seagulls, strutting and walking as if they owned the world, some gliding in from the river, others flying out to the water, filling the air with their unique, raucous sound.

Jarred out of her reverie when her friend touched her shoulder, she spun around. "Blossom, you startled me." Alethea gave her a peck on the cheek. "You look wonderful. That turquoise color suits you. Where is the *ice princess* hiding in all that glamour?"

"You know that's part of my image." Blossom adjusted her seat, "I have to look cold to keep the wolves away, otherwise they'd eat me alive." Shaking her head, her long dark hair flying around her, she frowned. "It's not easy having my own consulting business and dealing mostly with men. I have to be frigid and aloof, so they can't take advantage of me."

"I know what you mean—it's a man's world, no doubt about it." Alethea looked at her friend with a slight smile. "We used to have such fun twigging their noses. Nobody knew what to expect from us. Me the *dumb blonde*, you the *ice princess* and Camila the *bookworm* right down to those awful glasses and oversized clothes."

"I heard you talking about me," a frazzled redhead, with curls escaping every which way from her chignon, joined them. Kissing each on their cheek, Camila slid into a chair opposite Alethea. "I've missed you both.

It's good to be together after all this time, fleeting as it must be."

She cast them a look from her amber eyes, hidden behind a pair of ugly glasses. "You were saying something about my oversized clothes, if I'm not mistaken," Camila prompted. "Don't let me interrupt, it started to get interesting. I can't believe the lengths we took, to keep the adolescent boys and their raging hormones at a distance."

"Boys or men, what's the difference." Blossom straightened her napkin. "They don't see us as people. They're just interested in one thing—a body for their pleasure." Staring at her friends, she widened her aqua colored eyes, and shook her head. "What? Isn't that a fact?"

"I agree, Blossom, but their pleasure can be your pleasure, with the right man. So don't give up. In fact," Alethea added, "I've had some strong vibes about you, and you know what that means." Looking her in the eye, she winked. "My intuition is telling me *Mr. Right* is soon coming into your life."

Blossom gave her a dubious look.

Alethea played with her spoon, uncomfortable with the terrible premonition she had about her own future. "I had that dream again. You know the one where I'm drowning. It really spooked me this time."

"You didn't tell me about any dream," piped in Camila.

"No, you told me about it." Blossom said. "The other day. You were upset because you couldn't understand what it meant."

"Yes, the dream frightened me. In fact, this whole trip unnerves me. Why do they need a psychic to find a stolen painting? And my cards predicted my life would change with this long journey."

Stretching her hands, she moved her fingers. "Anyway, we'll see. I'm going to Greece and I don't know how long I'll be away, or how soon I'll see you again," she took each of their hands, giving them a squeeze, "friends always."

Camila squeezed back and looked from her to Blossom, "That's right, friends always."

Pausing, she added. "I'm leaving, too, for a dig in Brazil. So I'm glad for this time together." Holding up her arm, she motioned the waitress over to give her an order.

Alethea recognized the server as a friend who had been a grade ahead of them in school.

"Jennie, this is a surprise. I haven't seen you since we graduated. Are you working here now?"

"I'm an owner. My husband and I invested in this eatery. I'm Jennie Ward Mitchell now," she said looking around her. "It cost us a pretty penny to redecorate and to make it into what we wanted.

We call it The *Seagull's Nest*. We're trying to attract the local talent and support them through our cafe."

She gestured with her head. "Our walls are filled with their paintings, we play their discs, and they recite their works on the small stage over there."

"It looks great." Alethea looked around. "We used to hang here, remember?

But this concept is original. It should work. With Vassar, Mount St. Mary, and all the other colleges in the area, you should have quite a turnout."

"It's getting there." Holding up her pad, she asked, "What can I get you?"

"I'd like a green tea, and an order of cinnamon rolls." Alethea inhaled deeply. "Their aroma is hard to resist."

"Let me see, I think I'll have the chamomile tea and some of those scones," Blossom added, perusing the trays.

"I'll have the orange pekoe tea. My waistline can't take anything else." Camila gave the desserts a yearning look.

"You're paranoid about your shape," Blossom turned to her. "I can remember your crash diets, and your exercise drill. You got rid of all your baby fat and never put it on again."

She leaned back in her seat. "I don't know why we try so hard to make ourselves attractive when we keep swearing off the opposite sex."

"I think it's a matter of pride—looking good doesn't mean we're man hunting. We want to look our best for our own self-image." Alethea quirked her eyebrow. "And I don't remember swearing off men. I love it when they're looking at me. It's such a power thing—to know they're attracted."

"You like the power, do you? Hmm." Camila gave Alethea a wink. "You can look knock-down gorgeous or as plain as a doormat. It's the way you carry yourself."

She looked her up and down. "You don't need disguises, you just seem to change before one's eyes."

Camila looked at her friends and pushed her glasses closer to her face, "I don't have that problem. Men avoid me like bees avoid vinegar. I guess I look too brainy. You know my bookworm persona, it just scares them away."

"It's all right if they just look." Blossom bit her lip. "It's the groping I have a problem with." She closed her eyes a moment and shuddered. "I can do without the octopus hands, and being treated like a dish for their supper."

Blossom snapped her fingers. "I remember—the guy from Vassar who asked you out to win a bet— that's when you swore off men." She leaned forward and folded her hands.

"After that, you tried to hide your stunning face, those sensuous curves, and your golden cat eyes."

"I loved him but he only wanted a beautiful woman to impress his friends. He never cared about me. I felt degraded. That taught me a lesson, so now, I don't attract attention. If a man's interested, I know it's for *me*."

Camila tapped her fingers on her cup. "Be honest, we're just reluctant virgins. We want a man, but he has to be the right man."

"Oh, here are the tea and the pastries," Alethea said. "Well it's convenient not to be noticed. I prefer to blend into the scenery." She brought the Wedgwood cup to her lips and sipped.

Blossom nodded. "He has to be the right man. I'm tired of being a virgin, but they're all such losers—trying to take when you refuse to give."

"I've tried, I just can't." Alethea held out her palms. "Something must be wrong with me."

"I doubt that. You just haven't found the right one." Looking at Alethea, Camila tapped the table with her fingers. Sipping her tea, she raised an eyebrow. "Anyway, how did this writer know about your talent?"

She looked from one friend to the other, and decided, as foolish as it made her sound, she had to tell them the truth.

"When I first went to the city I dated this good looking reporter, and he kept badgering me to tell him how I helped the police." She looked at both her friends.

"So I confided in him about my talent and swore him to secrecy." She shrugged and lifted her hands. "He

23

was more interested in a scoop than me, abused my
trust by not only printing the story, but by making fun
of me in the process, like it was a big hoax. I didn't tell
you about it because—I was too embarrassed by my
stupidity."

"That's terrible," Blossom exclaimed as she devoured a scone heaped with whipped cream. "You
probably came on as a dumb blonde without a brain in
your head so he thought you were joking. You know
sometimes our impersonations work against us. We are
some trio…."

"Sure, we're some trio—smarty, dummy, and icy.
God that's so dumb!" exclaimed Camila.

"Anyway, this new assignment worries me. They
read that article about my psychic talents, and asked for
me. Why is my gift important in finding a painting?"

Chapter 4

Alethea stared out the window, while Blossom and Camila talked. Her instincts screamed danger. She watched the seagulls strut fearlessly filling every available space on the wharf. The humans strolling by didn't scare them. Why should they, she thought, no one tried to hurt them, many brought bread to feed them. Fear was a learned reaction caused by facing real menace. She had a feeling she would be experiencing that emotion soon.

Giving her a particular look, Camila asked, "What's so interesting about the seagulls? You seem captivated by them. You're not getting one of your intuitions, are you?"

Alethea looked at her, dumbstruck. Why of course—something would happen, something involving seagulls, thus her absorption with them. "You're right, Camila. You know me better than I know myself." She paused a moment. "I don't know what they have to do with anything, but I'm sure to find out soon enough."

"This feels like old times," Blossom commented. Stirring her tea, she looked at her friend. "Well, what else are you feeling? This sounds important, so focus."

Camila stared at her a moment. "Seagulls, they have to do with water. What else have you been thinking about? You know your sixth sense is fragmentary, maybe you need your cards."

Alethea closed her eyes to concentrate. "Give me a few minutes of silence." She looked into her mind, then shook her head to clear it. "You're right about the water, there's a cave… it opens on the side of a cliff just above water level, it's dry on most days, but on stormy days it floods as the water rises. I can feel the cold and I'm frightened." She gaped at her friends. "I don't know what this means. I've had this feeling since yesterday morning. I thought it had to do with my trip to Greece, but now I wonder."

"Wait," Blossom said. "Two days ago a local paper printed a story about a missing child, a five year old."

"What does that have to do with water or seagulls?" Camila asked, puzzled.

"Nothing, absolutely nothing, it's got to be something else," Alethea stressed.

Leaning her head on her hand, she looked at her two friends, trying to connect these bits and pieces of her feelings. They knew from past experience something important would happen, and wanted her to solve this riddle.

Camila leaned forward. "Think, maybe it's something that hasn't happened yet, but is about to happen."

"I don't know. The signals are weak—my intuition isn't working." Holding her head in her hands, she leaned on her elbows and closed her eyes. She had to concentrate. She sensed an urgency, as if she might not be in time, but for what?

"Someone's in danger, but who? I sense fear. A carpet of seagulls fills the space. Seagulls, water, fish, air, and what else? Oh yes, the wharf."

Snapping her fingers, she said. "I've got it. There's been a boat wreck. The survivor found a cave to hide in, but the tide is coming in, and there's danger of drowning."

Camila looked at her, wide-eyed. "This is weird. Damn, we have to let the Coast Guard know." Thinking a minute, she asked, "But how—without telling them about this premonition?"

"How about an anonymous phone call?" Blossom advised as she sipped her tea. "They'll have to respond. Won't they?" Confused, she turned toward Alethea. "Where is this cave? We have to tell them where to go."

"No." Alethea shook her head. "That doesn't sound right. I can feel the cave—the dampness, the cold—it's seeping into my skin.

My hands are tied. I can feel the ropes around my wrists and around my ankles. Someone I trusted has betrayed me."

Looking from one to the other, "We have to go to the police," she insisted. "I'm sure a crime has been committed."

Camila stared at her. "This is serious. Are you sure about it? How are we supposed to get help when we have so little information?"

Alethea glanced out the window again, at the birds. "I'm not sure what these bits and pieces mean, but my intuition is shouting they mean something. I have to act; I can feel someone is in danger.

Captain Duffy, the Chief of Police is a friend. He's known us since we were in diapers. He'll understand. I'll call him, explain what I sensed. He might have a case that fits the clues."

"Well, I feel better you've decided on this course of action," Blossom finished her sweet and leaned back. "Your intuitions are rarely wrong. The puzzle pieces are falling into place."

Camila glanced at her watch, put her teacup down. "Hey, I've got to get home," she pushed her chair back. "It's getting late. What's on for tomorrow?"

Alethea took the last bite of her cinnamon roll and put on her jacket. "If it's a nice day, why don't we drive along the river—maybe it will give me some clues. Then we can stop for lunch." She turned to her friends. "I'll call Captain Duffy tonight and see what I can find out."

Camila looked around, then turned to her friends. "What happened to Jennie? I wanted to say good-bye. I guess she went home, but she should have said something to us before she left."

A puzzled expression on her face, Alethea stood motionless for a moment. "I hope this has nothing to do with Jennie or her family," she mused, "that would really be…No. That would be too weird."

Chapter 5

Captain Duffy, sprawled back in his chair with his feet out in front of him, eyed the officer sitting at the opposite desk.

"I don't know how it works, but as long as the bad guys end up in jail, I don't care. We had no evidence, no clues. Alethea helped us out, and we saved the child."

"It's not something you can tell people, they wouldn't believe it," admitted Paul Hersh. "It's even hard for me to accept. I'm one of those guys who deals in logic and fact."

"No, people wouldn't understand." Duffy shook his head and sat up straighter. "It's the most amazing thing. She called and told me she had a gut fear that someone was in danger, and did we have any cases that might fit her psychic visions."

Stopping, he gathered his thoughts. "Mind, we've had this happen before, with her mother, so I wasn't hasty to hang up, I knew it wasn't a prank call. The things she told me were the missing pieces." He ran his hand through what little hair was left on his balding head, and sighed

"A five year old girl, kidnapped and held for ransom, and nobody knows except the parents. The kidnappers threaten to kill the child if the parents inform the police. The parents had just contacted us, afraid to do so sooner. We kept a tight lid on this out of respect for their wishes."

He paused and stared at his deputy. "Alethea told me she saw seagulls, many seagulls. The family lives on Seagull Ridge, an exclusive area of million dollar homes, so I suspected it was about this case. She could see the child, in her mind's eye, in a cave that would soon be filled with water. The child was tied up; she could feel that too. White birds were everywhere."

He leaned back in his chair and swiveled it. "I called the Coast Guard, and the local bird watchers group, and got an idea where the cave might be located. Thankfully, we rescued the child before any damage occurred. Now we have to find who did it."

"How did you explain this?" Paul leaned toward him.

Duffy put a piece of gum in his mouth. "I didn't follow police procedure, just went with my instincts, and didn't worry about explanations.

You have to do what you have to do, no matter how unorthodox. If anyone pressed me, I would have said an anonymous caller tipped me off."

He got a serious expression on his face as he sat forward in his chair. "We have to protect the innocent, no matter what, and take any assistance offered.

Mostly I've dealt with her mother, we've been friends for years. She usually asks for a personal item to help her find a clue. Sometimes what she says makes no sense until the crime is solved, then it all falls into place."

"She was my first grade teacher, her daughter and I were classmates," Paul said. "I remember Alethea well. She hung out with two other girls, inseparable friends, real lookers, too."

Chewing on a toothpick, he stopped a moment. "All the guys wanted to ask them out, but they seemed too perfect, too unapproachable. Just thinking about them raises my temperature.

We nicknamed them—Logic, Fantasy, and Emotion. Blossom was the math team captain, the logical one. Camila wrote fantastic stories for the school paper, and was a walking fantasy. Alethea told people's fortunes with cards; she was pure emotion. Even then, thinking back, she always tried to help people."

Duffy cast him a stern look, then cleared his throat. "I don't care about your personal recollections. And I'd appreciate it if you didn't say anything."

Chapter 6

Alethea spotted her number and eased into the window seat. She had first class tickets. This VIP treatment, on this Olympic flight, would make it memorable. But why the expense? Well, she wouldn't worry about it. Settling into the leather seat, she relaxed.

She scanned the interior and saw somber gray and brown suits with attaché cases. A familiar pattern formed. They found their seats, opened briefcases, read papers, and waited for the plane to take off.

She spotted an attractive man among them. He looked familiar, but she couldn't remember from where. His hair, a rich brown, glittered with gold streaks. Tall and lean, in his twenties, he had a forceful look about him. He walked up the aisle, with a briefcase in his hand and a raincoat thrown over his shoulder, stopped next to her to verify the number, and put his belongings in the overhead bin without so much as giving her a glance.

He scrutinized his ticket again, then turned and gave her a troubled look. "I'm sorry but I believe you're in my place, I always have my secretary book a window seat." He stared at Alethea, waiting for her to move.

Alethea stared back, wondering why he was making such a fuss. She hadn't paid attention to where she sat, had been just too glad to arrive on time. She checked her ticket. He was right, she *was* in his seat.

Her eyes narrowed. "You look like the type of guy who never parks in a *No Parking* area." Alethea looked openly around at the vacant seats, some even window seats, then glared at him.

He gazed back and shifted his weight.

She moved to the outside seat.

"You're right, I don't. And I always stop at *Stop* signs." He arched an eyebrow. "Do you have a problem with that?"

"No, I guess not." Jeez, what an unpleasant man. He was a real stickler for the right and proper. She closed her eyes blocking him out.

Alethea still felt rattled by the kidnapping. Though they hadn't found the kidnappers, the parents had their child safely home. It always upset her when children became the victims of violent crime. They were so weak, so helpless, such prime targets for corruption. If she hadn't had this vision, the little girl would certainly have been found dead.

She wished she could control it better. If it hadn't been for her friends, she might never have realized what her senses were trying to tell her. She still felt uncomfortable about this trip, as if it was going to change her life. But the fear she had had wasn't with her, as if she had absorbed the child's fear.

Alethea blocked out her surroundings to reach her inner self, a plateau that brought sensations and voices.

Much to her sorrow, she even attuned to people's thoughts, to their emotions. These—she didn't want to know. Ugh, too gross. Like now, somebody's erotic thoughts inundated her senses, her ears burned with their vivid images.

Alethea snapped out of her reverie to hear the flight attendant start the standard safety lecture. More often than not, she seemed to be glancing their way.

Preoccupied with the plane's movements, Alethea didn't give it another thought.

The seat belt sign appeared. The plane taxied into position. Firmly grasping the arms of her seat, she closed her eyes, took a nervous breath and tried to calm the butterflies in her stomach, as she felt the plane accelerate for take-off. When she opened her eyes and verified they'd been thrust into the air, she whispered. "Well that wasn't so bad," and took out her book.

Lost in her reading, she didn't notice the flight attendant approach until she heard her voice.

"Mr. Artemidis, how are you today? Would you like your regular drink?"

He snapped his head up. "Yes, fine." He took the drink, and got back to perusing his work.

"And you... what would you like?"

Before Alethea could answer, she again sensed lustful thoughts, and wondered which one was having them. The flight attendant was the same pretty one who had given the safety speech.

"Oh, I'd like some white wine."

Alethea observed the attendant cast a secret smile at the man. He seemed oblivious to her flirting.

A disappointed look on her face, she moved to the next passenger.

Well I know who has the lustful thoughts, she mused, clicking her tongue. Or maybe it was 'Mr. Right and Proper'. She sipped her wine, leaned her head back, and closed her eyes. She loved people, loved helping them. People's emotions surrounded her, enclosed her, she suffered their pain.

Alethea tuned out everything and took out her cards. She shuffled them, concentrating, trying to find her inner core.

She laid out the cards in the familiar patterns. It surprised her to see the jack of hearts with the two of hearts. Blossom's cards had showed a romance, but here it was in her cards, too. The *black* card, signified turbulence; she wondered at it.

Absorbed in her reading, she didn't notice her fellow traveler casting covert glances at her, not until he cleared his throat to get her attention.

She turned and looked at him.

"I couldn't help but notice your card playing. Are you good at reading the cards?"

She gave him a curious side-glance. "How did you know I was telling fortunes? Most people think I'm playing Solitaire."

"Maybe in America, but in Greece, you would have half the plane begging you to tell their fortunes. Don't forget, you're coming to a country that believes, really believes in fortune tellers.

They might use cards or coffee grounds to predict the future, but predict they will." Warming to his subject, he started to explain about Delphi and the oracles.

She stared at him. Could this animated man be the same one, who was so stuffy about the seat, just a short time ago? He wasn't handsome, but charismatic, with a deep mesmerizing voice. He oozed masculinity, and fascinated her. She noticed a rugged face and an athletic build that indicated long hours spent outdoors.

When he took off his reading glasses, his golden green eyes glowed with excitement, as he talked about a topic he seemed to know a good deal about. He definitely fell into the scholar pigeonhole, she decided.

He went on and on, but she found her mind wandering. She heard "Delphi was built on the slope of Mt.Parnassus. The oracle would predict future events. People would come from all over bringing gifts, rich treasure houses were built to hold these riches, a booming place of commerce."

Then she was there in this ancient place.

Looking around she saw the place honored as the earth's center. A shepherd stood looking at his goats. They seemed to be acting strangely.

"Ho," he called to his friends walking by.

"What's the matter Kouretas... why are your goats acting demented?"

Kouretas pointed. "There are some fumes coming from this hole over here, maybe that's causing it?" The neighbors went over to investigate and fell into a trance; many went insane and jumped into the hole.

Startled by the unfolding drama, she came to herself. She watched the man's lips move, but couldn't understand his meaning. Putting a hand on his sleeve, she put a halt to his monologue.

"Sorry, I don't know much about these oracles. I just like to play a fortune telling game, it doesn't mean anything." Alethea lied. She sensed his confusion, sensed a restrained withdrawing.

"Right, I thought you were the genuine thing." He adjusted his glasses, then started looking through his papers, completely shutting her out.

No sexual attraction here, she noted. She might as well have been made of stone. Alethea wished she could say the same for herself.

Beyond anything that made sense, she felt drawn to him like metal to a magnet. His body drew her eye as he relaxed in his seat. He filled out his jacket in all the right places. She wondered how such a nerd could look so athletic.

Eating her steak, she pondered her best approach. Maybe she should tell him she was a true psychic. He'd showed interest. But, that could mean opening herself to ridicule. Maybe she should unsettle him in some way, but how?

Alethea cast him a sideways glance. She couldn't help noticing how absorbed he was in his folders. He browsed through one, then the other. He must be some type of professor. All that paper work was enough to make one dizzy.

He glanced up, and saw the flight attendant with his food. He took the tray, peeled off the cover, and started eating the salmon. He didn't glance at her or pay her any attention. She might as well have been invisible.

This will never do, she thought to herself. She waited for the flight attendant to collect their trays, and asked for water.

While the attendant filled the cup, Alethea managed to move just enough to cause her half-filled water glass to spill over onto the next seat.

"Oh, I'm so sorry. How awful! This is all my fault." She took a napkin and dabbed at the liquid that had dripped over his lap.

"Of all the clumsy things to do," he grumbled. Brushing Alethea's hands away, he pushed past her into the aisle.

The flight attendant rushed after him, offering help.

Alethea bit her lip. "Well that didn't go well, did it?" She murmured under her breath.

She watched her seating partner making his way back up the aisle. She braced herself to make an apology.

"I'm so clumsy, I don't know how that happened," she touched his sleeve. "Please forgive me. As a peace offering ... why don't I read your cards?"

Chapter 7

"I'm interested in what kind of fortune you'll tell me." He bent toward her and gave her an angelic smile. "By all means, let's see what the future holds."

Alethea shuffled the cards then handed them over. "You have to concentrate on what you want to learn, and designate different cards for your interests."

He shuffled them, put the deck down as she instructed, and cut it in three.

Alethea studied the cards, smiling. "You're having a love affair soon with a blond woman." She continued. "There's another woman who will try to break it up."

"That's interesting. You're like the oracles at Delphi. You give just enough information to whet one's appetite." He gave her another beguiling smile. "Please continue."

She gathered her cards together, and indicated for him to cut them in half.

She spread them out and examined them. "I see a great deal of travel and a great deal of money." She gathered the cards, and shuffled them again.

Zach raised an eyebrow. "So there's more?"

"We're just getting to the juicy part. That was an appetizer." She looked through the cards a moment, then picked one. "Now the real reading starts. We'll put you down as the king of clubs, and see what will happen to you." Handing him the rest of the cards, she touched his hand. "Shuffle them and concentrate," she instructed.

He did.

Alethea put them down in a cross pattern. Distracted by his eyes—golden brown with specks of green, she hesitated, then turned back to the cards. She looked up, shocked by what she saw.

"Danger and betrayal, how can that be? I'm afraid you're in for rough times."

"What exactly does that mean? Danger and betrayal from whom or what? Can't you be more specific?"

Handing him the cards, she looked into his eyes. "Shuffle again and concentrate. I'll put success down and see what falls. We'll see whether you'll succeed with your plans, these rather dangerous plans, according to the cards."

"You know, this is an interesting way to learn a person's secrets. Do many people confide in you while you're telling them their fortunes?"

"I told you they're for fun. I don't care about anyone's secrets." She shook her head. "But really, I can't believe all this danger."

She gave him a pensive look, trying to understand how his apparently bookish personality fit with the character of the person in the cards. The cards' personality lived on the edge; violence and mayhem were a part of his life.

She got the oddest feeling she had seen him before, but couldn't remember where. She felt his presence, and wondered at her strong reaction.

She wondered at the dichotomy of his personality - a sexy man who seemed uninterested in sex. A man who appeared scholarly yet lived a dangerous life. He gathered the cards and started shuffling them. "Let's try again. I'd like to know more about this betrayal."

Alethea peered at him, trying to decipher his enigmatic expression.

She laid out the cards, then glanced up. "A big door falls… it's a place of authority, like a government building. You're with a group of men. Here - these black cards show peril. A long road. Then the two of spades falls, indicating an accident. See—right here, they fall together."

"You're just giving me cryptic messages. Bits and pieces that are clues to the whole picture whatever that might be. How do you expect me to decipher them?"

He leaned closer to her, so close she could feel the breath on her cheeks, and took her hand. "You know, don't you, what's going to happen. I can sense it. Tell me what you feel. It's important."

Surprised at his perception, not knowing how to answer, she shook off his hand and picked the cards up from the table. She played with them, taking her time to get her thoughts together. Of course she knew. But how to tell him without giving her secret away?

"Let's work through it together. Maybe by talking about it, you'll see its meaning. The big door could be the police department. Does that make any sense?

You're in danger from somebody who works for the police, and the road shows an accident."

"It's starting to make sense now. Apparently I'll just have to be on my guard, and not take any car trips." He looked into her eyes and took her hand. "Let's get back to the part about the blond woman and the love affair." With a flirtatious smile, he asked. "Is that something that's going to happen soon? You have blond hair and beautiful eyes. Maybe the love affair is with you."

Zach caressed her hand, played with her fingers before giving them a squeeze.

Wary of his amorous side, she eyed him closely. Of course she'd like to have something with him, but wasn't sure what that something might be.

She pulled her hand away. "I didn't mean I was the girl in your cards; there are a lot of blond women around."

He shrugged his shoulders, then leaned back into his seat. "I'll think about what you told me, and try to make sense of it." He put on a mask and earplugs, and went to sleep.

She stared at him dumbfounded. She couldn't believe this. One minute he was friendly, the next minute cold and disinterested. "What the…." She opened and closed her mouth

Alethea disregarded him, took out her travel package and looked through it. Hotel reservations at the *Caravel* in Athens were included, and one for the *Blue Sea* in Mytilene, also the stolen painting's picture. She was to stay in Athens for several days, then she was booked on the express ferry to Lesvos which docked right across from the hotel.

She returned everything to the envelope keeping only the painting's picture out to examine more closely.

What had she gotten herself into? In the photo, she saw a man and a woman, dressed in clothes reminiscent of the crusades. *If this painting is so valuable why didn't they report it missing?*

Feeling tired, she put the picture away. She settled back in her seat, curled her jean clad legs under her, and pulled her sweater down over her stomach. She pushed the chair into reclining position, covered herself with the flight blanket, adjusted the pillow under her head and closed her eyes.

The plane's hum lulled her into a light sleep. As she relaxed, she started to see visions, erotic visions that caused her pulse to race.

He was kissing her, devouring her. They lay in a huge bed, in a room with glass doors that looked over the sea. Slowly he caressed her skin, moving his hands over her body while entwining his legs around hers. Skin to skin, they slid up and down, enjoying the feel of their limbs as their breathing intensified in time with the beating of their hearts.

He lifted his head and his golden green eyes consumed her. He played with her breasts, looking into her eyes. Wetting a finger, he brushed it over the tip of her nipple. She gasped, overcome with pleasure.

Shocked awake, she felt the plane shaking, dipping, and rising. She held onto her seat, trying not to think of what could happen if the plane lost control, and suddenly fell out of the sky.

Alethea took a deep breath. She turned her head and found her fellow passenger staring at her. Recalling the details of her vivid dream, she blushed. They didn't even know each other's names.

She twisted toward him.

"Excuse me. Please don't think me rude. I know your fortune, but not your name."

"I'm Zachary Artemidis, and you?"

43

"Alethea Karras."

"That's a Greek name you must be at least part Greek."

"My parents are both Greek, but we've been in the states for years. My father's great grandparents emigrated from Sparta in the 1890's. My great grandmother worked in the textile mills in Lynn, Mass. They met and married in Lynn. Neither family ever went back."

"Do you speak Greek, or has that been lost too?"

"My mother insisted I learn Greek, so I've had many years of lessons."

"That's good. You should try to keep the Greek traditions."

"What about you? The flight attendant knew you. You must travel back and forth often."

"We have offices in New York. So yes, I travel back and forth regularly."

"What do you do?"

"We have cruise ships, the *Blue Dolphin* line. They travel the Caribbean and the Aegean," he answered after a moment's pause.

She sensed his hesitation and explained. "I'm sorry I didn't mean to be nosey, but that would explain the travel and the money I saw in the cards.

"You're right. We make money from travel, there's no secret here. We've been in business for many years. Our line is well known."

"So where do you live—New York or Athens?"

"I have an apartment in New York and one in Piraeus, a major seaport in Greece."

He scanned her body, the slim waist, long legs and nice sized breasts under a mauve sweater. "While you're visiting Athens, I'll show you the sights. We can spend a few days together."

"Yes, I'd like that. I'll be at the *Caravel* in Athens, you can call me there."

"I'll be sure to call—I think I can postpone some of my meetings. You should see the Acropolis. Maybe we'll even take a day and go to Delphi, where all the Oracles made their predictions. With your psychic leanings, you should definitely visit Delphi." Zach gave her a sideways glance.

She didn't know what to say. "What psychic leanings? I told you I didn't have any."

"You can deny it if you want, but after your card reading, I know better." He took her hand, rubbing his thumb over her palm, back and forth, then in circles until her scalp started to prickle.

"You shouldn't hide who you are. The power you have is special, few are gifted with it." He let go of her hand leaned his head back and closed his eyes.

Alethea stared at this strange man. He was a mystery, one that she was curious to unravel. One minute all fire, the next all ice. It was hard to keep her balance around him.

She took out her journal and started to record her impressions. She came from a line of psychic women who kept journals—her mother had been in the habit of writing things down, like her mother before her. Alethea, also, liked to record her psychic visions, often coming back to her notes for clarification.

The plane quieted down, the lights dimmed, making it conducive for resting. She hoped she could do that. She didn't need any more of those disturbing erotic dreams.

She put her journal away and snuggled down in her seat. Emptying her mind, she pictured a deep, blue sea lapping at the shore, its steady rhythm lulling her to sleep.

Chapter 8

"Zach. Look—the plane's approaching the Greek coast. I can see the sea and land clearly." Staring out Zach's window, she took a breath. "It's impressive." She leaned forward to get a better view. "Wow, it's stunning.

That aquamarine sea—you can see clear to the bottom. And the sun's so bright, it's reflecting off the surfaces—everything sparkles like jewels on a crown." Touching his arm, she pointed.

"Look, it's like a miniature golf course—the roads, the white buildings, and the cars – they're all so tiny... even the swimming pools. And they're so many boats—small fishing boats to large liners."

Zach glanced out the window. "Piraeus is a large shipping port with vessels from all over the world coming and going. That's why you see so much movement in the sea."

"I can't wait to land." Alethea said, leaning back in her seat.

"Oh, did I bore you with my conversation?" Zach asked, lifting his eyebrow.

"How could you bore me? I shudder when I think of your large family. Five sisters can cause major disorder. And you the only male - that must have exhausted you."

"You were an only child, that's why you're dazed by such a large family." He adjusted his seat and leaned toward her. "My three older sisters treated me like a child, especially when they lived at home. When I got older, they tried to run my life. But, I can't say it was ever dull. My sisters kept things lively."

"What about your two younger sisters?"

"Zena, my twin, was always competitive and tried to do everything better than me, forgetting she wasn't my size. Maro was protective of Zena. They always got into scraps together.

The worst was when they all banded together determined to get me married."

"I think that's sweet. Your sisters trying to find you a wife."

"Sure, once they all married they decided it was my turn." He grimaced. "They've put me into some awkward situations."

"But now you can avoid them, can't you?"

"Mostly I stay away from them, but I still have to contend with my mother and my twin sister Zena. She's my worst rival and my biggest ally—the only female who keeps my ego in check."

"I hear a voice over the loud speaker," she said, interrupting him.

"They're giving instructions for landing. You'd better buckle your seatbelt." He turned toward her. "Hey, you're getting that look on your face. You're scared."

"You're kidding, right? Me, scared—no way. I'm never scared. Why. I rush into danger all the time." Swallowing, she buckled her seatbelt and straightened her seat.

"Don't be nervous. These pilots are experienced

and have done this a thousand times." He narrowed his eyes and took a good look at her. "I noticed you seemed anxious at take-off. Trust me, there's nothing to be afraid of."

She felt reassured when she felt his fingers holding hers. Not that she was afraid, mind you, but…. "Thank you for those words," she added, "it's always good to have your two feet on the ground. I'll feel better once we land."

"Is someone coming to pick you up? Sometimes it's hard to find transportation, especially now, with all the last minute preparations for the Olympics."

"The Olympics," she nodded, "that's right. They're going to be held here in August. I forgot."

"How could you forget? This is Greece's shining moment. Finally we have the games back where they originated. It's a real triumph." Looking at her, he asked. "You will be here for the games, won't you?"

Alethea didn't know how to answer. She didn't want to reveal her work, and in truth, didn't know how long she'd be here. "I'm not sure, I'm doing some research and don't know how much time it'll take. I hope to be here."

"I'm inviting you to stay and will be glad to be your host." Zachary said.

"That's nice of you. But, shouldn't we get to know each other better first?"

"By then, we might be on intimate terms," he said. "Isn't that what your cards foretold?" He gave her an impish wink. "Your reading did predict a love affair."

Alethea skimmed his body and wondered. She desired him. But was he the one, or was he another one who showed interest only because of her talent? She had to take the chance. She wanted a relationship. She was tired of dating angry, uninteresting, disgruntled men. She decided she needed to encourage him.

"I think I'd like that. You working on it, that is."

He gave her a slow smile. "My car is parked at the airport. I'll drive you to your hotel. The Elefterious Venezela's International is a new airport with all conveniences. We'll get our bags and go through customs in record time."

His smile looked so appealing, she couldn't help but respond with one of her own. She wanted him, but didn't want to be exposed as a psychic again. Maybe she should try her damsel in distress act. That should convince him she needed his help.

"I always feel so powerless. It's hard being a woman alone. I'd appreciate your help. You're so - male." She lowered her eyes, then sighed.

"Imagine me trying to find my bags and then having to deal with customs and then finding a taxi." She lifted her hands in a helpless gesture. "I shudder to even think about it." Leaning toward him, she touched his arm. "You're a sweetheart for offering."

"My pleasure," he said. As he braced for the descent, he glanced over at Alethea, who sat with her eyes closed, clutching the armrest.

Maybe she was more helpless than he thought.

Nudging her shoulder, he snapped her out of her trance. "We've landed. You can open your eyes and release the armrest."

Startled, she looked around. The seat belt sign was off and the passengers were gathering their things. "Oh, we've landed."

"You looked petrified. I guess you're not used to air travel."

"I'm not. I much prefer traveling by car."

Zachary guided her through customs and through the airport to his car. He unlocked the cobalt blue Mercedes s55 AMG and loaded the suitcases.

Alethea got in and watched Zach slide into the driver's seat. Talk about attraction - pins to a magnet couldn't be more attracted.

Maybe it was his voice—it was deep with a resonance that shot straight to her nervous system. Deep and dark, filled with emotion, she could picture him whispering suggestive words to her as they lay together.

Such disturbing thoughts—she couldn't imagine why she kept having them. From the moment she saw him coming down the aisle, her emotions had soared, and still hadn't landed.

This reckless streak of hers was way out of line. Could she control it?

"Welcome to Athens," he settled back into his seat, giving her a sideways glance.

"An ancient city filled with modern problems, and the home of your ancestors," he said, winking. "I plan to make it an unforgettable experience for you."

"I'm sure it will be." She gave him a little smile and fastened her seat belt.

Zachary stared. She looked radiant when she smiled, her face lit up taking her from pretty to drop-dead gorgeous.

He started the car and shifted into gear. He paid the parking ticket then eased onto the highway toward Athens. From the corner of his eye, he caught her giving him secretive looks and decided he liked this interest she showed.

"I'll drop you off at your hotel and give you a chance to rest. Later we can see the sights."

"Yes, I'd like that." She gazed out the window. "So this is Athens. It's so modern. I expected to see temples and togas, and not a metropolitan city full of cars and people."

"That's the text book Athens, the one that deals with its ancient glory. Today, the cities are more or less the same." He turned into a side street and drove down a hill.

"There's the *Caravel* up ahead. Now that the new roads are finished, it's easier to get around Athens. A few months ago, you would have been crawling, stuck in one traffic jam after another."

Out on the busy street, he took Alethea's arm and led her toward the hotel.

At the desk, he asked for a room with a view of the *Acropolis*.

"Wait here a moment while I get your bags."

"Thank you, I'll see you soon." She held out her hand and smiled.

"It was my pleasure." He drew her close, giving her a light kiss on the cheek. "I'll clear my schedule so I can concentrate on *just you* for the next few days."

Chapter 9

Zachary went out to his car with a light step. Usually he had no time for romance, but Alethea was a lure too tempting to ignore. She intrigued him. She tantalized him, and he wanted to know her secrets.

At the police station, though distracted, he had noticed Alethea watching him. He had wondered about her. With her long legs, her blond ponytail bobbing as she talked, and her eyes flashing in his direction, she had been lovely sitting there.

He could picture her trim figure gracing a man's bed. She had made an instant impression as she sauntered away, her backside jiggling, unconscious of his attention.

He had forgotten about her, had never expected to see her again, so he was startled to see her on the plane. Since the meeting officially didn't happen, if she ever remembered seeing him at the station, he could deny it.

His trip to New York had gone well. Secretly, at a local police station, he had met with top Home Land Security officer Carlos Ramirez who was as anxious as he was to stop these criminals, these people who got rich from other people's troubles.

Ramirez told him they had the name for one large dealer. Rumors reported a rich shipping magnate with connections all over the world had involved himself in this nasty business, but not much else was known.

Zachary pulled out of his parking space and drove to the traffic light. There he made a right and passed the newly renovated Athens Hilton. Anxious to talk with Mitch, he sped along processing in his mind what he had learned on this last trip.

Mitch Petridis, his sister Maro's husband, worked for Greek Interpol. A large man, over six feet tall, he had wheat blond hair and blue eyes that seemed to peer into your soul. When he wanted something, he usually got it.

Zach found it hard to say *no* to him. Before he realized what was happening, Mitch had enlisted his aid in trying to break up a human trafficking ring transporting people from third world countries. With the Olympics only a few months away, security on all borders had been tightened. So many people were expected to attend this prime-sporting event, it was an ideal time for would be terrorists or illegal immigrants to breach the borders.

Zach shifted gear and sped past the light before it turned red. Thinking about this problem, he drove past The Grand Britannica Hotel and went on toward Omonia square.

Greece, because of its location on the Mediterranean, its nearness to Cyprus, Turkey and Eastern Europe, had become a thoroughfare for the smuggling of refugees into other E.U. countries and even into the United States.

The Greek government, afraid of attacks from terrorists posing as illegal immigrants, had recently broken with international treaties on *Rights of Refugees*. Asylum seekers were likely to be treated as potential terrorists, not as people trying to escape harsh conditions at home.

Because legitimate refugees could not find sanctuary, the immigration problem had worsened. Mitch, respecting Zach's problem solving abilities, had persuaded him to get involved.

Through his ties in the shipping world, he believed Zach could ferret out information and find the people responsible for this key smuggling ring.

Taking a right at the National Library, he ascended a labyrinth of small streets.

Zach thought on this problem as he reached his sister's house in *Kolonaki*, an expensive area of Athens, built on one of its several hills.

The house was old and aristocratic, it stood out like a relic among the new apartment buildings around it. Three stories high, on a corner lot with an oasis of green, it bloomed in an otherwise cement-gray city. An elegant fountain flowed in its enclosed flower-filled courtyard.

He rang the bell and waited, his hands loaded with gifts. Ushered in by a servant, he put his packages down on the foyer table before being led to the salon where the family was gathered.

Two energetic nephews came running to greet him. He hugged them and gave each a wink. "You'll find some surprises in the hall. Enjoy them, I'll answer your questions later." They dashed out and were soon heard squealing over their presents.

His sister Maro, thirty-five and eight years his senior, had chocolate brown hair and lively brown eyes. She stood to give him a sisterly hug.

"I'll get refreshments." She turned to her husband. "Don't say anything—until I get back."

Mitch who scared everyone but his wife, watched her leave the room with a wary expression on his face. "See this gray hair? That's what I get trying to keep up with her." He greeted Zach with a handshake. "I hope this isn't a business meeting."

"Sorry," Zach said, "but your friend at Homeland Security gave me important information I know you want. I came as soon as I got off the plane, not trusting this to anyone else.

The man is too powerful, has too much money and ears everywhere." He leaned forward, put his elbows on his knees, and clasped his hands together.

"Carlos recently broke up a ring of traffickers. A truckload of people, some from the Middle East, were caught being shipped across the border between Mexico and the United States. One of them, to gain favor, gave up a name. I thought you could check it out." Zach straightened, and shook his head.

"These sad souls pay five to ten thousand a head, to vile men just to try to secure their families a better future. They're packed like sardines in a ship's hold, or in a truck or a bus, at the mercy of these crooks. Carlos was disgusted. The group they found was near death."

Mitch stared blankly into the air. "You remember what happened a few months ago? It was in all the papers." He rubbed his forehead and scowled.

"Over a hundred bodies were thrown into the sea by a ship's captain. Human rights groups raised protests throughout Europe. Now the law enforcement agencies, worldwide, are making a concentrated effort to stop these atrocities." He leaned back with his arms across his chest. "That's why I asked for your help." emphasized Mitch. "So what do you have?"

"The name is Nicholas Pappas. Does that ring a bell?"

"It's a common name. Is it real or an alias?" Mitch eyed him, waiting.

"I don't know, but I figured you'd want to know right away."

"Let's keep this from your sister, shall we? She and your twin, Zena are better named the *snooping sisters.* I can't believe how persistent those two are." He groaned shaking his head, "how did you manage to survive them?"

"The same way you have after being married to her for twelve years."

He leaned back into the couch. "You stay out of their way, allow them to do just what they want, and pray they don't turn things upside down too often. My father gave up trying to control those two."

"It's not easy to keep up with my wife's mischief." Mitch confided. "Your sisters are all exceptional, as is your mother. But Zena, when she goes after a story is unstoppable, and she manages to drag my wife with her."

"Yes, they're strong, determined, and devious. My father and I love them, but at home we escaped when they got too meddlesome.

We spent time in his library, which was off limits to them. There we played chess together, discussed books and his love of history. This male camaraderie helped keep us sane in a house full of women."

"With so many of them in your life, I'm sure you have a good idea of how the female mind works," Mitch said, "and how to avoid their schemes."

"I love women, but these women can be exasperating. Nobody is immune from their scheming. They're always one step ahead. You know Zena will do anything for a story. Her job as a television news reporter is her life."

"That's why I don't want Maro to know why you came. She'll run and tell Zena and then they'll nag us until we tell them what's happening."

Mitch leaned back crossing his leg. "These men don't fool around, they're dangerous. I don't want your snooping sisters near this case."

"I agree." Zach said.

"Carlos at Homeland Security warned me to be careful, we're dealing with unscrupulous men who deal not only with illegal immigration, but with the trafficking of women for a sex trade. They promise them jobs, then keep them as veritable slaves."

He shook his head. "Zena would die for such a story. She'd probably want to go undercover. I can just picture the trouble she'd get herself into."

"Too bad about her marriage, she married too young, and to a fortune hunter to boot." Mitch knitted his brows. "Maybe if she married again she'd stay out of trouble."

He glanced up. Seeing his wife entering the room, he stopped talking.

"That's not going to happen; she's become too cynical. She doesn't want to get involved in a serious relationship." Turning, he saw his sister and also quieted.

Maro carried in a tray of refreshments and put it down on the table. "Did I miss something? You're too quiet. What were you talking about?"

They gave her an innocent look. "Why, about Zena and her broken marriage." Zachary said.

She looked daggers at them. "I don't believe you. What about her marriage, anyway? She was only eighteen, too young to know better and too headstrong to listen to anybody. People told her he was a fortune hunter, but she still eloped with the jerk. Now she knows better."

"I have to leave." he stood up. "I told you I didn't want refreshments. You shouldn't have gone to the trouble." Afraid his sister would start an interrogation, he persisted. "It was a long flight, I need some sleep."

"Stay, I have *baklava*, your favorite dessert. I made it myself. You know you love my *baklava,* sit and have some." She pushed him back into his seat and handed him a plate.

He smiled at his sister and shrugged. "How can I resist your sweets?" He bit into the pastry. "Hmm, this is delicious." Satisfied, Maro served her husband a piece. He gave her a wary look but said nothing.

She sat down, crossed her arms and beamed at them. "Now, tell me all about your trip. I'm sure you accomplished a great deal, Zach, to come rushing over here straight from the plane."

Chapter 10

He shouldn't have brought their business to the house. Mitch had warned him. Maro could be like a bulldog with a bone, chewing and gnawing at it, reluctant to give it up. But Zach had avoided his sister's interrogation leaving her confused and fuming.

Satisfied he had escaped her maneuverings, he drove to his apartment. Jet lag didn't affect him; he didn't plan to rest.

Instead he phoned Alethea.

"Hi again, this is Zach. I promised to call. Are you tired? Athens at night is something to experience. I can pick you up at nine o'clock."

"No, I'm fine. I had a quick shower, but couldn't relax. I kept staring out the balcony doors at the Acropolis. Amazing, isn't it, how long it's been standing there, towering over the city."

"You'll be impressed, then, with the sights I'll show you tonight. We'll visit Plaka, it's the section which contains the ruins of old Athens. It's right by the Acropolis."

He stood speculating about her as he hung up the phone. Alethea—he knew he wanted to see her again.

He took his travel case into the bedroom, unpacked it. How would she affect him when he got to know her better?

They both arrived at the hotel lobby at about the same time.

He saw her across the room, and waved. She spotted him, and smiled.

She looked fantastic in a strapless lace dress that left a lot of leg to admire. Her blond hair rippled around her bare shoulders as she glided across the lobby.

"Wow." He took a deep breath, just looking at her raised his temperature. She radiated beauty.

He had dated many beautiful women, many stunning women and yet, something made her exceptional. She captivated him, but so had others.

His looks and money lured them, but he always controlled the game. Maybe it had been too long since his last relationship, maybe he just needed a woman.

The dress seemed to clasp her breasts, pushing them up and out, showcasing her assets.

Her dangling earrings sparkled as they grazed her bare shoulders. From her neck, Zach's eyes trailed down to an extremely small waist, then to a ruffled black lace skirt that ended at mid-thigh, leaving her gorgeous legs bare.

She was striking, truly imposing. Dangerously so. He couldn't keep his eyes off her as she approached.

"Hello Zach," she said, "I hope you haven't been waiting long."

"No I just got here." His eyes scanned her from top to bottom. "You look amazing."

She turned modeling for him.

"Oh, it's just some old thing I picked up in New York. I usually wear jeans and a shirt, but once in a while, I like to dress up."

"I certainly approve. I like a woman who likes to entice a man."

"Consider this your lucky day." She flashed him a sexy smile. "I'm afraid I have nothing else to astound you with," indicating her body with her hands, "but this."

"Honey, that's more than enough," he passed her a heated look, "believe me."

"Really? I'd never guess it." She raised her eyebrow, and tossed him an amused smile. "If you stared much harder, you'd drill a hole through me."

"I can't tear my eyes away."

"I thought you were too involved in books to notice women."

"Oh, I notice them." He put a hand lightly around her waist, stepped next to her and whispered in her ear, "I can't be bothered most of the time. But in your case, I'll make an exception."

She lifted her chin and winked at him. "Maybe I'll let you make an exception, if you're real nice to me," she grinned. "I like a man who makes me feel special."

Taking her by the arm, he added, "You are special."

They walked to Zach's car. He opened the door and got an eyeful as she slid into her seat.

She adjusted her dress and leaned into the soft leather.

Walking around to the driver's side, he wondered at her thoughts. She looked like the cat that ate the canary and enjoyed every bite of it.

"We're going to a small club in the central *Plaka Square.* " Zach explained. "Plaka will interest you with its maze of streets and stores." He drove from the Caravel, went up a few blocks and made a right into Syndagma Square.

"These streets are getting narrower and narrower," Alethea observed.

"Yes, we'll have to park here and walk the rest of the way." Zach pointed. "Those bars across the road prevent cars from entering the streets."

"Sydagma Square is as bad as any major city road with all these people and traffic." Alethea noted. "And just as noisy."

Stopping, she gawked and pointed, "Jeez, Zach those two men are pounding each other right at the traffic light. I can't believe it. And look, they just got back into their cars and drove off."

"Don't be too surprised, people show their tempers here. You're bound to see it again."

He took her arm and led her up a side street away from the square.

"I can smell frankincense. I think it's coming from that small church."

"Most likely," Zach replied looking ahead. "Here we are. You can see the streets are lined with stores. Plaka, is known as the 'neighborhood of the gods.' It's the oldest part of Athens, built next to the *agora* (old market).

Peddlers and dealers sell their wares here. It's a good place to find antiques and artifacts." They walked side by side, holding hands.

Alethea fascinated, looked around Plaka. "The peddlers and store keepers bring the aged streets alive. You can sense the people who walked here in bygone times, people who went to the bazaar or the temples or climbed up to the Acropolis." She stopped to watch the tourists. They moved from store to store picking out post cards, fondling ancient statues, and fingering worry beads.

Peddlers without shops sold jewelry right on the sidewalk. Alethea admired the jewelry, many pieces looked like replicas of ancient designs.

"Look—they've lit up the Acropolis." She spun toward Zach. "I'd get lost here by myself. It's such a maze of narrow streets and alleyways."

Alethea slowed her pace, "… it's so picturesque. The colored umbrellas on the tables, the house with the ceramic planters, and the one next to it with the wrought- iron balconies over hanging the street. It looks like a post card."

"These are neo-classic houses," Zach explained, "built around the 1800s." He pointed upward. "If you notice the tiled roofs you'll see designs depicting either the head of Medusa or goddesses or foliage.

You don't have to be afraid of getting lost in this labyrinth of streets, just remember uphill is the *Acropolis* and downhill Syndagma Square."

Zach took her arm to guide her along. "Breathe deeply, you'll notice the air is cleaner here, scented by the flowers all around you. Palm trees shade the streets, and there's no car traffic. It keeps the pollution level low."

Alethea was breathless from her uphill exertion, her face flushed and glowing. She looked so edible, he could picture her as a feast spread out for his enjoyment to bite, lick, and taste. He yearned to devour her with his lust.

He led them to another square. This one was crammed with tables and chairs spilling out from the small cafes. It buzzed with people, most of them tourists. The aromas from the *tavernas,* with their charcoaled meats, whetted their appetites.

Alethea charmed, looked around as they passed several ancient buildings.

"This," she pointed to the ruins, "is what I thought Athens would look like, and not the modern city that we saw while driving from the airport."

Zach stopped and glanced around, as if seeing it for the first time, through a visitor's eyes. "I come here searching for interesting things and rarely remember how old everything is. If you think about it," he paused, "it's mind boggling. These buildings have been here for thousands of years, the ancient Greeks walked these streets. *That's* what attracts the worldwide tourists."

He took Alethea's hand. They strolled together, until they reached a small exclusive dinner club, right on Plaka Square. The club's name, carved in wood, hung over the ornately carved double doors. Once inside they sat at a corner table with a good view of the stage.

"The show will start soon," Zach commented, "I'm sure you'll enjoy it."

"I'm sure I will." She let her eyes roam around the room. Large painted murals decorated the walls, depicting scenes from ancient Greece, with temples and statues of gods as a major theme. "We go to Astoria in New York when we want a taste of Greece. The places are much like this."

"Yes, the decor isn't original, but," he shrugged, "it creates atmosphere. The tourists eat it up." He spotted the waiter approaching with the order. "Here's the food, eat and enjoy. Strictly speaking, you can't call it Greek food, much of it is a blending of Greek and Turkish cuisine."

Alethea watched the server place the food on the table. "Hmm, I didn't know that." She held up her fork, "here's to food, whatever its origin." She speared a piece of eggplant.

Zach's scent, she had noticed, was a unique blend of cinnamon and patchouli, one reminiscent of the Far East. It mingled with the food odors threatening to overcome her senses.

He started on his salad while he watched Alethea. She radiated beauty, her innate grace captivated him. He ordered drinks, the room quieted, darkened and the show began.

The plucking notes of a bouzouki filled the air and three male dancers were spotlighted dancing the Syrtaki to the tune of Zorba. They finished to a roar of applause.

Alethea glanced sideways at Zach. She liked his broad shoulders and lithe athletic frame, liked watching him from under her half closed eye lids.

A man with two female dancers started performing Shake It a song made popular by the recent Eurovision Song Contest.

The singer finished the song; the waiter brought their drinks.

"Did you rest at all?" Zach asked. "You must have some jet lag." He looked at her over his glass. "We're seven hours ahead here. It takes a while to adjust to the time difference."

"I hadn't meant to, but yes I did." She sipped her drink. "After your call, I lay down for a few moments.

Before I realized it, I slept." She moved, managing to turn so that Zach got a better look at her profile with all its subtle curves.

"That happens especially after a long trip." He watched her noticing her maneuvers. "Do you like the show? There's more *bouzouki* music."

"Yes it's wonderful," she crossed her legs, then bent down to rub her ankle, showing a good deal of cleavage. "A mosquito must have bitten me." She finished rubbing her leg, drawing attention to her body.

Alethea leaned back in her chair.

He gave her an intent look filled with meaning. "You're an attractive woman, but I have a feeling you like to play games," he paused and sipped his drink, letting the tension build between them. "If that's true, I'll be only too happy to oblige."

Alethea toyed with her drink. "What game would you like to play?" She gave him a subtle glance as she lifted her glass.

"I'm not good at game playing—chess bores me, checkers too, and card games are tedious." She took a sip, "What else can we play?"

"Cat and mouse," he smiled. "That innocent girl act," he shook his head, "it's good, but you're a grown woman. You know what I mean."

"Maybe."

He thought a moment before taking her hand, all amusement gone from his voice.

"Don't provoke me. Don't tease me with your body and not come through with its promises."

"You're making me feel like I'm out of my depth," Alethea said. "A woman has the right to be sexy and

67

provocative. I mean, it's not my brain you're interested in, is it?" She looked at her hand resting in his and sighed. She pulled her hand away and lifted her drink.

"It's a dangerous game. Before you start a blaze, you'd better know how to quench it," he gave her a narrow look. "What exactly do you want from a man?"

The sweet notes of a Greek flute were heard then a drummer joined in. The music took on a lively beat. Both turned to the stage pausing their conversation. Dancers in traditional dress started performing—stomping, twirling jumping in the air to the music.

"I want him to appreciate me and to need me." Alethea licked her lips, and sipped her drink.

Zach raised an eyebrow. What a vision she was. Creamy white shoulders, lovely breasts barely contained, a small waist, and long, long legs. She was definitely appealing and exciting.

He moved closer, casually placed his arm on the back of her chair.

"All's fair in love and lust." Alethea remarked. She lifted her wine, breathed in its aroma, and sipped it.

"It's chilly in here—too much air conditioning. I should have brought a wrap." She put her drink down and slowly, seductively caressed her bare arms. She turned toward him.

"What exactly do you want from a woman?"

"She obeys me." He lifted his hand and placed it on her shoulder.

"If she commits herself to pleasing me then we might have a relationship."

"Then all you need is a slave."

"No, I want someone who respects me and doesn't play games."

"Respect and obey are not the same things. When you say obey, you're just ordering someone around. Respect has to be earned."

Ignoring his hand on her shoulder, she looked around the room and noticed most of the tables had filled.

"My older sisters tried to order *me* around or manipulate me in countless ways." He moved closer.

"Maybe that's why you're so wary of women."

"Not wary, no. I just don't want to be involved on an emotional level."

Gently he stroked her shoulder. "I love your skin—so soft and smooth, like silk." His voice was soft, seductive, but with a firm edge.

"What I want is a physical relationship, just sex, with no strings attached." He looked at her sitting there next to him, so cool.

"I'll respect you, spend money on you, take you on cruises, on vacations, buy you expensive presents and show you a good time."

"That sounds almost like prostitution."

He thought a moment. "It's not prostitution. I don't pay to have sex, I don't have to."

She lifted her head. "That's a fine distinction. You might pay indirectly, but you're still paying."

"Not if I give because I want to give. That keeps things from getting too serious. As long as I'm not using you, I don't have to feel guilty."

"I see," she raised her eyebrows. "I think I see."

On the stage a man was preparing to sing.

"He must be well known," she commented, as a sudden hush came over the place.

Aware of him next to her, she felt his hand like a brand on her shoulder. She smelled his scent and thought of the Orient, with all its intrigues. He mystified her and surprised her with his honesty. He didn't play guessing games. He had put all his cards on the table. If she wanted to play she knew just what to expect.

She wondered if she wanted to play. The singer finished his program to a loud roar of applause. The room quieted once more and murmurs of conversation started up adding a soft cadence of sound to the room.

"Who's the singer?" Alethea asked. "He seems popular."

"Paris Vassos. He came tonight as a special favor to the owner. This is where he got his start. He always finds time to stop by when he's in town."

"He's got a fine deep, voice. I can see why he's famous."

"That attracts you in a man, his voice?" Zach asked.

"Yes, along with the rest of his qualities."

"Most women are interested in a man for his affluence and status. That attracts them more than his physical appearance."

"Yes, well, women are not all the same. We have different needs."

"What are your needs?" Zach asked.

"I'd like a good time, no strings attached. I'm not looking to marry a man just because we go out. His bank account doesn't interest me."

Her eyes sparkled, and she smiled. "I think I like your attitude—you know, live for the moment, no deep thinking or deep emotions.

The novelty, the excitement, and the potential risk in a relationship, that's what I like. It stirs up the chemicals in my brain, exciting me. I'm not looking to fall in love."

Just then they were interrupted by a young dark haired girl in a long dress. She couldn't be more than twelve years old and had a basket of gardenias on her arm.

"Please *mistuh* buy a flower for *th* lady," she gave him a pathetic look with wide black eyes, and whined, "please *mistuh* they smell real nice, buy one for *yor* lady."

Zach selected a flower corsage. "You're too young to be out on the streets doing this. You should be home in bed." He narrowed his eyes and scowled.
"Is someone forcing you to sell flowers?"

"No *mistuh,* no, it's alright." She pocketed the money and glanced furtively over her shoulder. Ignoring customers at other tables, she hurried from the club.

Through the large glass window, they saw her get into a new BMW. She said something to the driver and they sped away.

Alethea stunned, turned to Zach. "What was that all about?"

"Gangs operate in Athens—they've brought a lot of children over from the Albanian border. The kids peddle goods on the street.

You can't stop at a traffic light without having two or three children trying to sell you something or trying to wash your window. They're exploiting these children, especially now, with all these tourists coming for the Olympic Games."

"That's too bad," Alethea shrugged pretending indifference. "She didn't seem to mind what she was doing."

"That's your reaction," he gave her an annoyed glance, "you don't care about them."

Thinning her eyes, she gave it a thought, "I try not to think about these things too much. Worrying gives me wrinkles."

"You're joking, right?" Zach exclaimed, appalled. "Feeling for another human being's suffering isn't about having an opinion," he pointed out, "or about being brainy. It's about having compassion."

"So if I disagree with what you're thinking, I'm opinionated, argumentative, and bossy. Like I said, the girl didn't look unhappy. She was driven away in an expensive car. So who's being exploited?"

She gave her head a shake. "Anyway, men don't like smart women, so since I'd rather have a man, than not, I can be dumb and helpless, and say what he wants to hear."

He shrugged his shoulders. "It's true. A helpless woman makes me feel more like a man. But I don't like stupid women, either. It's nice to have a balance, you know, brains and a body too." He glanced around. Most of the tables were emptying.

"I didn't realize it was so late. We'd better go. I'd like to take you to see the Acropolis in the morning. You got a glimpse of it on the way here, but we should climb up to the top. We have to start early, before the sun gets too hot."

Chapter 11

"Hello, who's this?" Alethea answered, groggy with sleep.

"It's Zachary. Wake up lovely lady, you can't come to Greece and not see the Acropolis. We're going sightseeing—remember?"

"What time is it?" She snapped awake, and sat up in bed. "It feels like I just got to sleep."

"Nine o'clock, jet lag must have caught up with you. My fault. I kept you out too late showing you Athens. Get dressed. I'll be there in half an hour and we'll have breakfast together."

"No make it forty-five minutes. I'll meet you in the lobby."

A little stunned by his forcefulness, she took a quick shower, then tossed on a shirt, a pair of shorts and sandals, and rushed out of the room.

Downstairs, Zachary was already pacing back and forth.

Damn, she thought she'd make it down before he came. "Hi, you got here fast. Do you do everything so quickly?"

"No, I'm slow when I have to be," he winked, "I can make the moment last."

She lifted her eyebrow, gave him a look, and wondered at his odd comment. "Let's have breakfast. I could use some coffee."

"Breakfast coming up," he took her arm and led her to the buffet.

Sipping her coffee, Alethea savored its rich pungent flavor.

"Why the rush? I thought people did things slowly here in Greece," She spooned yogurt into her mouth. "You know there's regular time, and then there's Greek time."

"I don't want it to get too late." Zach looked up from his food. "The way you talk, one would think you weren't Greek. Both your parents and grandparents were Greek, that makes you Greek, too."

"I love Greece, with its ancient history, and I'm proud of my roots, but...." She shook her head.

"What does it matter, we're all people. America is made up of immigrants from all over the world. Almost every nation is represented."

"It matters when people try to exploit these immigrants, or abuse them."

"Why do you say that?" she asked. "What do you know about it?"

"It's a problem here. Immigrants come, some legally, some not.

We're a melting pot. They come for a better life, or as a stepping-stone into other countries." He bit into his toast. "Not long ago, a captain caught in a storm, tossed the illegal immigrants on his ship overboard. Bodies started washing up causing horror all over the world, but especially in Greece. All the papers ran pictures of these unfortunate men, women and children."

"That's shocking." Alethea, paralyzed for a moment, saw it all.

The captain and crew push the migrants into two rickety life boats. She can see the terror on their faces.

The young children cling to their mother's legs, the older boys are with their fathers. One woman dashes free, and rushes to the captain, grabbing him and babbling. The drunken captain pushes her away.

Another man holds his head high, cursing them all as the boat shudders and groans. The wind lashes at it, causing it to tip dangerously. The crew lowers the life boats and grabs the remaining immigrants. They struggle, but it does no good.

They are flung overboard to their certain death. She can see the waves engulfing them—tossing them back and forth, submerging them. Some swim toward the boats, but the boats fare no better. They capsize and spew their load into the churning waters. Others struggle to stay afloat. The storm tossed sea claims its victims.

Alethea came back to herself, shaken, and found Zach watching her.

"You didn't hear a word I said, did you?" He shook his head. "I just told you how my brother-in-law involved me in this illegal entry business, using this event as bait."

"Sorry, my mind wandered for a moment." She played with her spoon, staring into space.

"You still look a little odd. Are you o.k.?"

Alethea nodded.

He cleared his throat, then took a breath.

"Anyway, Mitch persuaded me to assist on this case even though I no longer work in the Special Services." He drank some water. "He told me my knowledge of shipping and my contacts in the industry would be useful. I can be involved without giving the game away." He thought of the undercover detectives he had planted in the shipping world, hoping to expose those who were behind the atrocities.

"Now *you* seem distracted…is something wrong?" Alethea asked.

"No, it's all right." He shrugged his shoulders and put down his glass. "Just thinking about business."

He smiled crookedly. "As I said, I'd like us to see the Acropolis in the morning hours." He took the last bite of his roll and looked at her. "Finish up."

"You're in a big hurry, aren't you?" She put her spoon down and glared at him. "Since you woke me this morning, I haven't had a chance to breathe. It's been rush, rush, rush."

"You'll see the Acropolis, the view of Athens, and feel its history. It'll be worth it."

"You're *not* going to give me another history lesson, are you?"

"No, but after your visit, you should read about it."

"What do you like about history?"

"I like people and reading about how they lived years ago." He raised his brows, "don't you ever wonder what life was like in different centuries?"

"Believe me, I can see them first hand, in this lifetime," she commented cryptically, "and it doesn't make me happy."

"Really. Are you telling me you can see back in time?"

Startled, she looked up, afraid she had given away her secrets. "No …no of course not, who ever heard of such a thing? No one can see history as it happens."

Zach peered at her from under his eyelids. "That would be strange." He gave her a beguiling smile. "Let's get going before it gets too hot."

After a short drive through the narrow city streets in the older part of Athens, they started walking toward the ruins of the Acropolis which loomed overhead.

Alethea stared up, overwhelmed by the magnificence of the buildings.

"We're almost there. The stairs are at its west end, it's the only way to get in. This gate is the access point. The other three sides are totally inaccessible."

Alethea followed Zach.

"Careful," he took her arm, "we have all these stairs to climb."

They went through the ancient gate, and found themselves on top of the Acropolis.

They paused to catch their breath, and to gaze at the ancient structures.

Seeing the Greek flag flying at one end, Alethea went toward it and peered out over the view of Athens, spread out below.

Zachary came up behind her, pressed into her as he looked over her shoulder. "That's Mount Lycabettos, and over there, you can see the Aegean and the ferry-boats leaving for the islands."

For a moment, she was only aware of him, his body solid at her back, his arousal pressing into her.

She was too caught up by his presence to speak. All she could do was feel.

"It's something, isn't it?" She answered, once she had her emotions under control.

"You're something," he whispered in her ear. "You smell sweet, like flowers in the spring."

"You're giving me goose bumps." she giggled

"Concentrate on the scenery. On a clear day you can see the Isthmus of Corinth."

Zach turned her around, drawing her near. He couldn't resist. Like a lure she drew him closer. He stared at her, his eyes roaming over her face, stopping at her mouth.

He leaned forward as if mesmerized, licking around it, nibbling at its corners, until he finally pressed his lips on hers in an electrifying kiss.

Shocked to her toes with sensations, she stood dazed. Then she gathered herself together, not wanting him to know how much the kiss affected her. She smiled at him, brushed a lock from his face and licked her lips. "Cinnamon, you taste like cinnamon."

Breaking the moment, she took his hand. "I want to see the Parthenon and the rest of the buildings."

They admired the columns of Pentelic marble reaching into the sky, a marvel of symmetry still studied by architects. Among camera snapping enthusiasts, they wandered toward the Erectheon with its women statues standing guard.

"There's a story behind this building if you want to hear it. It's said that Athena and Poseidon engaged in a contest. The winner was named the patron of the city."

Alethea raised her eyebrows, afraid Zach would start on another lecture. To distract him, she purposely fell against him, pressing herself into his body. "Sorry I tripped," she grabbed his arm and straightened up.

Zach, sidetracked by her curves pressed into his body, stopped talking. "Why do I get the feeling I'm wasting my breath." He cast her a quick glance as she continued to lean on him.

"Take a look, the five maidens are actually copies-four are in the Acropolis museum and the fifth is in the British museum."

"Why is one of them in the British museum?" Alethea asked innocently, thinking. *He wanted to kiss me. Let him suffer a bit.* She turned toward some Japanese tourists, led by a tour guide, who was giving a similar speech about the maidens.

"It's quite an international sight," she observed. "There're tourists here from all over the world."

She tugged at Zach's arm. "What did the tour guide say about Lord Elgin? I couldn't hear it."

"Lord Elgin, the British Ambassador to Turkey in the early 1800's, made a deal with the Turks to buy parts of the Acropolis." He took a deep breath, his body heating up with her nearness.

"The Turks sold him one of the ladies, a frieze from the Parthenon, and many other artifacts.

Since they owned Greece at the time, no one complained." He stroked her hand resting on his arm. "Elgin turned around and sold them to the British museum and the Elgin Marble controversy was born." Sighing, he tightened his lips, "Greece wants her treasures back, and England refuses to give them up, straining the relationship between the two countries."

"Isn't that like someone stealing a Picasso then selling it to someone else who knows it's stolen, but doesn't really care because he now owns the Picasso?"

"That's why there's a controversy about the whole thing, and a big effort being made to get them back." He put his arm around her, drawing her close as he led her to the Temple of Nike.

Alethea felt his hard body against hers causing the most delicious feeling. "This is such a rocky road, I'd better hold on to you, I'm afraid I'll slip again."

She drew even closer as he led her around the whole of the Acropolis, taking the path followed by the ancients in their holy processions.

"I'm exhausted." Alethea sat down on a column and rubbed her sore feet.

Zach wiped the moisture off his brow. "It's starting to blister here, we'd better start back."

They made their way down the stairs, and entered a near-by coffee shop.

They ordered *frappe*, a Greek version of cold instant coffee and cheese pies *(tiropetas)*. While they waited, they admired the splendid view of the Acropolis, framed by the window.

"What an experience." Alethea leaned forward, pulling her shirt out to cool her sweated skin. "All those ancient buildings standing after so many centuries." She fanned herself with the menu.

"I warned you." He raised his brows. "The heat is overwhelming at this hour. That's why they have siestas here." A waiter placed their order before them.

Alethea sipped her *frappe*. "I'm used to Greek dishes, but this frappe is new to me."

"When Nestle first came out with frozen instant coffee, *Nescafe* was born. The *frappe,* is the Greeks' unique way of serving it."

She cast him a sidelong glance as she bit into her *tiropeta. He's delicious… that kiss mmm fine.* Damn that sixth sense of hers, she could tell he was going to be an important part of her life.

Zachary watched her, flattered by the attention. Something was building between them—she intrigued him, and he wanted her. Very much.

"We'll take a drive to Cape Sounion. We can explore the area and enjoy the cool briny breezes. It's famous for the ruins of two temples—one to Athena and the other to Poseidon."

Never one to say no to an adventure, she gave him her most beguiling smile. "More breathtaking sights… sounds delightful. Do I get another history lesson?"

"Probably," he grinned sheepishly, "you know I can't resist them. Finish up."

He navigated the busy streets, found the road that paralleled the sea, giving them a view of the beaches and clubs that lined it.

The road became more dangerous, with each sharp turn. Frightened by the curving roads, she almost panicked when they went through a narrow tunnel, with visibility almost nil. *How many accidents have happened here?* She wondered as she looked down and saw a steep drop into the water.

When they reached the cape, they could see the temples facing the Aegean. He parked the car. They climbed toward the ruins and started to explore.

"Zachary, look, Lord Byron left his name on this column."

Coming close, he ran his hand over the carving. "He came to Greece to help the freedom fighters who

were trying to liberate themselves from Turkish rule."
He waved his arm around.

"Unfortunately, he wasn't the only one," he walked around, scowling, "see all the carvings, left by scores of tourists. They've desecrated the place."

He looked down at her.

She sat on one of the columns, and observed the twin peaks of the mountains opposite.

"The colors are so vibrant," she exclaimed, "the aqua of the sea, the browns from the earth, the clear blue of the sky, the bright yellow sun."

"Sunset and sunrise are especially spectacular here. The whole area is splashed in brilliant shades of red, orange, and pink. The sea sparkles with it."

He leaned against a nearby column, and appreciated her profile against the dramatic scenery.

"There's a small *taverna* nearby, we'll go eat there, and then come back. It's something you don't want to miss."

They drove down a ways, and stopped at the eatery. Walking out on to a wooden platform they sat at a table covered with a red-checkered tablecloth. The platform jutted into the water and rocked with the waves, lapping rhythmically below.

"It's quiet—not many customers." She laid her hands on the table, and looked around.

"It's early. Most places fill up after nine." He called over the waiter. "Let's see what the specialty of the day is."

He perused the menu. "Do you like fish? They have what's equivalent to the red mullet, it's called *barbounia*. It's entirely unique. I recommend it."

"I like fish, especially if it's fresh," she looked out at the sea. "They must take one of those fishing boats out every day."

She took off her sunglasses, and stared into his hazel eyes. She wondered what he was thinking and wondered, too, what he thought of her.

"I ordered some traditional Greek appetizers that I'm sure you'll like—fried potatoes, fried squash and a fried cheese.

What would you like to drink?"

He speculated about her thoughts. They had spent the day together, but had avoided exchanging any personal information.

"A nice cold beer," interjected Alethea, "seems just about right."

"Good choice. Make that two cold beers. Mythos if you have it."

The waiter took the order down, then left.

"Good thing it's a tourist area," Zachary explained, "the charcoal's hot, ready for grilling. Otherwise we'd have to wait to eat."

"You did say they like to eat after nine, so I wondered why they were serving."

She gazed around her. "But I can see your point. Look there are some tourists here from the ruins. I guess they're going to go back to see the sunset."

"They'd be foolish not to, it's a memorable sight."

She had fastened her hair on top of her head with a clip, loose tendrils framed her face.

He noticed how it seemed to absorb and reflect the sunlight. Her skin was pale, delicate as porcelain, white but for a slight redness under her eyes.

"You should be careful, you've gotten a slight sunburn."

"I didn't even notice, it doesn't hurt." Alethea ran her hands over her face, and down her arms. She felt the heat radiating from her skin. "I'll put some lotion on it when I get back."

"It's becoming, you were too pale. You must work inside a lot." He leaned back in his chair. "What do you do? Are you here on vacation or business?"

She drank some of her water and gathered her thoughts. What had she said to him on the airplane when he asked her a similar question? She tried to recollect.

"Research, I came to do research." She remembered.

"What kind of research?" Zach asked as he sipped his beer.

Now what? She hated telling lies, hated having to remember what lies she told. She valued honesty, but didn't like people knowing she was a private investigator or that she was psychic.

Thinking quickly, she cried.

"Flamingoes, I've come to study the flamingoes of Skalla Kalloni, on the island of Lesvos. The salt pans in Kalloni are filled with Great Flamingoes, Red-footed falcons, gray and purple Heron and other amazing birds." Alethea elaborated. "The government has designated certain areas on Lesvos as protected territories. Birds can't be trapped or hunted, thus preserving the natural habitat of many migratory birds that are also of interest to me." Luckily, she had gotten a guide book about Lesvos so she could be better prepared for her trip, and remembered reading something about flamingoes and birdwatchers.

"You're a birdwatcher?" He gave her a skeptical glance, then raised his eyebrow. She was rambling, a sure sign she was probably lying.

"No, not exactly, I'm doing an article on them for a magazine. I'm a free-lance writer and sell my work to different periodicals."

"So, you're a writer?"

They were interrupted by the waiter bearing a tray with their fish.

Relieved, she appreciated the scents of the food while ignoring his last question.

"This food smells so good. Let's see, there's oregano, onion, a strong garlic smell, and the charcoal aroma from the fish is making me hungry," she remarked, watching the waiter place the plates on the table.

"You have a good nose for scents, not everyone can separate them as you do."

"Yes, I guess I do." She gave him a radiant smile.

Secrets, he could smell them with the aroma of the food. A hungry man, he was determined to satisfy his appetite.

Interested and intrigued from the first minute he saw her, he wouldn't let her truthfulness, or lack of it, stand in his way.

He started serving the food.

"This is some coincidence. Lesvos is where we have our summer home. We live in Petra, which is not far from Kalloni, so we'll certainly see each other. In fact, you can take me bird watching with you."

He placed some fish on her plate, and waited for her reaction.

Now what—caught in her lie, she'd have to play it by ear, if and when the time came. "Yes, I'm sure you'll be thrilled to death to go bird watching," she said, mockingly. She knew he was baiting her.

"Only, I'll be watching you instead of the birds." Zach said.

I'm in trouble, she thought, giving herself a silent warning, *each lie is getting me in deeper*. "This fish is fabulous. I've never tasted anything quite like it. You were right." She paused with her fork in the air, "You know one thing I like about you?"

"What?"

"You asked what I wanted, most men just order without caring if it's something I'd like. They just make the decision and that's that."

"I've been well trained. I'm familiar with the female mind and don't disregard it." He took a bite of his fish. "Don't get me wrong, I love women. They excite and exasperate me, as well as exhilarate and exhaust me in that order."

Alethea, surprised, gave him a questioning look.

"I'll explain." Zach added, putting down his fork. "A woman uses her body. She excites me with her glance, her dress, and her movements. She allows a peek at her breast, a glimpse of her thigh."

Zach leaned toward Alethea. "She tempts me to begin the chase, and I, the hunter, oblige. I pursue, she retreats. Exasperation sets in." He leaned back, and lifted his hands. "She plays coy as if she's not interested. She tantalizes without allowing a touch—when she feels she's hooked me, the fish, she reels me in by surrendering." Smiling, he nodded

"That's when I become exhilarated. I finally get her where I want her—in my bed, with all her luscious charms, to enjoy. And believe me after all my efforts, I enjoy. Until I reach the last stage—exhaustion." He sipped his beer.

"I'm satisfied, sapped of all my strength, and sanity returns. The hunt begins again, only hers, not mine. She uses her body as a lure. Until I'm exhausted, again, trying to escape the trap she's laid, with her sexuality as bait."

Zach popped some fried cheese in his mouth.

"You certainly make yourself clear on this man - woman thing." Alethea said, amused by his little speech.

"I'm not looking for a man to marry if that's what scares you, but I do like attracting men. I love the idea of romance, I'm not ashamed of that. It makes me feel *bad*." She raised an eyebrow and drank her beer.

Zachary studied her.

Alethea glanced up from the fish on her plate and caught his eye.

She decided to have some fun. She swallowed her fish, fitted a small round tomato into her mouth and bit into it, licking the juices off her lips. She watched him.

She picked up a long slice of cucumber, and dipped it into the garlic mix. Sucking on it, she drew out its juices and looked into his eyes with a teasing glint.

Zach gave her a sharp look—*she's tempting the tiger, deliberately stirring me up, getting me aroused. She can't be an innocent, if she's so blatantly baiting me.* He took a sip of his beer, finished his fish, and silently dabbed his mouth with a napkin.

The waiter came over with a complimentary plate of seasonal fruit—watermelon, grapes and peaches, along with the bill.

"This fruit is refreshing. Do they always serve complimentary fruit after the food?"

"Usually, either fruit or a *halva* made by the house."

"Nice custom. I appreciate it." She passed her tongue over her lips, savoring the last lick of watermelon.

He watched her tongue. Wishing it were licking him, savoring him in all his interesting places. He wondered how he was going to lure her to his apartment.

Alethea watched the heated, hungry looks he gave her. No doubt about it. She had woken the tiger.

She closed her eyes.

What happens now? Jeez, psyche, some advice would be welcome about now, or some warning.

Chapter 12

Zachary's penthouse apartment was located on the top floor of an office building his family owned, across from the dock of Piraeus.

"I'd like to show you my etchings."

After seeing the spectacular sunset, back at the ruins, with its striking colors, Alethea had mentioned what a beautiful picture it made, how she would love painting it. She felt addicted to art, loved going to museums and viewing the masters.

He suggested they have a drink at his place. He had some interesting pieces to show her.

She didn't object.

At the door to his apartment, he wondered at her easy surrender. Did she make a habit of going to strange men's flats?

"Well, here we are. I collect only originals, mostly new artists of exceptional talent, but as you can see there is a Monet, a Picasso, and a Renoir."

He walked toward the glass doors and drew the drapes open allowing the breeze from the sea to cool the rooms.

Alethea stepped out onto the balcony. "What a remarkable view. The night's filled with lights. Look how the moonbeams twinkle on the sea."

They stood at the rail looking down at the scene below. Cars and buses moved like snails in the night, boats filled, and embarked to destinations unknown. He took her hand and led her back inside.

"Take your shoes off," Zach said, "you'll be more comfortable." He removed his own shoes and placed them together.

"What a lovely antique Chinese screen." She stroked it lightly. "The carvings remain remarkable after all this time."

Barefoot, she toured the room, stopping to look at the lit paintings on the walls. A cushioned burgundy sofa beckoned her. She nestled into it, appreciating its softness.

Zachary, amused by her obvious pleasure, walked to the bar. "What would you like to drink?"

"Vermouth, sweet vermouth with ice—if you have it."

A model of a finely crafted clipper ship sat on the mantelpiece. Above it, she saw a painting of a ship outlined by the setting sun done in muted tans and golden browns

"It's hard to look around this room without the unusual, or rare catching your eye." She leaned back, and sighed. "It's like having your own museum."

"Yes, I'm a collector, antiques are my passion."

Drinks in hand, he sat next to her, his thigh pressed against hers. He placed the drinks on a table made from an old ship's wheel. Reaching under it, to a hidden shelf below, he pulled out a book covered in black cloth.

Alethea watched, curious, as she sipped her drink.

He opened the bag. "I've made some unusual finds, like this book." He took it out of its velvet sack and laid it on the table in front of her.

"It might interest you. It's about a hundred years old, and has some unusual drawings."

Alethea stared at the ancient book. The tooled maroon leather cover was embossed with gold. She admired its craftsmanship, as she ran her hands over its intricate designs. She turned the gold-edged pages, her eyes widening with each picture. Her head shot up in shock.

"Why, it's an old book of pornography! The sketches are skillfully executed, but they're so detailed, so lewd." She tried not to show her embarrassment, but she could feel her face heating.

Despite this, she couldn't stop looking. Driven by curiosity, she turned the page and scrutinized the carefully drawn sketches, each richly penned and lustfully illustrated. "Such strange positions." She widened her eyes, "they don't look possible."

Althea turned the last page, looked up and caught his eye. "Is this the way you seduce your dates… with a pornographic book? This is," she shook her head, "…so not worthy of you."

Slamming the book shut, she stabbed him with her eyes. "Is this supposed to heat my blood so I'll fall all over you?" She shook her head. "This is *not* going to happen.

I'm sorry if I gave you the wrong impression." She scanned him. "I don't have sex with strangers, no matter how appealing. You're out of luck, chum. I just thought you should know, up front, so you don't call me a tease. *"*

"But you are a tease. You did everything to give me the wrong impression." He bent toward her and narrowed his eyes. "You enticed me—your body language excited me. You moved - boy did you move, so I'd get

91

a glimpse of your breasts, your legs, your tempting curves. That dress last night… you knew what it would do to me. In the plane you even spilt the water on me to get my attention. And what about that act at the *taverna?* Don't tell me you're not interested."

His brows knitted in a scowl. "Are you saying you didn't encourage me," he put the book under the table, "that I misunderstood the signals you gave me?" He moved closer.

"Not exactly. I find you attractive, and maybe I did encourage you," she shrugged. "So what?" Backing into the cushions, she gave him a little smile. "I like it when men find me desirable. It doesn't mean I'll have same day sex with them."

She placed her arm on the back of the sofa. Posing, she gave him the once over while she showed off her body. "I like the sexual tension—the smile, the touch and heated looks. And, I like to neck and pet, but you were just too blatant with your erotic etchings."

Alethea flickered her eyes, put her hand to her chin, and puckered her lips. "Honey, you got me so hot, I can't wait to jump you." She simpered in a stage falsetto. "Really… what did you think?"

Angered by her sarcastic tone, he grabbed her by the shoulders. "You like to prod the tiger. You're playing a dangerous game by coming to an unknown man's apartment in the middle of the night. How do you know that a man will respect your wishes, and not take you anyway?"

"I know. I can tell."

"Bullshit! You can't tell anything. Of all the asinine things I've heard, that's the stupidest. How old are you anyway?" Not waiting for an answer, he answered himself. "The age of consent I'm sure." He took her into his arms and started kissing her.

Startled, she kissed him back, allowing his tongue to play with her mouth until she opened giving him entrance, wanting more of those marvelous feelings.

Distracted by his kiss, she barely realized his hand had slid under her shirt, unfastening her bra until she felt the cool air on her breasts.

His hands caressed her, played with her.

"Damn—that feels good." She wiggled, trying to get closer. "Please-don't-stop." She felt the excitement burgeoning inside her with each caress.

"Your breasts are beautiful." He leaned back and looked her over. "You're beautiful—perfect in every way." He took each breast, held it. Bending, he took her nipple, licked it, enfolding it between his lips. "You like that."

Her insides clenched and she closed her eyes. Her sensitive nipples burst with feelings.

He's making me crazy. He's doing such amazing things...Oh my God. Inundated with sensation, she stopped fighting him.

He undressed her, and himself, in record time. Naked, their bodies entwined, he continued to caress her, not giving her time to think or protest.

His animal side evoked, blood pumping through his veins, he'd turned into a predator, and she his prey. Her lips glistened, her eyes filled with passion.

Too hungry to stop, he devoured her with kisses. He moved like a locomotive, going full speed, unstoppable.

Spread out on the couch under him, Alethea tried to catch her breath. His hands were everywhere. She panicked.

"Stop! Get off me. I don't want this. I just met you." She pushed hard against his chest, and tried to shove him off her.

"*Fuck (GAMOTO)!*" Stunned, he lifted himself up on his hands, and looked down at her face, her excited face, flushed with desire.

"You're kidding, right. You can't lead a man on, then say— Stop." He gritted his teeth. He didn't know if he had the strength to release her.

He looked down into her angry amethyst eyes, felt himself getting annoyed. Combined with his sexual frustration, he was at a volatile point

"You're a tease."

"No I'm not."

"Yes you are. You start something that you have no intention of finishing… *that* makes you a tease. What is it with you? Do you feel a sexual thrill when a man slobbers over you, and you control the game? Stop, start - like pushing buttons - is that how it is?"

He got off her, and threw her a contemptuous look. "At least you're a real blond."

"Of course I'm a real blond." She covered herself with her hand, embarrassed. "I don't understand why you're so angry. Why are you looking at me like that?"

She sat up and reached for her clothes. "I told you I like men and their attentions. So what's the problem?"

"There's no problem." He straightened, folded his arms and arched an eyebrow. "In fact you're normal, it's normal to want to be kissed, and petted.

What's not normal is stopping when we're both so aroused, and having a philosophical discussion about it when we're both nude."

"Sorry—this is awkward, I know, and I - always mean to finish what I start," she hesitated, then gave a little shrug, "but at the last minute a little voice in my head says - don't. So I stop, but it has nothing to do with you."

She leaned her head to the side, examining him from head to toe. "You look splendid nude, you've muscle in all the right places. You're one fine specimen."

He narrowed his eyes, not believing the idiotic thing she had just said.

"Women—none of you have any sense when it comes to men. When a man's aroused he thinks with his dick and not his brain.

You don't know what a man's capable of when aroused. But since I'm a gentleman, you can either go home or sleep inside." With that, he put her over his shoulder and carried her into his bedroom.

"Put me down you jerk. Stop manhandling me." She tried to get control as she pummeled his back. "Let go of me, you lummox."

Tossing the spread off his huge bed, he threw her on it. Outlined against his black and white sheets, she made a fetching picture as moonlight played over her body in all its naked splendor.

"What are you doing?" She grabbed the sheet and pushed herself up on her elbows.

"Leaving you alone. I'll get your clothes. You can dress yourself and take a taxi home, or stay and I'll take you home in the morning. Close the door. You'll have the privacy you need."

"Wait!"

"Darling, I've suddenly become deaf and dumb."

"But you're angry—that's not what I wanted."

"What did you want?" He asked. "Never mind." Threading his hand through his hair, he closed his eyes. "Sorry, but you bring out the worst in me. I'm tired of this game of yours." He glared down at her. "And we're not having this conversation with you sitting there na- ked. I'll get your things."

Zachary turned his back on her and went to get her clothes.

I didn't want him to stop. What's wrong with me? At this rate I'll be a career virgin. Alethea, dazed, shook her head. *Is that what I want? No way. I want to have hot, crazy sex and—with him. It's about time things changed. I'm such an idiot.*

Zachary walked back into the room wearing his shorts. He put her things on the bed and turned to leave.

"Wait, let me explain."

"What's there to explain? You said *no*—that's it. No other explanation's needed. I thought you were a woman of experience, who wanted me. I guess I read the signals wrong."

"That's the problem—I do want you. But you went too fast and I panicked," She lowered her eyes. "I've never done this before—I mean I'm still a virgin." Lift- ing her eyes, she watched him to see his reaction.

"You didn't act like a virgin." Zachary raised his eyebrows, and gave her a skeptical look.

"I got the impression that you knew what you were about."

"Well—I've had experience, but technically—I'm still a virgin."

"In other words, you've done everything but have sex." He shook his head. "I see I'm not the only poor fool you've tempted beyond reason." He stood and stared at her. "You must leave a lot of frustrated men behind."

"I don't mean to." She sat forward, and gave him an appraising glance. "But I do want you."

"You want me, your body wants me." He scanned her from head to toe. "I can see that. You're licking your lips and your eyes—they're glazed with passion. Your cheeks glow and your body's ready." He raised an eyebrow. "But why me?"

"I can feel a strong connection between us. You understand me, accept me," she leaned forward and took his hand, "most don't."

She surprised him with her statement. He looked down at his hand in hers. "Are you telling me you want…?"

"Yes." She touched her hand to his knee.

"Hold on—I'm not sure about this." He spread his arms wide, and backed away. "You're not … I mean I thought you were. Hey, I'm not good with virgins, especially ones like you."

What a mess - denying myself this? I knew he was the one when he suspected my psychic powers. Damn— what do I do now? She tried to stay calm, to concentrate. A sense of *déjà vu* swamped her. She remembered her erotic dream in the airplane—it was the same bed, the same view out the glass doors, and the same sensual appeal.

As she sat there, she became acutely aware of him. His unique male smell engulfed her. She heard his erratic breathing and it excited her.

She could sense his erotic thoughts, and they overwhelmed her. She realized their minds had attuned to each other. So why had she stopped?

And how did she make him want her again?

"Pretend I'm not a virgin." She licked her lips. "Please, I want you." She lay down and held her arms out to him. "Come."

Staring at her, laid out in front of him like a feast for his consumption, it was hard to say *no*.

"You're not going to change your mind again, are you? After all I'm only human."

His eyes roamed over her as he moved forward, stripping his shorts off in one smooth gesture. His heartbeat throbbed faster with each lick of her nipple. Its roughness tickled his tongue as he suckled and bit. His body heat increased. The blood raced through his veins. Zach bowed his head, rubbing his cheek against her belly, enjoying its smoothness. He touched, and fondled as if she were made of glass. No anger in his touch, he skimmed and stroked, delving down into her core, building a heat in her that seemed to explode into flames.

"Are you sure."

Gasping, she tried to breathe. "Yes, I'm sure. No— don't stop. I want you to ...go on."

He groaned as she licked his skin, her tongue sliding over its sensitive surface.

Zach nuzzled her neck, then kissed her eyes, her chin. Her mouth opened for him. It was sweet, welcoming.

"Did you like that?" He looked down at her face. "You're flushed." He stroked back her hair, nudged her ear. "I hope you're pleased with yourself, you turned me from a gentle man into a raging beast."

He gazed into her eyes, into their purple depths, and was lost. Closer, he brought her closer. He turned her on her side and caressed her back.

Stroking slowly, he enjoyed its smoothness as he passed over it again and again. Her buttocks were firm and yielding under his touch. He kneaded and pinched.

"Ouch ... too hard." She put her hand back to stop him.

"Sorry, but your ass is so luscious, I couldn't resist." He caressed her legs, bringing his hand higher to touch her folds, sleek with moisture. He opened and stroked her. Played with her and built her excitement. Waves of lust ebbed and swelled, reached a peak, then crashed. Her eyes lost focus. Her body shuddered and stilled.

Blood boiling, heart beating alarmingly faster, he felt ready to burst as sweat beaded on his skin. Her reddened face before him, made his heated blood hotter. He turned into her open thighs. Too hungry to allow further delay, he slowly, carefully entered her. He felt resistance, but he pushed through into her virgin passage.

Alethea tensed. She felt the invasion. A slight pinch then a slow plowing as he pressed into her core. Her muscles surrounded his length, his largeness. They pulsed, they stretched to their own rhythm. She gave him pleasure as he pleasured her.

Her passion revitalized as his passion built. She could sense his elation, could feel him tense, and then release as he reached his climax.

He felt pleasure, possession. His - no one else had enjoyed her lush body. Moving in and out, with her leg over his, he built the friction, the heat. And felt a surge of ownership as he exploded.

"Mine, only mine." Breathing heavily, he curled her body into his.

Smiling up at him, she moistened her lips. "Hey, caveman."

Lying quietly, he looked off into space thinking how complicated his life *had* just become. "Darling, I wanted a simple *affaire*, and instead I got you."

She turned to him. "Hey, there *are* no strings attached. I'm old enough to know what I want." Tapping his chest with her finger, she slowly turned the tapping into caresses as she felt every tactile inch of him.

He closed his eyes. "You shouldn't taunt a man when he's sexually aroused." He hugged her, squeezing her, "but I have to admit, you were attuned to me like no one else." He looked down at her sensual body, and wondered what kind of saint she thought he was.

"But sweetheart, you can't come to a man's apartment looking like you do, let him undress you and expect him not to pounce. You were asking for trouble."

"Why, I'm a modern woman. I make my own choices." She sighed, framing his face with her hands, "I'm not sorry, so don't you be."

"I'm not sure what to do with you."

"Don't sweat it. I have a job to do. When it's finished I'm out of here and back to the States."

"We'll see. It's not going to be easy getting rid of me. You're an intriguing woman."

"You're an exciting man." Alethea brought her hand up to the back of his neck and pulled him to meet her lips. "I want you. No strings attached." When she kissed him, she felt him tremble.

Zach took the initiative. He turned her so she lay under him. Her blond hair framed her face as it spread around her. Pushing up, he leaned back on his bent knees and looked his fill. Plump breasts, firm but graceful legs, a narrow waist and full hips, completed an erotic picture etched in his brain. He stroked to stir her passions. Lifting her knees, he placed them on his shoulders and pushed into her.

Again he sensed their connection. Her heat mingled with his, her heart rate matched his, and their breaths synchronized along with their bodies. Her pleasure, her joy, her emotions meshed with his as they rode the sexual waves.

This time he took it slow making sure they climaxed together. Satisfied she had found pleasure in his arms, he brought her close and entwined their legs. They could worry about the future tomorrow.

Chapter 13

Lost in sleep, Alethea started dreaming, not a sensual dream, but one fraught with danger.

A red-headed man was running, he kept looking over his shoulder, positive he was being followed. Sweating, panting he tried to hide, but to no avail. Somebody chased him, who wanted him dead.

"Pain, piercing pain. A pang, a twinge, a red hot iron burns with every thrust. Screaming, I'm screaming. My voice rises in pitch—louder, longer with each plunge of the blade. I can feel a jab, then a stab.

Gaping wounds cover me, they're deep, throbbing. I'm in agony. Help me someone." She bowed her back, curving it as if to avoid a blow. "It's terrible, I can't stand it. I'm covered in blood, I'm terrified. My life's seeping away."

"Alethea wake up! You're having a nightmare." Zach shook her again. "Honey, snap out of it, you're screaming in your sleep."

She blinked her eyes, took a breath, and got herself under control.

"Oh my God someone's being murdered." Trembling, she pulled her knees up, and clasped them tight to her chest.

"It's terrible. I can see him—no," she closed her eyes, "not exactly "I see his reflection. Red hair, black clothes - the name Deliverance printed on a ship in the background. He's panicked, breathing heavily. He stops—tries his cell phone, but there's no signal. He drops the phone. A man with a switch blade comes out of the shadows. Yuh filthy snitch, yuh angered boss man, the man speaks, then the stabbing starts."

Shocked, Zach at first couldn't understand what she was saying and then, made out her words.

"What do you mean? You're not stabbed, there's no blood. You're here, in bed, with me."

"No, you don't understand, it's a vision. I saw a man get stabbed, felt his pain, his fear.

These visions are the blight of my life. I can feel the person's thoughts, I become one with them, but it's not always clear. Most of the time, I can't stop what's going to happen."

Alethea gasped more air into her lungs and looked at him, "I'm sorry, I wish this hadn't happened."

Zachary placed his arm around her and brought her close. He rested against the headboard of the bed.

"Talk to me. Do you have these visions often?"

"No, something usually triggers them. It's scary because they're often not clear. I know they're important—life and death in the balance, but there's nothing I can do."

"Don't think about it." He stroked her arms, trying to soothe her.

Still panting she turned to face him. "Could I have a glass of water? My heart's racing. I can't talk anymore. Just please, water."

"Of course. I'll be right back."

"Thank you." Taking the glass, she gulped down the contents. "What an awful thing to happen. That poor man - he didn't have a chance." She closed her eyes.

"Try to relax—you're too tense." He put his arm around her.

"Damn it! I'm not tense, I'm horrified." Alethea snapped. "How can I be calm? You don't understand. All of a sudden, it's in my head—just there. But why? I don't know."

"You're rambling." He pulled her close. "Tell me what you saw. Be specific - it's vital."

She gave him an odd look, then tried to gather her visions, to remember. "I become this man. I can sense his thoughts. He's restless, unhappy about something that happened earlier in the day."

Pausing, she closed her eyes. "He's at a ship, I can clearly see the name Deliverance. The man's suspicious. I can feel," concentrating, she put her hand to her head, "something had bothered him when he was unloading it earlier in the day.

He told someone he trusted, but decided to come back at night to investigate. He's followed. Scared, he runs for his life."

Zach kissed her on the head. "You're amazing. Thank you." Looking off toward the balcony doors, he saw the sky start to lighten. "Try to get some sleep." He stood up. "I have to make an important phone call." He pulled on a pair of jeans, walked into the living room to get his cell phone, and not wanting Alethea to hear, went out onto the balcony to dial Mitch Petridis number.

The sound of the phone intruded into Mitch's deep sleep. Maro was still sleeping. He slithered out of bed, got his cell phone from his jacket pocket and went out to the kitchen, carefully closing the door behind him.

"This better be good," he whispered. "It's six o'clock in the morning. I can see the sun rising."

"Just listen and don't ask questions, I wouldn't have called if it wasn't important. "Zach ran his fingers through his hair, "and I hope my nosy sister isn't listening." He tried to put his thoughts in order.

"Leonidas is in danger, either he's been murdered or it's about to happen. You'd better send a squad car down to where the ship is docked. Do it immediately. It's going to happen on the wharf, right at the bow of the Deliverance."

"You're so sure of this that you want me to send out the police?"

"Yes, I'm sure."

"All right, I'll get on it." He hesitated a moment, "I'm not going to ask questions now, but you'd better be ready with answers later. I'll be in touch."

Mitch pocketed the phone. Maro was standing at the door.

He held his finger up to his lips. "I think your brother has gone completely mad, but in case he hasn't, I have to call the precinct to get a car out to the pier." He gave her a sharp glance. "O.K? No questions."

She shrugged her shoulders, "I can wait. I'm not unreasonable."

Chapter 14

Zachary was surprised to see Alethea up. "Hey. Why are you pacing like that? After what you just went through, you should be resting."

"I'm worried. My gift is meant to help people, and I always worry. Sometimes I'm in time, sometimes not." She turned, piercing him with her eyes. "You know what this is about. Tell me. It's because of you I had this vision."

"I was right about you. You're psychic. Don't say no. It's obvious. You gave yourself away. We're lovers now, you can confide in me." He leaned against the doorframe and crossed his arms over his chest.

"I don't publicize my psychic ability. Don't you see? People get weird about it. Some think I'm crazy, and make fun of me. Others, who believe, want to use me for my gifts.

Anyway, this isn't about me. We're wasting time. What do you know? Come on- spill it? A man's life depends on it." Muttering to herself, if he hasn't already been murdered. She turned on him. "And just because we had sex doesn't mean you own me."

"Temper! I didn't say I own you, I said we're connected. You can trust me."

"I know we're connected—that's why I had the dream. It's because of you. Something's worrying you. What is it?" She tapped her foot impatiently. "Quit stalling," she narrowed her eyes and gave him an icy stare, "tell me now."

"It's too dangerous, I really don't want you involved. Will you promise to not interfere or try anything behind my back? I already have two bothersome sisters, who don't know the meaning of fear and safety, so I insist on it." He straightened from the door and took her arm. "Do you agree?"

Alethea shook his hand off. "You're kidding, right? I am involved. You've had proof of it. I can't promise not to interfere. My gift makes me accountable. Accept it, or get out of my life."

"I'm sorry—I didn't think. Come sit with me, I'll tell you what I know." He ushered her to a lounge chair near the glass doors, and pulled another chair close. "You're not the only one who wants to help people. I got into this because I can't stand seeing innocents abused."

She read the concern in his voice. "I remember you mentioned it. A drunk captain- men, women and children tossed into the sea. That can certainly make some people want to get involved." She looked uncertain as she peered at him.

"But how are you involved?"

"I told you—I help my brother-in-law Mitch with some of his cases. I'm in shipping, so I have inside information about what goes on.

I can get facts when something suspicious happens. This man you saw is one of ours." Zachary gathered his thoughts. "He worked on one of my cruise ships to establish his identity, and hired on as a dock hand to unload the Deliverance. Our man suspected that the ship carried illegal immigrants as part of its cargo, that they smuggled them into the country that way.

107

Due to the crowds expected for the Olympic Games, Greece has tightened its border security. But our waters are still vulnerable. Desperate people will pay any price to find a home for their families." He tightened his lips. "They're in the hands of corrupt operators who bring them into the country illegally. They exploit them, turning them into virtual slaves."

Alethea lifted her hand to his face. "It's upsetting. Their hunger for money makes them monsters." She looked out the window to a calm sea reflecting a spectacular sun coming over the horizon. "I hope it's not too late to save this man."

She stood up. "I'd better get dressed. I'm still naked under your shirt." She gave him a self-conscious smile and went to get her clothes.

He watched her rear jiggle and smiled.

"How about coffee and breakfast?" He hurried to join her, and couldn't resist giving her a kiss.

"You're amorous this morning." She pulled on her blouse. "I thought all this drama would have dampened your urges." Joining him in the kitchen, she rested against the wall. "Do you need any help?"

"No, you're a guest. Just sit over there and talk to me." He indicated a small glass enclosed alcove off the kitchen.

Zachary filled the coffee maker and leaned on the counter. He gave her a blatant stare. "All I have to do is look at you and my impulses are in full swing."

Alethea gave him an enticing smile. She sat down at the table, took in the view of the sea. Watched him prepare coffee, appreciating his half - nude male torso as his muscles flexed with each movement.

He wasn't the only one with itches out of control.

Zach brought the coffee to the table and poured her a cup. He got his mug, sat across from her and took a sip. "Whew, this is strong and hot just the way I like it."

"Coffee is all I have in the morning." She started to say more, but was interrupted by the constant ringing of the doorbell.

"Aren't you going to open the door?"

"No," he said grinding his teeth, "whoever's there can just go away. It's too early for visitors."

Alethea covered her ears. "How can you ignore it? My ears are ringing from all that buzzing. Someone's shouting, can't you hear them?"

"Honey, if I let that person in, trouble will blow in with her. Believe me, we're better off this way." He shrugged his shoulders. "As far as I'm concerned, she can stay there all day."

"You said she. You know who it is?"

She lifted one eye brow. "Maybe it's a girlfriend, coming back for more. Is that why you don't want to answer it?"

He tightened his hand around his mug. "No. Only one person, one obnoxious person, would ring my door-bell so boldly this early."

"And who is that?"

"Zena my twin. She lives next door. Can't you hear her calling me by that disgusting name?"

"I can hear her crystal clear, now," she moved forward. "She's calling out Zacho"

"Damn, but I hate that name." Taking a hurried sip of coffee, he slammed his mug down. "She's the bane of my existence—she thinks she can run my life. I ignore her, along with my other four sisters—who also want to run my life."

Alethea pulled herself up. "Well, I can't stand this," she muttered, "I'm going to answer it." Glancing back, she raised her eyebrows. "After all, how bad can she be?"

"She can be intense," he leaned back in his chair, crossing his arms. "I warned you."

Opening the door, she found herself pushed aside as his sister came rushing in like a steamroller.

"I've been out here for ages. What took you so long?" She stopped when she realized it wasn't her brother who had admitted her. "Who are you?"

"I'm Alethea. I gather you're Zena." Alethea leaned on the wall, with her hands in her pockets, and looked her up and down. "Zach said it was you at the door. He's in the kitchen."

"Thanks," Zena pushed her aside and went in search of her brother.

Alethea, curious, followed.

"Zacho, I'm glad you showed some sense and let me in. I would have climbed over the balcony from my apartment, if you hadn't." She put her hands on her hips and squinted her eyes. "You know better than to ignore me. It's not nice to leave me standing out there, shouting. You're such a jerk."

"Stop the dramatics and tell me why you're here."

She pulled out a chair and plopped herself down. "Maro called, said something about trouble by the docks. I want first bids for my TV newscast." Zena pushed back her golden brown hair and stared at her brother.

Similar golden green eyes, with the same slight lift at the ends, stared back. "I should have known you'd find out. Mitch should keep better control of his wife."

Zena stood, her firm body moving easily as she walked to the sink. She grabbed a glass from the cabinet, filled it with water and gulped it down.

"Maro shouldn't have called you." He pressed his lips together. "Sit down, you make me nervous. I don't need your interference, or your prying. Why don't you just go home?" Damn—he just wanted her gone.

"Of course she should have. That's what families do—help each other." She shot daggers at him as she paced. "Except for you. You're my twin - we're supposed to have a special connection. So what happened? Where's your twin loyalty?"

Zach crossed his arms and glared. "I don't know what Maro told you, but whatever it was, forget it. Stay away from this case. I mean it. Zena's Hour can do without this story."

Alethea watched them from the door. They reminded her of two tawny lions, each ready to pounce on the other.

Zena, tall, with a lithe form, wore a stylish burgundy pantsuit. Her white silk top molded sensually to her figure, when she moved.

Joining them, Alethea managed a slight smile. "Who's Maro and why did she call her so early?" She glanced at Zachary with a puzzled expression.

"Maro is my next youngest sister. She's married to Mitch," Zach said. "He's the one who's in charge of this case." He gave his sister an intense look, then crinkled his brow.

"Those two are partners in crime, the one spies out all her husband's cases, then reports them to this one here. She runs to her news station to get ahead of her competition." He swiveled toward his sister, "There's nothing to report. I got an anonymous text, that's all, and called it into Mitch."

He and Alethea exchanged looks.

"That's not what Maro said." She noticed Alethea, and turned to her brother. "Who's this—a new girl-friend or a one night stand?"

"Mind your manners. You know better than to ask personal questions." He motioned with his hand. "Alethea, this is my interfering sister Zena, ignore her rudeness, she can't help herself."

Zena gave Alethea a quick glance, before glaring at her brother. "If it's nothing—why are you warning me away?"

"Just because." Zach lifted his cup and sipped. "I don't need to explain myself."

Zena, a bundle of energy, couldn't sit still. Her foot tapped under the table, her arms gestured while her head moved constantly from left to right. She looked from one to the other.

"I'm glad to meet you." Alethea replied. "As to who's this? I'm a new friend. Your brother and I met on the plane, and he's been showing me the sights of Ath-ens."

"Sorry about that. It was impolite to talk as if you didn't exist, but it's his fault." She pointed at Zach, and blustered. "If he wasn't so secretive, I would know what happened, and wouldn't have to pry it from him." She stared at her brother, narrowing her eyes.

"Tell me—what's going on? Maro said you called early in the morning, and Mitch left right afterward. Debating with her conscience all of ten minutes, she called me." She leaned her hand on the table, and started tapping her finger.

"Sit still, I can't take this nervous energy. And stop tapping." He brought over a cup and poured her some coffee. "I got a tip that one of our men was in danger, so I called. Nothing secretive about that."

"And what happened?"

"We're waiting to hear."

"Well, I'll wait with you," she looked toward Alethea." I'm not interrupting anything?"

"No, actually, I have to leave. I'm expecting a call from the States. I need to be at the hotel to get it." She pushed back her chair and left the room.

Zachary glared at his sister. "I owe you one. Next time you have a visitor I'll be sure to crash your party the way you crashed mine."

Zena held her hands, palms up, "What did I do? I didn't throw her out or anything. I mean, she said she had to leave."

Alethea came in. "I'll take a taxi, you stay here in case you're needed." She cast him a meaningful look, then opened the door. "I had a good time—so call me later."

Out in the hall, he pushed the button for the elevator. "Wait." He whispered so his sister couldn't hear, "this isn't the end of us. I want to see you, and soon." He grabbed her, giving her a long kiss.

Breathless, she backed away. "I know—we'll talk." She went into the elevator, "you don't have to come down. I'll get a taxi." She blew him a kiss, watching the door shut him out.

Zach scratched his head, then walked back into his apartment just as the telephone rang.

"Give me that," he called out, when his sister rushed to get it. He grabbed the phone from her hand and listened. "Let me understand this, Mitch. You found blood on the pier, but no body."

Chapter 15

Still upset after her traumatic dream, Alethea entered her hotel room and paused a moment before she walked to the bed. She kicked off her shoes, and lay down.

What an awful vision—murder was ugly. Why were there so many depraved people in this world? She placed her arm over her eyes and tried to relax, but the images of the last night came back to haunt her. To calm herself, she repeated her litany.

'Harm and hurt to bad adhere—Joy and right to good alight.' She had to believe this, to believe there was good in the world.

Alethea reached over to the night table to gather her messages. One from her mother, asking her to call. The other from her office, asking her to call. Not now—she didn't feel like talking to anybody. She turned on her side, put her hand under her head, and stared into space.

This assignment had altered her life in unexpected ways. Her cards had foretold about the long trip, and about the love interest. But she hadn't believed them. She should have. Her cards never lied.

She adjusted her pillow and lay on her back. Zachary, she could sense, was her destined mate. The sex with him was awesome, it surpassed her every expectation. She sighed, then smiled. About time things changed. She had nightmares of being an eighty year old virgin, of never experiencing her sexuality.

Her hands on her chest, she drummed her fingers. Who would have thought that such a studious man, a real nerd type, would turn out to be so virile? His mild-mannered exterior hid a will of steel.

She shook her head at her own naiveté. He was so calm, so clever, and so determined. She didn't stand a chance—she had been outmaneuvered.

Alethea never would have gone to his apartment if she had thought he was dangerous. She turned on her side and puffed up her pillow.

Her coy game didn't impress him. Her pseudo-resistance wasn't doing it. As he said, if she didn't want it, why did she come to his apartment? She turned on her back and stared at the ceiling.

Why indeed? She wanted it, for sure, with him. Her subconscious wanted him to force her hand, like the heroine in Rudolph Valentino's movie The Sheik.

She sat up and leaned back against the headboard. Well, she enjoyed it. No one before had seemed so right.

She could read his thoughts, feel his desires, and sense the psychic link forging between them. She rose and moved around the room.

It was there from the beginning. The erotic thoughts she felt on the plane were his, and he had appeared not to notice her.

Too restless to sleep, she undressed, and went into the bathroom. She glanced at the mirror, put her hair up with a clip, and noticed that indeed, her arms and face had a slight sunburn. She stood in the shower, the hot water pouring down her body, and felt herself calming with its soothing rhythm.

After she scrubbed, she washed her hair and thought about last night. She finally satisfied this appetite, this sexual hunger that lay dormant, unrealized until now. Better than a tranquilizer, it calmed her, and made her feel so 'bad.'

She dried herself with the large bath towel, looked again in the mirror, and tried to see a difference. You would think that such a mind boggling experience would leave its mark.

She threw the towel down, and started dressing. The phone rang.

"Hello, Zach—you must have news." Alethea said. "You called so quickly."

"Our man's living, but it's not clear if he'll stay alive."

"I can't hear you, there's static on the line. Where are you?"

"I'm out on my balcony." He moved. "Is this any better?"

"Yes, you're clearer now."

"Your warning saved him. He would be dead without it. Mitch searched the whole area, and just when they were about to leave, an officer spotted a leg sticking up from one of the garbage bins. They had taken him for dead, thrown the body in an alley hoping he wouldn't be found. He's lost a lot of blood, but thanks to your tip, he'll live. He might not make it, but at least, now, he has a chance."

He hesitated a moment, "Mitch is a problem. I told him that an anonymous caller tipped me off, but I'm not sure he believed me." He bit into his bottom lip. "Thanks to my sister, we didn't have a chance to talk.

She spoiled our morning. I'm sure you wouldn't have left so soon otherwise."

"No, I would have, I had things to do, my messages to get. I'm not here on vacation."

"And how are you?" Zach asked, a curious note to his voice. "I can smell the jasmine from the nearby trellis, it reminds me of you. Your subtle smell still lingers in my sheets."

"That's sweet. But I'm fine." She opened the drapes allowing the sunlight into the room. "And why do you think I wouldn't have left?" She paused a moment.

"Are you that sure of yourself? Jeez, did you think I'd be so impressed by your performance I couldn't unglue myself from your side? " She walked across her room.

"I'm not complaining—it was good," she said, "but not that good," she lied, not wanting him to get cocky.

"I'll have to try harder next time." He changed the subject. "I'm going down to my office. I have some work to do. We can meet for lunch." He paused.

"By the way, Zena left right after the phone call from Mitch. She went to the hospital determined to get an interview." He blew out his breath.

"Good luck with that—the man's still unconscious. I told her. But does she care? No—she's after the story. Blast, but she's hard headed. She said she'd wait there until he woke."

"You two look alike," Alethea commented, "but you're so calm and she's so nervous. Watching her wears me out." She sat in an armchair by the window and gazed out at the bustling city. "He won't regain consciousness today. She's wasting her time."

"Are you sure he won't wake up?" He asked.

"I'm sure."

"I bow to your psychic self," he mocked.

"Don't mock what you can't understand," Alethea warned.

"Sorry this whole thing is too bizarre," Zach offered, with a strange note to his voice. "I'm going to have to get used to it." He cleared his throat, "Be in the lobby at two o'clock, O.K?"

"I'll be there." She walked back toward the bed, and mumbled as she hung up. "He thinks it's bizarre. How about me? I've had to deal with it all my life."

"You better be there," he said into the empty phone.

Chapter 16

In a shabby one bedroom apartment near the Piraeus wharf, a large man with a patch over his right eye sat on a worn sofa cleaning his nails with a knife. Interrupted by a rapid knocking, he dropped the knife on the table, wiped his palms on his pants, and dragged himself to the door. He opened it a crack and peered at his visitor.

The door slammed hard against the wall and a fat man strode into the room. "Bruno, you messed up." Pushing hard against him with his stomach, the fat man forced Bruno to step aside. "The boss doesn't like stupid mistakes. You've made a big mess, mate." He moved his corpulent figure to the nearest chair, and eased himself down.

"Dockhand's not dead." Dark beady eyes raked over Bruno, making him squirm. "You know what that means. The boss warned you, mate. He knows about your family, about your pretty *bird*. If you don't do your job, he'll take care of them. After—your *bird* won't fly."

Bruno sat across from him, grinding his teeth. "Sure, man dead. I dumped his body." He rubbed the moisture from his bald head with a dirty handkerchief. "I kill, stab many times. No way he's alive! It dark place, empty, hard to find. Makes no sense, Mr. Oliver. Nobody saw."

"Oh yeah? Then what's he doing in the hospital? No witnesses—you're sure?" Oliver stared at Bruno, and tried to decide if he told the truth. "We've got a problem, if he comes to." He shifted in his seat. "He knows too much."

Oliver's diamond ringed fingers tapped on his chair. Suddenly he spread his large hands. "Go to the hospital, got to snuff him before he yaps." He brought his hands together, as if twisting a chicken's neck, "like that."

"Too dangerous Mr. Oliver, hospitals have strong security. They don't let anyone past the front desk without pass."

"Don't be daft. He knows too much. He unloaded the freighter, mate. You betcha he snuck a peek—got an eyeful." He pulled on his ear lobe. "He worked on Zachary Artemidis' ships, worked crew on *Deliverance*. He reported to my man - that's why I called you."

He adjusted his designer pants, and fixed Bruno with a beady stare. "You got one more chance to snuff him, mate. We got a fancy set-up, lots of green rolling in, real sweet deal.

These *immigrants,* they pay big bucks. He has them stashed - making the green, blackmailing their families for more green. They're stuck. The Boss controls the racket." Oliver pushed himself up from the chair. "The Boss got eyes everywhere. Don't cross him or me." He jabbed Bruno with his finger, *"kill the dockworker."* He strode out and slammed the door behind him.

Chapter 17

Zachary stretched his hands to loosen his cramped muscles, signed the last contract, and walked out to his secretary's office. "You can reach me on my cell, if it's a dire emergency."

His secretary adjusted her glasses more firmly on her face, and considered her employer. He never left early, never shirked his duty. He had top people working for him, but he was in charge.

"It must be a woman," she muttered under her breath, "there's no other explanation."

Zachary hurried to the hotel. There was no sign of Alethea in the lobby. His watch showed two o'clock. Where was she? Too anxious to sit, he checked at the desk. No messages. He smoothed his hair and started striding back and forth.

When he said two o'clock, he expected her to be on time. He found a corner, with a view toward the front doors.

"Women," he shook his head in disgust. These men-women games—they grated on his nerves. They maneuvered, he avoided. He had an aversion to women who plotted. His sisters knew all the tricks, mapped their strategies as if they were generals planning a campaign. Damn. They were so cold-blooded about it.

He wondered if Alethea was good at these games. Maybe that was her strategy, this act of indifference. He blew out a gust of air. "This is annoying," he muttered, "wasn't I clear enough about the time?" He knitted his brows. *Maybe she thought I'd be more interested in her if she kept me waiting.* Zach checked his watch, again. Half an hour had passed, with no sign of her.

Women - they got in the way of his life. He could be researching historical facts, or enjoying a book on antiquities instead of wasting his free time like this. Damn these physical needs that made men drool over women. Even though she was worth drooling over.

He leaned back, admitted he wanted it again - that ultimate experience they had shared. As she climaxed, he was in her mind, felt her ecstasy and knew she felt his. Their emotions blended into one, her excitement made his greater, made the moment even more power-ful. Hard to believe, but they had linked telepathically.

This psychic gift of hers, it fascinated him. He wanted to learn more. If he hadn't experienced it him-self, he wouldn't have believed it possible. She said she had lived incidents like this before, and hinted at other talents. He wondered what they were. She said she could go back in time and relive history, and that her talents were still evolving. Was this possible?

According to what he'd read, it was. Besides all that, she was stunning, a real beauty, with just the right looks and figure to satisfy him. As a connoisseur, he ap-preciated her uniqueness

He tapped his foot on the marble floor, checked his watch again and tried to calm himself, it wasn't work-ing. He was passed pissed off, now he was downright angry. He never allowed women to control him, even exquisite ones. Did she understand the exception he was making? He'd ignore her lateness for a little longer.

Alethea was lost. She sat on a bench berating herself for losing her temper and wandering aimlessly from the hotel. She hadn't paid attention to which way she had gone or to how late it was. Zachary—what must he be thinking?

In the morning, after her phone call with Zachary, she called her office where her friend Lucretia gave her a message. An invitation to a house party would be waiting for her at the *Blue Sea* in *Mytilene.*

Her call to her mother went as expected. Her mother had sensed her distress and wanted to know what had caused it. Alethea gave her an abridged version. When Alethea asked if they had found the kidnappers of the little girl, her mother answered in the negative.

She had time before her rendezvous with Zach. Alethea decided to explore the area around the hotel. She was shocked when Karl Hendrickson, her old enemy, entered the elevator one floor above the lobby. Now sitting here, she recalled their conversation.

"Well, well what have we here Alethea Karras, the fortune teller? Surprise, surprise what brought you to Athens-some psychic vision? You seem to have them often. Let me guess, you're on a rescue mission. Come on you can tell me."

"Work brought me here, what else?" She ignored his snide remarks. *"What's your excuse?"*

"I'm here because of the Olympics." Karl leaned against the wall. *"My paper wants the sights and sounds of a city organizing itself, as well as Olympic coverage."* He eyed her. *"I came early with my crew to get the best spots."*

Alethea, distressed by their meeting, had shot straight out the hotel doors. She walked and walked and walked. Dressed in casual clothes, with comfortable shoes to match, she had no problem in navigating the city streets. Before she knew it, time had passed, and she realized she was lost. When she tried to get a taxi, there was none to be had.

Now here she sat on a bench, in a small park, wondering what to do. Her wristwatch indicated two- thirty.

She looked up to see a small kiosk on the corner with a line of people waiting to use the phone. She stood and joined the line. When her turn came, she found the number for the Caravel Hotel in a brochure she'd stuffed in her pocket. She paid the old man in the kiosk, then dialed the number. Her fingers crossed, she hoped that Zach would still be there.

"Hello, could you page a Mr. Zachary Artemidis to come to the phone. No, he's not a guest, but I am. We were to meet in the lobby, so please call him."

Alethea tapped her finger on the wood shelf, and waited. After a tense few minutes, she heard his voice on the phone. "Who is this and why are you paging me?"

"Oh Zach, you sound angry. It's me, Alethea, and I'm so lost. No taxi would stop. I was hoping you were still there." She twisted the cord around her finger, and made a face. "Maybe this wasn't such a good idea. Hey, I'm sorry I called, but I knew you were waiting, so I thought maybe you could come and get me."

"I've been here for the past half-hour, couldn't imagine where you went." His angry tone dissolved with the sound of her voice. "I was worried about you." He heard swishing sounds over the phone, "Where are you?"

"I'm not sure, I think it's called *Syndagma.* There's a hotel called *Grand Bretagne* on the corner," she looked around, "there's a lot of traffic, tons of cars, but no taxi would stop. And I got this strange feeling each time a bus went by. "

"You picked the worst time. It's rush hour, and everyone is going home from work." Thinking a moment, he said. "There should be a *McDonald*'s close by. Go and wait there, I'll pick you up." He cleared his throat. "The traffic will delay me. Don't get impatient."

With the silent phone in her hand, she shook her head. "Who's impatient?" She spotted the *McDonald*'s across the street, and dodging the rushing cars, walked over to it. She waited for Zach at a table, and wondered if he had any news about the stricken dockworker. And wondered about the city.

What an amazing city. She had enjoyed her walk around the side streets, but every city seemed the same when it came to traffic. She heard such a din of noise, such a cacophony of sound, zipping, zinging, honking, and shouting. Everyone rushed around. Nobody appeared to be just walking.

She watched the tourists. They were all over and from everywhere. Some carried backpacks, and were dressed like bums. Others walked in groups with a guide. Those came expecting to see temples and togas, and stayed at expensive hotels.

And temples they did see, she thought, *and that's what made Athens unique. The sense of history that followed you as you walked the streets passing ancient relics of a great age. And the acropolis towering over it all in splendid glory.*

Alethea spotted Zachary's Mercedes in the approaching traffic. When he stopped, she quickly got in.

"I'm so glad you waited, I'm not sure what I would have done if you hadn't. I can't believe how lost I was. I should have known better than to wander around like that. I have a terrible sense of direction."

He smiled—he couldn't help it. Her rambling was so uninhibited. He was glad he had waited, glad he hadn't let his temper ruin things.

Hungry— that's what she made him, whenever he looked at her.

"I bet you're starved," Zach said. "You left so fast—you didn't have time for a bite." He turned toward her and winked. "I'm certainly starving. I can't wait to satisfy my appetite."

Alethea studied him. She had expected to hear him bellowing about her lateness. Instead, he was so calm, so pleasant, and so *suggestive*.

"I'm glad you're not angry. When we spoke on the phone, you sounded annoyed."

"Not with you."

He gave her a quick glance as he maneuvered them out of the city traffic.

"We're on the road to Pendeli, a place on the mountainside, well-known for its restaurants."

"I hope it's not too far from here. I am hungry."

From the window, she saw they were climbing a mountain road lined with pine trees. The curved road snaked uphill until they reached a level plain, where restaurants surrounded a central square.

127

"Here we are." He took her arm and led her to the closest taverna. Seated, he gazed around. "Look at this view. It's lush and green, like a forest."

Alethea took a whiff of the air. "Smell that charcoaled lamb. It makes my mouth water."

"They're noted for their grilled baby lamb chops, so we'll have those for sure." Zach moved his chair back. "I'm going to see what else they have today."

"Pick anything, I'm not fussy. But mountain dandelions are a favorite of mine, when I can find them, and I love thick fried potatoes."

He quirked an eyebrow. "I'm glad you're *not particular* about your food."

Zach returned from the kitchen, smiling. "We have to wait for the lamb chops, but they're going to bring the side dishes right away. I also ordered *retsina*."

"A Greek wine? That's fine." Alethea looked up at the trees towering overhead. "After the smog of Athens," she breathed deeply, "the air here is clean, fresh. You can smell the pine."

"It was greener," Zach gestured around. "Fire ruined acres of trees. If you look, on our way down, you can see charred stumps from the burnt forests." He lifted his fork and frowned. "These forests cover valuable land. People have erected million-dollar homes on forestland ravaged by fires." His lips tightened. "They don't care. There's a law preventing it, but...."

Alethea arched her brows. "You don't approve?"

"No, I don't. We need the forests to keep the mountains from falling into the sea, to keep our air fresh. At this rate, with these fires, there won't be any trees left." He waved his fork, jabbing the air.

"Even re-foresting isn't the answer. The trees don't grow fast enough to solve the problem. Stronger safeguards are needed. Stronger prosecution of those caught starting fires. And, we need to control building on this land."

Alethea stared at him. "You impress me. You're so passionate about your convictions. I've never met a man who feels as powerfully as you do about things."

"My convictions are not the only thing I feel strongly about." His golden eyes roamed over her, with a charged intensity.

"Are you telling me you're falling for me?" Her scalp tingled with sensual awareness. She drummed her fingers on the table, impatient for the food to come, for Zach to bring her back to his apartment and fulfill his erotic promise.

"I'm famished for you. I intend to show you once we finish dinner." He sipped his wine. "You did say you wanted to have an affair with me, or did I mistake you?"

Alethea leaned toward him, and whispered. "No, you didn't. I want you. No strings attached."

She loved his voice. It was so deep, so compelling. She liked the cleft in his chin and the masculine set to his body. Memories from last night engulfed her, making her heart beat quicken. *Take hold*, she scolded, *this will never do. He'll notice your fascination, and try to control you. Don't let that happen.*

Zach noticed her distraction, and wondered at her thoughts.

Alethea kept hearing a voice in her head. *Help me, somebody help me.* She shook her head to clear it, but the voice was there sobbing in her head. She put dande-lion greens on her plate, added fried potatoes and waited for the voice to leave her. She drank some wine.

"That was excellent," Alethea looked up and spot-ted the waiter. "Oh, and here comes our lamb."

"You've never tasted this in the States." Zach served the aromatic charcoaled meat.

"So what happened with your brother-in-law?" She was looking at her plate and didn't notice his troubled expression.

"Mitch wanted to know about the stabbing—about what happened and who informed me." He sipped his *retsina*. "I told him it was a mole, and not to probe fur-ther. I had privileged information I couldn't reveal."

With the wine glass in his hand, Zach tightened his lips. "I can understand your dilemma now, why you don't tell people about your psychic ability. Mitch would never believe me if I told him what actually hap-pened."

"If I told you I'm hearing a voice in my head right now, what would you say?" Alethea asked.

"Are you serious?" Startled, Zach looked closely at her.

"Yes, I'm afraid I am. Someone is calling for help. She keeps saying *help me!* Over and over, it's in my head."

"What are you going to do about it?"

"Nothing. I can't do anything until more is re-vealed. I get bits of emotion, sounds in my head and then the visions start." She took a breath, closed her eyes and sighed. "It's upsetting. I know I'm needed, but I'm powerless to act. Yes, now you understand *me*, and the problem I have.

And I'm starting to understand *you*." She picked up her glass and looked into his eyes. "I don't want to know you, though, to know who you really are. I just want us to enjoy each other."

"Hold a minute, you can't just ignore this call for help." Zach looked at her in horror.

"What am I supposed to do? It's just a voice in my head nothing else at this point." She cast her eyes down and played with her fork.

"You have to do something. How can you sit there so calm?"

Alethea threw her fork down and shot her head up. "I'm not calm. I'm frustrated and angry."

"Okay, I didn't mean to upset you. What do you usually do in this situation?"

"Wait, I can't do much else."

He stared at her, interested to understand who the person Alethea was. "You're not like other women." He took her hand. "If you need my help, let me know."

"Thank you, but unless I get more from my psyche, there's not much I can do."

Zach bit into his *moussaka* and stared at Alethea. "We were discussing our future before your bombshell of a psychic intrusion. You sounded as if you would rather not have a husband. Men are the ones who want to be free, to have sex without responsibilities."

"That's hogwash! Are you a woman to know how a woman thinks?" She frowned, moving her fork across her plate. "I'm my own person. I like it that way. I don't have to answer to anyone. I enjoy my job. My money is mine to spend as I wish. What do I need a man for?" She noticed Zach's upraised eyebrow, and clarified, "besides sex, of course."

"That's a big of course." Zach said as he spooned some fried zucchini into his mouth.

She faltered under his steady gaze. "Having sex with a man doesn't mean I have to marry him or that he owns me. And don't look so smug. It means nothing that you were the first."

"Is that what you think?" Annoyed by her attitude—his possessive streak aroused, he tried not to show it. They had just met. He couldn't say too much, yet. He would give it time. "You're probably right about it not mattering. I'll try not to give it *too* much importance."

He took her hand and caressed it slowly. "You know you're beautiful sitting there. I can't wait to get you alone. I satisfied one craving and am more than ready to satisfy another."

"You're stirring me up," Alethea looked at him, "and I can't wait to get to your place."

Zach paid the waiter and reached for her hand.

"Let's go?" And then his cell phone rang.

Chapter 18

"Hello. Mitch, what's happened?"

Alethea watched Zachary's facial expression change to a hard savage look. The transformation was so shocking, she hardly recognized him.

He stood and grabbed her arm. "Let's go, we have to hurry and get to the hospital. It's nearby. Another attempt was made on my man's life.

My snooping sister saved him, lucky man. Come on, I'll tell you the rest on the way." He pulled her toward the car.

Alethea stumbled and ran to catch up.

"Hey, you don't have to yank me around like that. I'm quite capable of following on my own." She wrenched her hand free and got into the car.

"Sorry about the rush, but Zena's been hurt." He opened his car door. "She noticed a man going into Leonidas' room, that's the man in your vision. She followed and caught the would-be assassin smothering him with a pillow.

The killer tried to escape and crashed into her, knocking her against the wall. The doctor had to stitch her head."

Hands tight on the wheel, he checked his mirror, then pulled out onto the road and sped down the hill. He was furious with Zena.

"Of all the foolhardy things—he should wring her neck. The man might have stabbed her, then finished the job on Leonidas, thus killing them both." He gritted his teeth and started mumbling. Ignoring Alethea, he cursed his sister for her hardheadedness, for her ability to get herself into trouble without thinking.

"You're angry. I'm getting all these hostile thoughts from you. You're making my head swim." She rubbed at her temple. "Try to tone down your temper, I'm sure your sister recognized the danger. At least she saved the man's life."

"That made it right, to act without thinking?" Zach raved on, not realizing Alethea had read his mind. "She's always been so damned impulsive—she acts first, then thinks later. That's how she married a loser when she was eighteen years old." He breathed deeply, striving for control, "That's how it's been since we were young. I've had to get her out of one jam after another."

Zach was still mulling the incident around in his mind when he pulled into the hospital parking lot. Clearly, they had an informer in their midst. He turned toward Alethea and leaned his arm on the back of her seat. "We have a problem," his brows knitted in a frown, "someone inside the police is giving the enemy information."

Chapter 19

Startled by his comment, she looked at him. "What makes you say that?"

"Somebody followed Leonidas. Attacked him before he could reveal what he found. He had to have talked to someone, and that person arranged his assault." He opened his car door. "That's been bothering me since this morning."

"I should wait for you here." Alethea got out of the car and walked over to join him. "I can sit in the shade, over there, until you finish."

He grabbed her arm and pushed her along. "No, we're in this together. You're going to stay by my side. I might need your insights."

"This isn't a good idea." Alethea cast him a disgruntled glance and tried to squirm from his grasp. "I don't want to meet these strangers. My reactions are unpredictable. You might be caught in a difficult situation." She pulled her arm free and faced him.

"People confuse psychics with witches. I'm telling you for your own good."

"Witch hunts are out dated. Besides—you're not a witch." He gave her a hard stare. "And nobody would dare hurt you when you're with me."

She tilted her head and frowned. "If that's what you think, then you're deluded." She warned.

He felt helpless standing with her in the middle of the parking lot. "You're mine, and I protect what's mine. Haven't you realized it yet?"

"Jeez, get real. I don't need you to protect me. And," she shook her head, "I don't belong to you, or to anyone else." She closed her eyes tightly and sighed. "Look, I need to use my gift. I have it for a reason, but I don't have to publicize it, and I don't need you hovering over me."

"Just come with me and meet Mitch, my brother-in-law. I won't tell anybody about your dream." Not giving her a choice, he grabbed her elbow, walked with her into the hospital.

She allowed it. Squirming from his grasp again would draw unwanted attention.

"Wait here, until I find out where everyone is. We can check on Leonidas, then find my sister and Mitch. I don't know how badly Zena was injured."

Alethea made herself as unobtrusive as possible and waited near the entrance. She couldn't help notice how the receptionist eyed him, as he walked to the desk.

"I need Leonidas Kontronis' room number, and to see if a Zena Artemidis has been admitted."

"Wait a minute I'll check for you." She smiled sweetly at him, and turned aside. She typed the name in the computer, looked up and frowned. "You can't visit Mr. Kotronis, he's under police protection. As for Ms. Artemidis—I don't see her name."

I'm glad someone did something right. Zach mumbled to himself.

"Excuse me, what did you say?"

"Never mind, please page Mr. Mitch Petridis. I'll wait for him in the lobby."

He motioned to Alethea, indicating for her to join him.

She walked over reluctantly and cast him an indefinable look.

They sat side by side in silence.

Alethea stared into space, unhappy with the situation. Zach kept pushing and pulling, telling her what to do and when to do it. She wasn't her own person, she felt subject to his will, like a circus animal performing on cue. At the first opportunity, Alethea was out of here. It was a good thing she was leaving for Mytilene soon.

"What do you mean about being unpredictable?" Zachary asked. "You used that as an excuse to avoid coming inside. I don't understand."

"Can you believe in the unbelievable? Complicated doesn't begin to explain it. I feel things others can't, or see things others don't, like at the taverna. I heard this woman's cry for help, I felt her pain, but you didn't. Sometimes you talk to me and my mind is, literally, in another place, or another century."

Exasperated at being in this situation, she didn't know how much to spell out. "While I was walking, before you picked me up, I'd get this strange tingle when a bus passed or when I saw a house with red shutters. They'll mean something, but I don't know what."

He tried to take this in and draw some logical conclusions. He had researched the phenomenon of psychics, and, together with his father, had tried to find real psychics. They found many fakes instead. They had started to believe that true psychics didn't exist, that the concept of psychic power was a myth.

He had read that some true ones could perceive things. They could shift waves into the alpha and theta regions of their brains.

They had a natural born ability. He hadn't believed this was possible until he met Alethea. He knew a true talent when he saw one, had experienced her psychic ability, first hand. What else could she do, what was she capable of?

"This other century thing is weird. How do you get there and what happens?" He leaned forward and watched her, not wanting to miss her response.

Alethea crossed her legs, put her elbow on the arm of the chair, and played with her hair. "During the flight, while you lectured me about Delphi, I had a vision about a shepherd named *Kouretas*. He had found a hole. Fumes from it made his goats, his friends act weird."

She studied him for a reaction. "When I came back, you were still talking, but I hadn't heard a word."

"That's astonishing." He lifted his head and sat up straighter. "They built the temple of the oracles at Delphi there. The original story of Delphi's founding includes this *Kouretas*."

"I've shocked you." She rubbed her cheek with a finger.

"Yes, to be honest, I'm stunned." He closed his eyes, breathed deeply. "Give me a minute." He let out a gust of air. But couldn't help his body's reaction. For him to be excited physically by a woman wasn't unusual, but to feel this mental stimulation was rare.

"This has nothing to do with magic, right? You're not a witch casting spells or stealing a man's soul?"

"You're being ridiculous. See, that's why I don't tell people about my abilities, because of reactions like yours." She looked daggers at him.

"I don't cast spells or practice black magic, and I don't twitch my nose or ride on broomsticks, either."

"Sorry, but I need a logical explanation for this obsession I have. It's so bad I can't think straight." He let his eyes roam, searching her face. "This reaction to you, it's unusual. I've always had an iron control over my sexual impulses, until now."

"Don't sweat it. We agreed. Only an affair, nothing more." She didn't want any deep conversations, here, in this hospital.

A man in uniform and a plain-clothed man strode up. Alethea stilled and blended into the background.

Mitch went over and sat next to Zachary. "I'm glad you came. Your sister had five stitches put into her thick skull. And my wife's here. Once Maro found out what happened, she rushed right over." Mitch shook his head.

"Zena shouldn't have been here to begin with. The man's unconscious, for god's sake. Granted, because of her Leonidas lives, but she could have called out to an officer, instead of rushing in herself.

Why do those two find it so difficult to take orders?" Mitch suddenly narrowed his eyes and pierced Zach with a look.

"Tell me." Mitch raised an eyebrow. "How did you know what happened, and where it happened, before anybody else? All day I've been mulling it over, and can't come up with anything." He looked Zach in the eye. "And don't tell me it was an informer."

139

Zachary tried to think up a logical explanation, without revealing Alethea's involvement. Not able to come up with anything creative, he stuck to his story.

"Sorry, but it was one of my *moles*. I can't be more specific because it seems we have a spy in our midst. Since I might need him again, I don't want him to be compromised."

"What do you mean by that?" Mitch stood up.

"We'll talk later." Zach motioned with his head indicating the officer. He rose from his seat, went over to where Alethea stood, and brought her over.

"Mitch Petridis, this is Alethea Karras. We met on the plane a few days ago. I had started to show her Athens, but this business came up and interrupted our sightseeing."

Alethea saw a tall man, not fat but full of muscle, a large man with an air of authority about him. He looked like he didn't suffer fools gladly. They shook hands.

"A pleasure to meet you, we don't often see Zachary with a date," Mitch arched his brow. "He keeps his private life private."

"I'm not actually a date. I'm more in the line of a travel companion." She cleared her throat, muttering under her breath, *I can understand why he wants his privacy with a sister like Zena.*

Mitch scrutinized her with his light blue eyes. Burning with curiosity, he turned toward Zach. "You're keeping secrets from me, but I trust you have a good reason. I won't say more." He took each by the arm, and together they walked to the elevator.

"Wait for me here at the reception desk," he turned to the officer who accompanied them.

"And if anybody asks for the room number of the dock worker, notify me at once."

As they exited the elevator on the second floor, they heard a commotion down the hall. Zena's distinct voice could be heard clashing with Maro's.

"You almost got yourself killed," shouted Maro, "reckless that's what you are. You came to the hospital—for what? The man's unconscious." She threw up her hands. "That's it. Don't count on me for any more information. You're a walking disaster."

"Stop shouting, my head hurts," Zena put her hands to her ears. "He had a pillow over Leonidas' face, suffocating him. What was I supposed to do, walk away? Nobody else was here."

Mitch paused at the door and smiled at the two sisters bickering.

Alethea, walking with Zachary, didn't want to hear their conversation. She shook her head. *Not a good place to be right now—surrounded by his family.*

"I don't want to stay," Zena wailed, arguing with her sister. "I have a story to write."

"The doctor wants you here for observation. He's waiting to admit you. There are five stitches in your head, you dummy, you could have a concussion." Maro glared at her sister, "Just be glad it was your head and not your face, or you'd be scarred for life." She hesitated, then coaxed anew. "I'll even stay with you. We'll be nearby if Leonidas regains consciousness. This way you'll have your scoop."

"I didn't think of that." Zena mulled this over, "you might have a point." Somewhat appeased, she stretched out on the bed. "All right—I'll stay, but just for one night."

Preoccupied with her headstrong sister, Maro didn't realize anyone had come into the room.

Startled, she turned at the sound of her husband's voice.

"What are you two plotting?" Mitch stood in the doorway and observed them. His wife, dressed in red, sat in a chair next to the bed. Zena, dressed in a hospital gown with a bandage around her head, was lying down.

Alethea felt out of place. She hung back, trying to stay out of sight.

"What are you doing here?" Mitch, pointed at his wife. "You should be home with the kids. When I called you about your sister, I expected you to come check on her and then leave. And," he warned.

"You can't sleep here. What a stupid thing to say."

Maro narrowed her eyes and gave her husband a disgusted look. "Now I know you didn't mean that the way it sounded."

"Of course I meant it." Mitch, rocked back and forth on his heels. "A woman belongs at home, taking care of it, and not sticking her nose where it doesn't belong."

"Yes master, I'm your obedient servant." She bowed. "Your wish - my command."

"That will be the day." Mitch remarked under his breath, coming into the room.

"That was an awful risk you took," Zach berated his sister, as he sat on the bed, "you could have been killed… you're just as brainless as ever."

"And you're as much of a male jerk as ever. What makes you guys think you're the superior sex?" Exasperated, she tried to shake her head, but it caused her too much pain.

"I only did what you would have done." She held her hand to her bandages, and winced, "stop shouting at me— my head hurts."

"I'm a man—I can protect myself. You can't. You are a fe...male." Upset because she got hurt, and because she looked so helpless, with bandages around her head, his concern turned into anger.

"You're not as strong as me. You can't go up against a man's strength. You think you can but you can't. So why are you always taking risks with your life?"

She surveyed him, then narrowed her eyes. "Who are you to judge me and tell me what to do? Save that for your wife. I had one bad experience with a man. And I assure you, woman are much smarter and more resilient."

"That experience should've taught you a lesson," Zach shouted, "females might be the superior sex," he raised an eyebrow," but that didn't help you when your brawny husband was using you as a punching bag." He closed his eyes, could still see his sister, his proud sister, sporting a black eye and a cut lip cowering when she opened her apartment door.

That was the last time it happened. He had found her husband, and brutally convinced him he should agree to a divorce—beat him black and blue until the man saw reason. He would remember Zach for a long time after that, think twice about beating any woman again. Zach shook himself out of his reverie, and gave his sister a warning look.

"You're no match against the strength of a man. You're not me, so stay out of a man's way."

Zena looked fiercely back at him, refusing to make another comment.

They were so involved in this drama, they didn't notice Alethea had slipped away.

Down the hall, she saw an officer sitting by a closed door. This, of course, had to be Leonidas' room. Pretty dumb. If she could guess this, so could others. He stood as a beacon to anyone wanting to cause harm. To make it worse, the officer was asleep.

She gave him a passing glance, then opened the door and slipped in.

She recognized the red-haired man instantly. He looked the same as in her dream.

Inundated with emotions, she took a breath, and re-membered his pain, his fear. He looked so pale, so help-less struggling to stay alive with the help of these bot-tles and tubes hooked-up to his body.

Alethea stood next to him. Could she help? She took a deep breath, then closed her eyes. If she didn't try, she'd never know.

She put her hands on his chest. Concentrating, she tried to visualize his inner body, could see torn tissue, severed ligaments and open wounds.

Blocking out her surroundings, she looked into her mind and brought forth energy. Slowly a familiar heat streamed from her hands, a healing heat that passed into his battered body. She stood still, willed his wounds to heal and his organs to start functioning.

The mental waves poured from her and drained her. She felt, dizzy, weak her arms couldn't hold her and she collapsed on the edge of the bed.

Staying still, her fast breathing the only movement, she slowly pushed up, blinking her eyes. Satisfied she had done all she could, she examined Leonidis. A little color was coming back into his face.

The officer still slept when she sneaked out of the room. She didn't notice Zachary standing in the hallway, until she bumped into him. Not sure how much he saw her do, the door was closed after all, she shrugged her shoulders.

"Hey—are you finished in there? That was quite a family drama. Damn, I never heard anything like it."

"You shouldn't be roaming the halls." Zachary searched her eyes... *Why was she really out here?* "The killer might come back. Stay close to me, I don't want anything to happen to you."

"I just took a walk. With all that shouting, I didn't think you'd notice."

"Oh, I noticed, I seem to have a sixth sense where you're concerned, one minute away, and I can sense it."

"Stop that. You're getting out of hand."

Alethea turned on him. "I don't like people smothering me. Don't hover or try to dominate me."

"Sorry!" He put his hands up as if to keep her back.

"Let's not argue. I'll try—that's the best I can do. I need to protect you, that's who I am. That's who I was taught to be. A man takes care of his woman."

Not wanting to annoy her further, he changed the subject. "Come in and meet my other sister."

She hesitated. "I should be going. This is a family affair and I feel awkward."

"Don't be silly. Maro wants to meet you. Apparently Zena told her some things."

"Just what I need. I can't wait to hear what she said."

"Nothing bad, I'm sure." He stepped closer, and caressed her hair.

"She probably told her we're having an affair, that you're my new love interest."

"How am I going to face her after that?" She felt her cheeks start to redden. She saw the grin on his face, and realized he was teasing her. He wanted to play, did he? *Well Alethea,* she thought, *get your act together, and put on a good show.*

She flipped her hair, put a wad of gum in her mouth and moved into the room. Nearing the bed, she spoke in a low sultry voice.

"Hi, I'm Alethea. You're Maro, Zach's other sister? Oh, I'm so glad to meet you. Aren't foreign men just gorgeous? They're so sexy, so yummy."

Zena's head ached too much for her to remember Alethea from her morning visit.

Maro didn't know what to say. She sat there stunned. "Yes, Zena did mention Zachary had a visitor. You're from America," she eyed her guardedly. "I can tell by your accent. Terrible isn't it, this war, so many women and children getting killed."

"I don't know anything about it," she assumed an indifferent stance, "is there a war?" Alethea blinked her eyes and sighed. "I never get involved in politics or religion. They're just too deep for me."

146

Zena and Maro sat there with opened mouths.

"Excuse me, don't you have any opinions about what's going on in this world?" Zena turned to her. "After all you do live in it." She held her head, and tried to alleviate the ache.

"No, I let others worry." She pasted a self-satisfied smile on her face and sat in a chair across from the bed. "I live in my own world. The greater picture doesn't concern me."

"What you're saying is you don't bother with world affairs," Maro glared at Zach, from her seat next to Zena, "that it's better left to others."

"Absolutely," she settled back, chewed her gum, and crossed her arms under her breasts. "It's a man's world. What can little old me do to change it?" she looked from one to the other. "Don't you agree? After all—your parents made a fuss over Zach, the son and heir. They treated him special, didn't they? You must have resented it just a bit." She raised her thumb and finger and showed a tiny gap. She rubbed her cheek, leaned her arm on the chair, and studied them.

"No—we never resented him. We love Zach." Zena and Maro exclaimed together.

"Yes, I'm sure you do." Alethea left the subject and spun toward Zena.

"You risked your life to save another that took guts. And men think only they can be brave?" She blew out a bubble.

Zach watched Alethea's performance in puzzled silence. She exuded sex as she sat there talking. Those breasts had been his to touch, her legs, his to feel sliding up and down on his own, her waist, he remembered joining his fingers as they wrapped around it. He shuddered and tried to get a grip on his libido.

What was this dumb act? Why try to convince his sisters she didn't have a serious thought in her head? That she depended on the male of the species to tell her what to think? That would be the day.

What was she up to?

Mitch observed, but didn't know what to make of her. He lifted his eyebrow in question and looked at Zach.

Suddenly the door flew open. The officer guarding Leonidas rushed into the room. He crossed himself and exclaimed.

"It's a miracle. The dockworker—he's regained consciousness. He's sitting up moaning. I went in to check on him and I couldn't believe it. He'd been almost at death's door, now he seems well, come see for yourself."

"Have you been relieved? Get back to your post," Mitch commanded.

Zach peered at Alethea.

Did she have anything to do with this miraculous recovery? After all, I did see her by his door. What other abilities has she kept secret?

Zach turned to the women. "Don't any of you leave this room."

He looked at Alethea. "And you—we'll talk when I get back."

He and Mitch rushed out with the officer.

"Damn, he's bossy." Zena closed her eyes. "Does he expect me to leave my bed?" She leaned back into the pillows, groaning. "I wish. My head's hurting too much."

Maro looked at her. "Is this an act? Half an hour ago you wanted to go home. You complained about staying in the hospital." She stood and straightened her sister's sheets.

Zachary and Mitch hurried toward Leonidas' room. Halting, Zach looked at his friend. "I should warn you—someone is privy to our plans. Someone Leonidas trusted ratted him out"

Mitch stopped in the middle of the hall. "I thought it strange he was attacked for no apparent reason. No one could possibly know he worked for us, unless they recognized him or had inside information."

Chapter 20

"Amnesia? I don't believe this." Maro tilted her head. "He says he can't remember anything before his attack?"

Maro and Zena exchanged glances, stared at him as if he had sprouted horns.

Zach chuckled as he neared Zena's bed, "if you could see your faces. Mitch and I just finished talking to him and he's a complete blank." He shook his head at their distress. *What were they up to? A spying mission as soon as he left?*

Alethea looked at Zach. "Other than his memory—how does he feel?"

"He's good." He fixed his eyes on her, "he had been near death, but now his stab wounds are almost healed."

Zach took her hand and pulled her toward the door. "We have to go. There isn't much to do here."

He turned to Zena. "Are you going to stay the night or do you suddenly feel well enough to go home?"

"Of course I'm staying," Zena grabbed her head. "I have two hammers banging in my skull."

"I'd better go. Mitch is waiting for me." Maro inched toward the door.

"I thought you were going to stay." Zena made a moue with her mouth, "fine desert me."

She played with a corner of the sheet, then glowered at her sister.

"I'm *so* glad there's no man running my life."

Alethea said in a low breathless voice. "Well, I have to go, you know how it is." She wiggled her fingers at them. "See ya."

Both women waited for Alethea to leave the room, then said in unison. "She's one dumb blonde. How did you get involved with her?"

Maro clarified, "sorry it's easy to see why you got involved with her, but she's not your type. If I recall you go for the more intellectual kind."

"When I met her this morning, she seemed different," Zena concentrated a moment, "actually she left quickly so I don't remember we said too much to each other. But she certainly didn't look so *hot*. I would have remembered."

Zach stood at the open door. "You shouldn't jump to conclusions. Looks can be deceiving."

"Your wife's waiting for you." Zach warned Mitch when they passed him in the hall. "But she's leaving a peeved sister behind. So move it, before Zena persuades her to stay."

"I'll make sure she leaves." At the door, he looked back. "I put extra men on duty tonight, in case we have another visit, so don't worry."

Zach and Alethea headed for the car. Neither spoke until they were out of the lot.

"Why the bimbo act?" He looked askance at her while he steered the car down the hill. "Not that I didn't enjoy the display. You've got one sexy body. But, why? I don't understand."

"Why not? I gave them what they wanted to see, you with a bimbo." She adjusted her blouse, drew it down to cover her waist and peered at him over her sunglasses. "Didn't you like it? I thought it was one of my better performances."

Sighing, she leaned back into the seat and watched him take the curves. "I'd much rather draw the wrong kind of attention, than have people look too closely at me. Your sisters are too perceptive. This way, when they start to wonder, they won't look in my direction."

"You protect yourself." He observed her out of the corner of his eye. "I respect that. But your act - whew!" He concentrated on his driving while taking peeks. At the light, he casually caressed her thigh, her breast. "My place or yours?"

"You're free with that hand." She pushed it away. "Really." She moved around looking down at her bodice. "They're such a bother." She took a few deep breaths.

"Are you trying to unsettle me? Because I assure you, I'm uptight enough as it is." He turned toward her. "So my place or yours? And don't tease."

"Maybe a little unsettling is in order." Alethea gasped as he took a sharp turn. She eyed him and pointed straight ahead.

"Your eyes on the road, Mister, and your hands off me. Got it?"

But warning signals flashed in her head.

He liked to control her. Her hand and arm were numb from the many times he had pulled or grabbed her today. She felt like a sack of grain picked up and dumped wherever he wanted. And now, he felt he could touch her intimately whenever he chose. Not a good idea to allow him such freedom, at least in public. If they were alone—well that was another story.

The good thing, she reflected, was her hospital visit. She found the opportunity to help Leonidas. She suspected he wasn't just a dockworker.

"What are you thinking?" Zachary asked. "You're too quiet."

Alethea made no reply.

"I'm driving to my place," he decided. "The hotel is too public. I would rather keep our relationship private."

"So would I," Alethea quipped, "believe it or not, I met an old acquaintance, here, in the elevator, someone I wish I could have avoided."

She looked at him, and she decided to let things roll. If he became more controlling, she would just have to manage him. "He's a journalist here to cover the Olympics. I trusted him once, and he made a mockery of me."

"He wrote about your abilities?" Zach guessed.

"Yes. He made me seem like a charlatan, faking it to fool unsuspecting souls."

"Is that why you're so guarded?"

"That, among other things. Look, let's drop the subject." She looked out the window. They had left the small roads, and were on a super highway to Piraeus.

Alethea considered him. The physical attraction between them felt right, he felt right. But he hadn't seemed interested until he suspected she had hidden talents.

His studious side, she could tell, wanted to delve into her mind, to dissect and analyze, to see what she was about. And now she was being drawn into his life style. She didn't want that.

153

He took control. He had taken the dangerous back road curves easily, meticulously even at the hair-raising speed he was going.

The measured moves indicated this intellectual man had a wild streak, but one he restrained. He craved adventure, but adventure that he managed. Watching, she saw his lips turn up in satisfaction as he executed a particularly dangerous move.

Zachary enjoyed driving, and once he reached the new highway, he could speed and maneuver as if on a racetrack. He loved this feeling of power.

Lost in his driving, he stopped thinking, stopped feeling, and stopped guessing at things for which he had no answers. Exhilarated by the surge of the engine under his hands, he deftly steered the car over the road.

He slowed down, took the exit toward the port and relaxed. He took a furtive glance at Alethea. He caught her observing him with an absorbed look on her face, and smiled.

She captivated him. She had amazing gifts. And she used these gifts to help others without a thought to herself.

He was sure she had helped Leonidas heal. He didn't know how she'd done it, but she had.

He glanced at her again, determined to find out her secrets. He would keep them safe, but he had to know them.

The rules he followed for his liaisons seemed made to be broken with Alethea. He needed all of her, not just her body. Though his family was pressuring him to get married, to have sons to carry on the family name, he didn't care. Marriage was not what he wanted, at least not yet.

She said she wanted to have an *affaire*. He wondered if she meant it.

The building he lived in had a clean, modern look. He drove into the subterranean garage, and parked in his reserved place.

"Well, we're here. What an exhausting day— one drama after another." He took Alethea by the elbow, and guided her to the elevator. "I can't believe how Leonidas recovered."

She shrugged her shoulder, unperturbed by his stare. "I can't believe how much has happened since we met. It seems a lifetime ago." Her senses sparked at his nearness.

In the elevator, his body moved with a lion's grace, moved slowly not giving much away until he'd cornered her. He pushed her against the wall, captured her mouth in a searing kiss.

She hadn't seen this coming, wasn't sure if she wanted it. But her unruly body told a different story. She yearned for him, as if she knew him from another lifetime. She took a deep breath, got a whiff of his stimulating, unique scent, a combination of spice, frankincense and man. She loved his calm composure. It acted as bane to her highly charged person.

They rode up, with only the sounds of the elevator filling the space.

Inside his apartment, she took off her shoes and looked right into his eyes. They needed little conversation as each felt the urgency in the other.

Scooping her into his arms, he carried her into his bedroom. The open drapes framed a fantastic view of the sunset. They watched, sitting on the lounger, as an orange color inundated the sky, reflecting off the water as the sun set into the horizon, darkening the sky.

The emergence of night brought its own beauty, as the stars sprinkled the vast darkness with points of light. Neither one spoke while they appreciated this miracle.

Aware of each other, they lay on the settee. Their bodies responded to each other's nearness, escalating their temperatures, causing their pulses to race.

He enjoyed her weight in his arms, He caressed her, explored her, slipping his hand under her clothes. Until, annoyed with the clothes that barred his way, he pulled off her shorts, then her top, then undid her bra, letting her breasts fall into his hands.

With her back lying on his chest, he could feel every inch of her. He lifted each breast playing with them, squeezing and stroking.

He liked to touch, she liked to be touched. Curving her body back into his, she showed her assent. She felt his hands all over her naked body.

Her joy increased as he whispered in her ear.

"Feel my hands, know me through my hands. Close your eyes. Just feel them running over you."

She closed her eyes and gave her silent consent.

He petted and probed.

Instantly, she was immersed into levels of sensation.

She trembled under his touch, swayed into him. And bit-by-bit relinquished control.

She offered him complete power as he felt, fondled, and gently explored her body. He teased her nipples with his fingers, then sucked them biting, then soothing them again and again.

She gasped, then turned in his arms, no longer thinking, while his hands, his knowing hands, glided over her body stimulating, and soothing until she was a mass of emotions. Her world had become his hands, his voice whispering in her ear, sexy whisperings that stirred her blood.

He told her what he would do to her, what he would make her feel once inside her, pounding into her, giving them both the release they needed. As he talked, his hands delved inside her, over her, and around her making her lose what little sanity she had left.

Still dressed, still in charge he whispered, "Fly. Spread your wings and fly high."

Mesmerized by his voice, she succumbed to the building tension, the gliding and caressing hands opening her up, touching her intimately until she soared, lost in wild sensations.

Breathing rapidly, her body took over, her heart beat faster, heating her skin. Her head felt ready to burst— until an overpowering pleasure hit her, like she had never known before.

Blinded by passion, she heard his voice near her ear. "This is for you, just for you." Gradually her world started coming back into focus.

Alethea sat up, looked around, saw the room in darkness and Zachary fully dressed, watching her. She turned, leaned over and kissed him.

"That wasn't fair, I had all the pleasure and you had nothing.

I can feel your need nudging up against your pants." She stroked him and continued in a sultry voice. "Let me ease your ache?"

She unbuttoned his shirt peeled it down his arms and off his body.

Watching him, she unbuckled his belt then un-clasped his pants and pulled his zipper down with her teeth, feeling his hardness against her cheek. She pulled his pants off with his briefs, leaving him naked. She brushed her tongue over his impressive erection, on her way to licking his chest.

Lying on top of him, between his legs, she nestled, while she focused on nibbling on his nipples, hard ridges on his chest.

He tried to take control, to assuage his hunger, but he was putty in her hands, being shaped by her, not al-lowed to interfere, as she played with his body as he had played with hers.

Control had shifted, she took advantage, not giving an inch, as she probed and caressed him. Finally, a mis-chievous look on her face, her touch confirmed what she already knew.

He burned with desire—hot to her hand, ready to explode any moment.

She sheathed him then taking pity, sat astride and gentle took him into her core, riding him, squeezing him to feel every inch of her.

Unable to endure another moment, he took over the mounting, put his hands on her hips and started pump-ing in and out. He built their pleasure as he increased his actions.

Watching her as she rode him, her hair flying around her face, her passion-filled eyes lost in an erotic haze, his lust increased until it burst into a flame and both collapsed in exhaustion.

Entwined together, their sweated bodies cooled, their heartbeats steadied as awareness slowly returned.

Exhausted from their union, never feeling this complete satisfaction before, Zach realized that this was more than just sex.

Too tired to think, he put this thought aside, gathered her into his arms, and carried her to his bed.

Sated, she snuggled into him, and sighed.

Chapter 21

Alethea woke and gazed around the room. She saw books, books and more books. She was right about his studious side, but his streak of wildness had surprised her. Pinned to the bed by his arm across her waist and his head prodding her breast, she felt trapped.

Chewing her lower lip, she tried to think.

What should she do about Zach, about the way he complicated her life? He had become too important, her life too much a part of his. She had lost control.

She sank down into the bed and tried to ease herself from under his body. Her bare skin against his caused an instant erotic reaction. Her skin sizzled with every movement, her scalp prickled, and heat rushed into her core.

She was truly caught, and couldn't free herself. She held her breath and tried again. Just then he woke and stared into her eyes.

"Trying to get out from under me, are you?"

He nudged her, nuzzled her neck with kisses stopping at her mouth. He teased her lips with his tongue.

She opened for him, and he savored her, feasted on her.

He gathered her close, turned her so they faced each other and the heaviness from his body wasn't weighing her down.

He looked into her expressive eyes, lured by their sexual summons. Still hungry for her, he pressed into her and stopped, exciting her with his teasing.

She felt the passion building as he rode her, with increasing urgency, until a mutual explosion stilled them.

Her pulse racing, she took several deep breaths then cast him a smile.

"That was some wake- up call." Closing her eyes, she lay still trying to get her balance back.

The visions start. She sees a two story house, old, with red shutters.

The voice—"help me please." She hears a scream, then sees a woman— dark haired, full-figured, naked, being held. One man is hitting her, another is holding her. She hears—"if you don't obey this is what will happen to you."

A pretty house with flowers hanging from the balcony.

The woman is forced down onto the bed, tied to the bed's frame, tied so she could move neither hands nor legs.

A house surrounded by contorted olive trees weathered with age.

"This is what will happen to you if you try to escape." She sees a man climb onto the woman. He hits her, bites her, pinches her breasts and hurts her over and over then forces himself into her.

The woman screams then another woman screams.

Alethea comes back to herself and looks up into Zach's concerned face.

"What happened I lost you for a minute?" He smooths back her sweated hair. "I was talking to you, but you couldn't hear me. Did you have another vision?"

"Yes, I'm afraid I did. Please, I need you to hold me."

Zach pulled her into his arms, hugging her until she calmed. "Agapi mou (My love), do you want to tell me about it? You seem upset. It wasn't a good vision?"

"When someone needs my help, it's never a good vision. I saw a woman being abused by two men. I think another woman was being forced to watch. It was terrible. They treated her like an object, not like a person. And—they kept hurting her."

"Can we do anything to help?" Zach scratched his head. "We have no clues as to who are where they are. What do you do when you have these visions?" He held her and caressed her, trying to sooth her.

"Wait until something's revealed that gives me clues as to the where or the why of it." She snuggled closer to him. "I'm so glad you're here with me and I didn't have to endure that vision alone. It was horrible."

She pushed hard, trying to move him. "But now I have to get up, nature calls."

Chapter 22

Alethea peeked out the bathroom door, saw him brazenly displayed. Comfortable with his nudity, he leaned against the backboard of the bed, with a self-satisfied look on his face.

Jeez, what to do now? What an awkward situation. She wrapped herself in a towel, walked out the door and got her clothes. She dressed quickly conscious of his eyes on her.

"Are you going to stay like that all day?" She looked him up and down. "Not that I mind, but it's going to be hard to have a conversation with you looking so sexy. And we have to talk. I'll meet you in the kitchen." She put the coffeemaker on and waited for the coffee to brew.

Zachary dressed only in jeans, soon joined her. "I'm addicted." He came up from behind and circled her with his hands. He brought her close against his body, his erection pressing into her back. "I can't seem to get enough of you."

"That's sweet. And I need your sweetness after that terrible vision. But I can't spend all my time in this apartment. I've got obligations." She poured coffee into a cup and took it to the table.

Zachary, his own cup in hand, sat down across from her.

She scanned his face. "I wish we could have more time together, but we can't." She took a sip. "My office called. I have to leave for Lesvos."

"No problem. We can see each other on the island. As I told you, we have houses there. My sister Stella's husband owns a distillery on Lesvos. It's well-known for its ouzo. In fact, my sister and my parents are at their homes now."

He drank his coffee, and asked off-handedly. "Where will you be staying in Mytilene?"

"My boss' secretary made reservations for me at the Blue Sea hotel, right by the pier."

He raised his eyes. "You have a boss? I thought you were a freelance writer selling your story wherever there was an interest."

Damn, she thought, *that's the problem with telling lies. I always get caught in them.* "Actually, I meant my office made the reservations. There are a few magazines, which buy my articles, and are technically my bosses. *"How am I going to do my job with him trailing after me?* She bit her lip. *And I know nothing about birds. What a mess!*

"Why leave so soon? Let me tie up some loose ends, then we can travel on my yacht to Lesvos.

"I can't." She smoothed down her hair and avoided his eyes. "I already have my ticket. I leave tonight," she shrugged her shoulders. "I have deadlines to meet. I might even be gone before you come."

How long can it take to find the painting? Not long, I hope.

He narrowed his eyes. "Are you giving me the brush off? I hope not. I haven't finished with you yet."

"What do you mean?" Alethea eyed him suspiciously, "what exactly are you saying?" She thought a moment, chewing her lip. "Am I like a delicious dessert you want to savor a little longer, stretching out the moment, and that's why you haven't finished with me?

Or, you can't dump me because I'm the one who does the dumping, so I'm not finished with you?" She arched an eyebrow and waited.

Annoyed at himself for getting too openly aggressive, Zach tried to pacify her. "I like the first interpretation, you as the dessert. You're the most delectable woman I've ever met. I want to sample you, taste you, again and again." He took her hand. "I'm not finished exploring you, your stunning body, and this remarkable ability to see and feel things, a normal person doesn't have. I suspect you have other talents yet to be revealed."

"So what intrigues you more—me or my psychic gift?" She looked down into her cup with an engrossed look on her face.

"Let me explain. You stimulate me, physically and mentally. That's not normal for me. You're one sexy lady, even before I got to know you, I wanted you. Then it became more, much more than sex." Zach leaned back in his chair, and gave her a searching look.

"What do you mean, more than sex?" She met his eyes. "Answer my question. Is it me or my talent you want?"

He took her hand. "I like women and I've had my share of them, but never anything serious." He quirked his eyebrow. "But you have become, more to me." He played with her fingers in a distracted way. "I didn't want the responsibility of an *affaire,* just now. I'm committed to this case, I intend to find this gang and stop

the illegal immigration. I didn't want anything to interfere. But then you came along, and now I want you. Not
your talents—you. That's why I'm putting my cards on
the table."

"I don't know what you're trying to say." She
moved her hand away, crossed her arms, and stared.
"You want me, but don't want the responsibility of a relationship with me." She shook her head. "You're one
confusing dude."

"I want you." He looked out at the sea, as if getting
his thoughts together. "I don't want you to walk out of
my life. I'm charmed by this psychic ability you have,
but I'm fascinated by you."

"Zachary, I can't. I've told you this from the beginning. I can't stay here. I have a job to do." She rubbed
her arms. "I want us to be together, but we'll see how it
works out."

He lifted his eyes to hers and smiled. "It meant
something to me—taking your innocence. I'm really an
old fashioned guy." He nodded his head.

"I want to cherish you, to protect you, to provide
you with the best of everything. Don't disappear on
me."

He pushed his chair back. "Let's give us a
chance." They went out to the balcony. "Except for my
sister Zena, I have no other family obligations. Zena, I
worry about. She's my twin. We have a special bond
and I have to look out for her, whether she wants me to
or not."

"I think she resents the fact that your father doted
on you." She leaned her back against the wall and
stared into his eyes.

"I never realized that until you mentioned it. But how can you blame him. He had sisters he dowered, and then five daughters." He sat on a wrought-iron chair.

"My father wanted a son. He wanted his legacy to continue as well as his name.

We also share an interest in antiquities." He glanced at her and raised an eyebrow. *We also have a mutual interest in finding a true psychic, but you don't have to know that yet.* "So, we read together, did research together and became collaborators and best friends.

My sisters shouldn't resent me. I have the burden of being the heir. While they're free to do as they please. That's freedom."

Alethea gave him an amused look. "You sound like a whiny child. You're his heir and it brings responsibilities. I get that." She went over and sat across from him under the awning. "I can also sense this bond between us. But let's wait and see."

"If I was too forceful with you, I didn't mean to be. I'm so used to being in charge, maybe I forgot myself." He looked directly into her eyes.

"I understand that. And I know at times you're too serious, too controlling, but I also know I want you." She took a deep breath, and let it out. "But whatever happened between us, I made happen. You didn't take, I gave. So lighten up."

Chapter 23

"It's not that simple. I want you in my life. My father created a shipping empire. When his illness forced his retirement, I took over. But it's not *me*, not what I want to do. I'd rather work with Mitch helping him solve crimes." He drummed his fingers on the table.

"So now I do both. I work long hours, but I can leave and know everything will still run efficiently." Leaning toward her, he took her hand. "I can make time so we can be together." He tightened his lips.

"And I admit I'm curious about your dreams. Are all your dreams so accurate? You saved our man's life. You heard this woman calling for help."

Alethea glanced down at her hand in his. *What does he want?*

"I have these dreams. Yes, they're accurate. They're given to me to save lives. It's my responsibility, much as your family is yours." She pulled her hand back.

"If I understand you correctly, you want me, even though it's not convenient." She gave him a quizzical look. "Your family obligations don't allow you anything more serious, or you're enjoying your freedom too much to change. Which is it?"

"Let me explain. I take my responsibilities seriously, but I don't allow them to interfere with my personal life. I joined an elite combat force in the Greek Army against my father's wishes. I didn't listen then and did as I chose. My family has been hounding me to get married. I refuse to even consider any of their candidates."

"So, it's the second reason. You want just an *affaire*, because you're enjoying your freedom too much to change." She looked over the railing to the sea below.

"Yes, I'd like a relationship with you, as long as I can fit you into *my* schedule." She smiled at the stunned look on his face. "Why do you look so shocked? It's a modern world. Women are equal to men. They aren't censured if they have sex outside of marriage.

Let's be civilized about this," she picked a Jasmin bloom from the trellis and smelled it. "As long as I'm free to say '*no*' to you when I want, I say '*yes*' let's do it."

He looked stressed. "What exactly are your terms?"

"Honey, no controlling, I need my space." She watched him as she added, "and mutual fidelity for the length of the relationship. There are health issues. And, I don't share."

Zach smiled. "I think I like those terms. Of course we should write this down, just so things are clear."

He sensed she was in a reckless frame of mind. She might change her mind later. He was a detail person, he'd rather have everything spelled out. Once she agreed, in writing, he was sure she'd honor her commitment.

"Let me get a piece of paper, then we can both sign it." He pushed back his chair, and went to his office.

Uneasy, Alethea wondered what she'd started. She had wanted to shock him, not become his mistress. Was she being too reckless? *But why not.* She thought. *It doesn't mean anything, it isn't a binding contract.*

She admired his naked back, the well-defined muscles rippling as he moved, and widened her eyes. He was delicious. She decided she'd play along and see where this led.

Pen and paper in hand, he came back out onto the veranda and pulled his chair close to her. "Write your conditions first. Then I'll dictate mine."

Straightening the paper in front of her, she wrote down her terms and looked up.

"That was quick. Now write this down." He drew his lips together.

"Our affaire will be kept private, we won't disclose our intimate moments for financial gain. Any Secrets learned won't be revealed to anyone."

"No honey, you write it down, I'm not your secretary." She pushed the paper back to him.

He lifted an eyebrow. "O.K. Then." He took the paper and started writing. "Is there anything else we should add?"

"Yes. We should keep separate households, and if by accident, there were to be a child it will be my responsibility." She played with the pen, refusing to meet his eyes.

How much weirder could this get. What kind of man wrote everything down? A careful man for sure. He definitely had a gold digger as a girlfriend, at some point in his life, probably when he was young.

"I'm a careful man." He confirmed her thought. "I don't think it will be an issue. As to living apart, it's for the best. I travel a lot. You'll be more comfortable in your own place." He looked at her and couldn't help thinking.

I don't want to lose you. You're the best thing that's happened to me in a long time. Writing things down makes it more than a casual affaire

"Well, that wasn't too complicated." She took the paper from him, and added the last line, before signing it. Turning it toward him, she pointed. "Your turn, sign here, and make a copy. This way we'll both know this is more than a casual affaire"

Damn—did she just read my mind? Stunned, he shook his head. "I'll make one later, and give it to you before you leave. I'm curious though." Zachary couldn't help asking. "Why are you so secretive about your abilities?"

She took his hand. "I'll tell you my story, now, since you've told me yours." She paused.

"When I was eight years old playing in front of my house, with my friends, two lunatics snatched me. They'd heard rumors. It's a small town. People talked."

She stared down at his hand, took it with both of hers and squeezed.

"These men wanted to use me to become rich. They grabbed me, wrapped me in an old blanket and put me in the trunk of their junk car.

I was scared. Darkness surrounded me, the blanket had a rancid, moldy smell. I felt suffocated. I shivered not knowing what to expect. We stopped. They let me out and led me to an old house with peeling paint, a broken door and cracked windows." She shook her head, remembering the scene. "They weren't mean to me, they kept apologizing. I stopped being scared. Here

I was, sitting in this shabby room, bribed with ice cream and cake.

I felt sorry for them. Racing forms, lottery tickets, any game of chance—they kept bringing them. I couldn't do it, I couldn't pick the winners."

She shrugged her shoulders. "I mean I was eight years old, what did they expect?"

She smiled at Zach. "I can see them clearly. One was short and stout with a wart on his nose, a scarce amount of hair on his head and sweat stained clothes that hadn't been washed in ages.

They reeked of onions and garlic and grime. The other, a little less disheveled, was taller, extremely thin, almost emaciated, and toothless. I can only guess at their history—what they had been and what they became.

They weren't bad, just desperate. They spoke well, as if, in another lifetime, they'd had a different life. Now they saw me as their way to becoming millionaires.

I couldn't do what they wanted. They gave up and brought me home. I don't know where they came from, and don't know where they went. I never saw them again. My parents were worried, my friends were frantic but my mother refused to call the police. A few hours later I walked into my house to everyone's relief. I had learned a valuable lesson.

Since that incident, my parents have been overprotective, my friends overzealous—guarding my secret as if it was gold. And I refuse to allow people to exploit me. I don't admit to anything, do what I have to do without a lot of fanfare. End of story."

She pierced him with her amethyst eyes. "You excite me. You're a responsible person who cares about helping people. I respect that. But are you going to pick my brain to find out how it all works? Or are you going to be happy just to be with me?"

Zach took a deep breath, and let it out slowly. "That was some story. It must be hard being psychic." His eyes roved over her.

"I'm a curious person, my mind wants to know the why of everything. Who wouldn't? But I would never exploit you. You interest me, all of you, abilities included, more than anyone I've ever known."

Taking her chin in his hand, he looked into her eyes. "We begin here. I'm glad we talked and hashed this out. I'll follow you to *Lesvos*," looking directly at her, "you can count on it."

Chapter 24

Zach stopped in front of the Caravel and handed Alethea a key. "When you finish checking out, take a taxi to my place. There's the address. After I finish with Mitch, I'll join you." He cradled her hand, putting the paper and key into it. Then drew her close and kissed her.

Alethea blinked and shook her head. "You're one bossy fella, you're lucky you're a great kisser." She stroked his cheek, giving it a final pat before she got out.

Zach watched her enter the hotel. Putting his car in gear, he merged going into traffic toward the Greek police Central Headquarters on Alexander Boulevard.

Still flustered after her eventful night with Zachary, Alethea gathered the few things she had unpacked, and put them into her suitcase. Finished, she sat and looked out at the Acropolis, awed by the ancient civilization that had created such beauty. She leaned her head back on the chair and closed her eyes.

Zach stimulated, but drained her. She had to raise mental barriers to save her from the erotic waves he gave off. She had to shut him out to focus her energy. When they made love, his feelings and vivid images flooded her mind, increasing their passion.

They had a unique connection. Somehow he had felt her thoughts too. Her body quivered, flooded by memories. She could sense his goodness, his desire to right the wrongs of the world—unusual in today's world where money often overruled morals. He seemed like an anachronism, a throwback to another time, when knights practiced chivalry and rescued damsels in distress.

He had money, position and a loving family. Why should he bother with confusion and chaos?

Her suitcases ready, she took one last look around the room and realized she hadn't spent any time here after that first night. Mostly, she had come to change clothes and pick up her messages. She'd hardly even unpacked. Her time in Athens was over.

Zach's apartment was near the dock. The high-speed ferry left late at night. They had a few hours to be together.

Zachary, she mused, proved an unexpected bonus on this trip.

It amazed her how fate played a hand in each of their lives. She could still hear his last words. "I'll follow you to *Lesvos.* "

We'll see about that. She thought.

On her way to check out, she heard a commotion. She saw a crew from the Omega T.V station setting up their cameras.

Zach's sister Zena was in the middle of the hubbub. She was so busy directing the crew, she paid scarce attention to anything else.

Karl Hendrickson, Alethea's nemesis, was just coming out of the dining room. He stopped and stared at the cameras.

Now what? Two people she would rather avoid stood between her and the door.

She went into action. "Zena, how are you—I hope your head isn't still hurting." She motioned with her hand.

"Why all this equipment, is someone famous staying here? This is really exciting. Tell me what it's about!"

Catching Karl's eye, she waved.

Zena looked at her, raised an eyebrow, then shook her head. She turned her back and resumed working with her crew.

Karl, pleased at Alethea's welcoming gesture, sauntered up to her.

"What a pleasant surprise. You greeting me, I mean. You usually give me the cold shoulder. Why the change?"

"You deserve it, but never mind." She turned toward Zena, who was untangling her microphone.

"I want you to meet Zena Artemidis, she works for Veba, a Greek T.V network. She's a newscaster as devoted to her work as you are to yours.

And Zena, this is Karl Hendrickson, a reporter on the Daily Globe, a New York paper."

"To answer your question, I'm here to do an interview with Shah Raoul Zin.

He's from Unda, a small African country, rich in oil, and a personal friend of my brother Zach. They were in the *Special Services* together, and have remained friends."

Zena frowned at Alethea. She pulled her aside. "Don't tell my brother, but I used his name to get an exclusive. Raoul absolutely refuses to give interviews, but he made an exception for Zach's sake."

She narrowed her eyes at Karl, "and I'm not interested in meeting popinjays, and that's exactly what he is."

Alethea cast Karl a critical eye. "He's really not a popinjay more like an obnoxious sparrow, but I thought you might have some fun with him.

She checked her watch. "Well, I have to go, nice seeing you both, enjoy." She took her suitcases and started for the door.

Chapter 25

Zachary passed through the security check with no trouble. He had an appointment to meet Mitch in his office at Central Headquarters. The colossal building contained the offices of the hierarchy of the Greek police. The offices of Interpol and Europol occupied the top floors.

He entered Mitch's office, and shut the door. He intended a private conversation. He had a strong suspicion someone was monitoring their every move. They had searched for bugs, but found none. Still, somehow, their each action was known.

Mitch, immersed in paper work, didn't hear him come in.

"Mitch," Zach said, making his brother-in-law drop his papers. "Why so surprised? I told you I'd be stopping by."

"I'm sorry, you're right. I had forgotten."

He looked exasperated as he gathered the papers. "We're being bombarded by critics on all sides because we refuse to give sanctuary to refugees. But it's too close to the Olympics. We can't risk a terrorist infiltration. We won't risk it."

Mitch straightened in his chair and stretched, trying to ease some of the tension from his shoulders.

"I was scanning the report about the drowned immigrants. There are no survivors, and no information—one blank wall, countless deaths to process." He leaned forward, picked up the file and tossed it to him. "Here, take a look. You might see something I didn't. Try to figure this out. With the preparations for the Olympics, I haven't been able to give it much time."

Zach picked it up. "Let me go through this later. I have an idea that may help us find the ship." He glanced through it, then gave Mitch a conspiratorial wink.

"By analyzing where they found the victims, I can trace their route, and find which ship traveled it." He touched his finger to his lips, motioning him to silence. "The data should give me the information I need. Once we identity the ship, we'll have who the captain is, and the gang leader."

**** **** ****

Down in the basement, in a small storage room, each word passed down through the air conditioning ducts that connected the rooms. The janitor recorded their conversation. He pocketed the paper and stepped out into the hall. He listened carefully, heard a door slam, then nothing. At a near-by pay telephone, he dialed a number, recited the information and hung up.

Mr. Oliver, on his way to his rendezvous, heard his cell phone ring. The apartment was in an old sordid neighborhood where only the poorest lived. The buildings riddled with World War II bullet marks. He stopped and answered." Yes, what? Right, I'll pass it along." He pocketed the phone, then knocked on the door. It opened slowly. The crack widened.

"Bruno, mate, you messed up. Again." Mr. Oliver looked him over with his beady eyes, before he entered the apartment. "The boss isn't going to be happy—so stupid," he sneered, shook his head, "that's twice now you didn't do it. That's not good."

Oliver pushed past him, and went to the open window. An alley strewn with garbage, crawling with rats blocked his view. He heard people scuttle by and a jumble of languages reached his ears. This cacophony of sounds, mixed with the smells of sewage, made him scowl. He remembered well the cold and dampness, the constant hunger of his Liverpool childhood. He shuddered.

He turned from the window, and stared at the one-eyed man called Bruno. "One more chance you got to snuff him. If you don't, we got to get somebody else. And," looking at him closely, "you'd better vanish or you know, mate, things won't be good. The boss," he shrugged, "is getting impatient."

"Not my fault, Mister," his gruff voice, heavily accented, whimpered. "Told you, he's too well guarded," he played with his knife, "a woman came, spoiled the kill."

Bruno threw his knife with force, and just missed a cockroach climbing the wall. "He should have been dead. I stabbed many times," he took his knife out of the wall, "now, too dangerous."

Oliver's black eyes pierced Bruno. He folded his diamond-ringed fingers over his substantial girth, looked down at his shiny shoes and pointed a pudgy finger in Bruno's face. "He squealed to someone before you stabbed him— he's got to die. The Black Spider, he says so. That's how it's gotta be. Do it right—you fucking understand?" With that he went to the door, looked back once, and then went out. Mr. Oliver paused a moment outside and hefted his pants over his bulging belly. Careful not to touch the walls, he prodded down the urine saturated stairs.

Outside, he took a deep breath, and checked his watch. He had a half an hour until his next meeting. He patted the wad of Euros in his jacket pocket. It had taken a while, but the temptation for easy money had won. It had overcome the last scruples of the newest member of the team, a close associate of Zachary Artemidis. Zachary's every movement would now be watched. The phone call he just got made Zach a key player.

Chapter 26

Alethea used Zach's key to enter his apartment. She smiled, pleased with herself, remembering Zena's annoyed grimace when introduced to Karl. It had been a priceless moment. Zena, she was confident, would give Karl some well-deserved grief. She placed Zach's key on a hall table, and stood thinking.

Being an opportunist, Karl was sure to chase Zena. After all, she worked for a major station. He liked to play the charmer and felt no woman could resist him. He would be certain of his own success, taking advantage where he could. And Zena, burnt by a scheming man, was bound to guard her heart

Alethea swung her bag off her shoulder, dropped it on the coffee table, and sat on the sofa by the fireplace. Revenge would be sweet when Karl got his comeuppance.

Satisfied at this bit of plotting, she took her journal from her bag. Before she forgot, she had to write down what had happened in the hospital. Apparently, she had the power to heal. Closing her eyes, she tried to remember. She started writing.

When I placed my hands on him, I could feel them heating up. Concentrating, I went deep into my mind and saw a white heat. It gathered inside me. I guided this healing energy, sending it into Leonidas. I closed my eyes. I could see his sliced ligaments and torn tissues mending, growing together—sealing themselves. The blood pumped harder, pulsing under my hands, pushing throughout his body. I stopped, too exhausted to continue. Drained of energy, it took me a few moments to recover. As I did, I noticed color coming back into Leonidas face. It was the most satisfying thing I have ever done, and the most amazing.

As she wrote, she recalled the many other times that she, like her mother and grandmother before her, had written in her journal, analyzing her psychic skills. She had been trained, at a young age, to write down her abilities as precisely as possible. She had also been made to understand this gift was an obligation.

She closed the book. Put her journal away and took out her cards. She shuffled them and closed her eyes to concentrate. Zach had kept her too busy these past few days. She hadn't had time for card reading or for herself. She had been swallowed whole into his life. She still hadn't made up her mind if this was a good or bad thing.

When she examined the cards, she saw danger lurking. She put a card down for Zach. Two jeopardy cards fell on his head. Not good at all. There—a death card on someone. She wished she hadn't read them. Now she would worry. She gathered up the cards, stood and started pacing. How could she leave for Lesvos if Zach was in danger?

His fate hadn't changed much from the plane. This assignment would place him in peril. Somebody would die. Why did he have to risk his life? This wasn't his problem. He should save the heroics for someone else. But he wouldn't. She scowled, and folded her arms tightly around herself. Jeez—to improve the world - okay, to lend a helping hand - okay, to try to fight evil, alright she got it. But to risk his life? No, not a good idea. People like him, though, made the world a better place. She had to admit she liked his selflessness. But at what cost?

She was startled to hear the door opening. She turned.

Zach stood outlined in the doorway with a bottle of wine and box of chocolates. He pushed the door shut, looked at her with a satisfied smile before slowly coming over for a kiss.

Alethea couldn't help responding. She smiled back, took the things out of his hands and placed them on the table. They sat together on the couch, not talking.

Finally, Alethea couldn't restrain herself any longer. "How did you make out with Mitch? You said something about setting a trap for the spy."

"Whoa - slow down." He squeezed her hand.

"If anybody was listening to our conversation, I certainly gave them something to think about.

We've checked Mitch's office for bugs, with a fine-toothed comb. We couldn't find anything, but they still seem to know what we're doing. This time, they got an earful."

"And put yourself at risk. I can sense it, so tell me what you've done."

Zach managed a smile. "I wouldn't say I placed myself at risk. We let it be known—by analyzing the data, and mapping out where the bodies were found—we could surmise which ship went by there that day. This way we can find the ship and its captain."

"And who's going to be the puzzle solver—you?"

He nodded.

"I knew it." She glared at him. "I just knew it! So if anyone was listening and I'm sure you suspect someone was, they'll be sure to come after you. This is stupid."

She gave him a quizzical look. "Can you really find the ship from the location of the bodies? And where is this supposed information?" He hadn't brought in any files.

"We left the file in the office as bait. I didn't take anything with me; I'm supposed to go back for it. This way they'll have time to break into Mitch's office to steal it."

"I don't want to criticize the police." Alethea, chewed her lip. "I know that ninety per cent are dedicated people who want to lessen the chaos in this world, but you have to be careful of the ten per cent who aren't. The greedy ones, the perverts." She watched him closely. "Money can tempt even the most honest."

"I know," Zach said. "We've taken the first step in finding the informer. This file has become an important file. And you're right, I've become a player. They'll focus on me." He leaned back with a satisfied smile. "They always seem to be one step ahead, but not anymore."

"I hope you're right." Alethea placed her hand over his, stared into his eyes. "This is because of Leonidas, the dockworker. You're trying to draw the attention from him." She took his hand. "By the way, you never told me who Leonidas really was. I got the impression you knew him and not as a dockworker."

"Mitch, Leonidas and I were in the *Special Services* together. After that Leonidas joined the police.

Mitch asked him to go undercover for this case. He's a close family friend, completely trustworthy. We put him to work on my ships to establish an identity."

"I see." She raised her eyes, "that explains your family's concern for him. It kind of backfired on you when he got stabbed, didn't it?"

She bit her lip. "He wasn't supposed to be in danger. Obviously, he stumbled across something. I hope he regains his memory."

"I hope so too. But the fact remains he called someone in the department, someone he trusted, someone he considered a friend, and this person almost caused his death. When I find out who it is," he looked at her sharply, "and I will—I'm taking him down."

"I have a bad feeling about this." She rubbed her hands up and down her arms.

"He's still in danger. Mitch said he had men protecting him, but I don't think it will help. He's stumbled onto something bad. My intuition's telling me it has nothing to do with these illegals, and something to do with the Olympics.

Death is near. There's death in the cards. I wish I wasn't leaving. Who's going to protect you?"

He put his arm around her, drawing her close.

"How can you protect me, there isn't much to you." Letting her go a minute, he drew out a cell phone and handed it to her.

"This is for you. My number's programmed into it. Call me for any reason. I need to know you can find me.

This terrorist theory is farfetched, but I'll let you know. After I see you off, I'll stop at the hospital and check on Leonidas."

She opened the phone, pressed the contact button. His cell phone number came up.

"Thank you, this helps relieve some of my worry, but not all of it. You have to go to the hospital."

"I said I would." He opened the wine, and gestured. "What time does your boat leave?"

"Really late—it leaves at midnight and arrives early in the morning."

He noted the time, took off his jacket and laid it down on a chair before going to the bar to get two glasses and a bottle opener.

She watched him get comfortable and raised her eyebrows. "We still have a few hours. What would you like to do?"

He sat next to her, reached for the opened wine, and poured. "Give you two guesses." Winking at her, he handed her the wine glass, then opened the chocolates, placing one in her mouth.

"To us," he toasted, his glass to his lips.

Alethea, touched, finished her chocolate. "To us," she saluted, then sipped.

Not wanting to rush the moment, Zach took the remote control from the table and turned on the set.

With his hand around her shoulder, her body snuggled next to him, they watched the screen. After the foreign news reports, the narrator switched to local stories.

Zena, in a smart red suit, sat across from Shah Raoul Zin in a hotel lobby. She thanked him for taking the time out of his busy schedule to allow for this interview. The Shah, condescending and polite, answered her questions, but avoided giving any direct replies to her politically volatile queries.

"Why that minx," Zach said, "she must have used my name to get an interview. She should have told me he was here. Raoul and I were friends, we still keep in touch. I'll have to call him."

She shrugged her shoulders. "She didn't want you to know you were helpful to her in any way. She certainly carries this independence thing to an extreme.

I saw her at the hotel, she was setting up for the interview. I promised I wouldn't say anything."

She raised an eyebrow. "He's got quite a regal presence." Watching the screen, she added. "He's good-looking—with that black curly hair and mahogany skin and those green eyes. Where did he get those eyes?"

"He's part Greek, on his mother's side. His father went to the University here in Athens.

They met at school. I believe it was love at first sight." He nodded at the screen, "from what I heard from Raoul, there was quite an uproar when they decided to marry. Raoul's father was next in line to rule his country."

Shifting his weight, he made himself more comfortable. "Both families felt the cultural differences would bring conflict once the bloom of first love wore off. They urged them not to marry. The couple insisted. His mother's family agreed but only if the couple spent time in Greece. This wasn't a hardship. Summer in Greece is magical."

He pulled her closer. "We first met at Harvard. Then we went into the *Special Services* together. We filled our mandatory Greek military obligation in an area of our choice, instead of being drafted and being put who knew where.

Mitch, Leonidas, Raoul, and I were well trained in sabotage techniques, among other things, and sent on special missions all over the world. Through me, Maro met Mitch. They hit it off from the start."

Zach rubbed his chin. "I wish Zena had told me Raoul was in town. She got her interview for Zena's Hour, but it would have been better if I had talked to him. She's too proud to ask for help and wants to do things on her own—Miss Independence herself."

A muscle twitched in his jaw. "There's not much I can do for her outlook. Her gold digger husband abused her, and left her with scars."

"I'm sorry to hear that. She obviously doesn't want to need any man, even you." She picked up her glass and sipped her wine.

"Why do you do it? You have everything a man could want, why get involved with these criminals? Why help your brother- in- law to solve crimes? It's not your job. You could be out partying with a different woman every night, enjoying yourself. Why aren't you? I mean—this doesn't concern you."

"That's a curious point of view, from someone like you, who says your gift makes you responsible to mankind. That's a selfless stance. Why do you do it—try to help whenever you can?"

Playing with the rim of her glass, she watched him lean into the couch. He looked sexy in his shirt with his chest hairs showing.

Fate had played its hand, and they had met. She eyed him up and down. How to explain?

"Self-satisfaction, that's what I feel. I was given this gift to help, and I have to help. It's a compulsion. I have little control over it."

She played with the buttons on his shirt, then looked up. "I might be afraid, but I put fear a side when I know someone's in danger. You don't have this gift, so why do you care?"

"I care. I always have. From a young age, I've helped people in trouble in whichever way I could." He ran a hand through his hair, and shook his head. "If we don't help each other, what are we?

Bad people don't care about a person's human rights, about their right to live a free life." He leaned forward, poured some more wine.

"That's why I got involved. These people - they're fleeing poverty and oppression - they're trying to better themselves. But there are too many rogues making money from their misfortunes.

Nothing else matters—just the money." He paused a moment.

"Maybe I like to think of myself as a man of action, maybe being surrounded by women all my life, it was important to identify with my masculinity, maybe I court danger for this reason. Who knows?"

"Well, there's no doubt that you're a man. But I can understand how you feel. I don't think you court danger. It's not your masculinity that you're testing. You're just a responsible person." She stared into his eyes. "A person who refuses to turn his back on someone in trouble."

"Maybe you know me better than I know myself. You're not only a psychic, but a psychologist as well."

He nodded. "You're right. I am responsible. I'm not reckless. I don't jump into danger without thinking things through.

After my Special Services days, I'd just as soon stick to my books and my research. I've had enough adventure for a lifetime. But if needed, I want to help." He meditated a moment. "Maybe I enjoy the challenge.

Mind games of any kind attract me, I like solving puzzles."

She pushed back into the cushions, tucked her jean-covered legs under her. "That's what I like most. Your honesty with me, and with yourself, from the start. No pretense. I hate dishonesty, lies, more than anything. Next to that, I hate being used for my abilities. I don't like people taking. That's why our relationship suits me."

Alethea slowly sipped her wine. "This white wine is excellent. I've never tasted anything quite like it. It's sweet."

He pulled her feet into his lap and started massaging them.

"I got a case of it last Christmas from an Alex Vladis, a friend of my oldest sister Sylvia's husband, Peter. They're from Cyprus.

He's a business associate whose home base is England. These wines are produced in Kakheti, Georgia," he paused to play with her toes. "They've been making wine there since 7000 B.C."

He looked up at her. "He's a shipping tycoon, owns Vladmire lines. He has two daughters. My sister Sylvia, a notorious matchmaker, hoped to get us together. I think the wine was meant as an inducement to get me to meet and marry one of them. He and I met at one of my sister's parties."

Lulled by his rubbing, her body supported by the couch, she felt completely relaxed.

"Did you ever meet them, or see pictures of them? They seem like perfect candidates for you." Noticing his glare, she shrugged. "Sorry, I'm beginning to see what you've had to put up with."

I'm not the marrying kind." He shook his head. "Except for satisfying my biological urges, my life's going to be women free. Don't get me wrong. I love women. But in their place, preferably not in my place." He closed his eyes a moment and took a deep breath.

"I don't like to be manipulated. People make me angry when they try to coax, wheedle or threaten me into doing what they want. They piss me off, even more, when they're determined to change my life." He clenched his teeth.

"I like my freedom too much. I'm not ready for marriage yet, maybe later, maybe never."

"That's what I like most about you—your honesty. We have the perfect relationship, mutual satisfaction, hopefully friendship, with no obligation."

Feeding him a chocolate, she smiled. "Aren't you glad I'm *also* not the marrying kind?" *Honey you don't know it yet but your freedom is a thing of the past.* She went into his arms and licked the chocolate from his lips. "That's a lovely taste. I think we've talked enough."

Chapter 27

"Well, it's time." Alethea put her arms around his neck and kissed him. "I can't seem to get enough of you." Hearing the warning whistle, she gave his cheek a final caress. "I'd better hurry before the boat leaves."

"Not a bad thing. We'd have more time together." Zach leaned over, and kissed her again. "I'll see you soon. I have a few loose ends to take care of, then I can join you." He pushed a lock of hair out of her eyes. "Sure you won't wait and come with me on my yacht?"

"No, as much as I'd like to stay, I have to leave today. My sixth sense is telling me I have to be on this boat." She opened her door. "Don't forget to check on your friend, it's important."

"There's the final whistle." Zach hurried to get her suitcases, walked with her to the barrier and watched as she boarded the lighted high-speed ferry. It pulled out, sea-horn blasting. He followed the boat with his eyes. How had she become such a necessary part of his life?

Zach eased into traffic and headed for the hospital to check on Leonidas. He had too much respect for Alethea's psychic insights to discount her warning.

He parked his car at the hospital just as an ambulance whizzed by, sirens screaming, tires squealing.

He quickened his steps. There was a pounding of footsteps and a chorus of voices shouted orders. Attendants rushed out to the vehicle to transport the injured to the emergency entrance. Right behind them, another ambulance came to a screeching halt.

Everybody rushed around taking the stretchers out of the vehicles. Getting closer, he heard fragments of their conversation, enough to gather there had been a serious three car accident on Kifisias Ave.

He walked into the hospital, and into the elevator without anyone noticing. The guards on duty had disappeared. Not good at all, he thought, it left the area free for any assailant.

On the second floor, the police officer was still at his post, outside Leonidas' room. The officer recognized him, and opened the door. Zachary paused in the doorway and looked at his friend. Leonidas was wrapped in bandages, but the IV drips and life monitors systems were gone. A few days ago he had been near death. Now his life threatening wounds appeared nearly healed.

Alethea had pretended innocence, but he suspected she had something to do with Leonidas' miraculous recovery. Zach had not wanted to spoil their last day together, so he hadn't questioned her about her part in this development. The next time they met, though, he was going to, for sure.

Leonidas, eyes alert, watched him.

Zach drew a chair up to the bed. "I thought you'd be sleeping." He shrugged. "There've been two attempts on your life, and we still don't know why. You're still in danger." Zach lifted his eyebrows. "You look better than you did when you first came in. How's your memory - has anything come back to you?"

"An angel came. I woke up, thought I had died and gone to heaven." He rubbed his eye, as if trying to ease an ache. "My soul was leaving my body when she put her hand on my chest. A surge of energy went through me, shocking me as if I'd touched a live wire. Everything darkened. When I came to, she was gone. But I felt renewed.

My body's better, but my mind's still a blank. Visions and sounds bombard me, but they don't make sense. They're like flashes, a glimpse here, and a glimpse there. Before I can grasp what it is, it—disappears.

I'm tormented by a feeling of impending doom. This thing's bigger than discovering who's bringing illegal immigrants into the country or who's trafficking in women." Leonidas shifted in his place, and tried to make himself more comfortable. "I ache all over. My memory's shattered. The harder I try to remember, the more difficult it becomes. Vague thoughts nag at me. There's danger. And it concerns the Olympics."

"The Olympics? What can the *Deliverance* have to do with the Olympics? It's a cargo ship." Zach scratched his head, "this doesn't make sense.

When you were stabbed, we checked the ship from top to bottom, looking for clues. We found nothing. No illegal immigrants stowed away, no hint as to why you were attacked, just a cargo of used car parts from Bulgaria." He shook his head. "The ship came south a few days ago, by way of the Black Sea. There has to be something important enough on it to warrant your death. We just haven't found it."

Zach gave him a questioning look.

"Who did you talk with at Central Headquarters, before you were attacked? If you remember anything, no matter how minor, tell Mitch or me. No one else.

We're sure there's a mole on the staff, feeding the enemy information."

Leonidas moved his arms and turned on his side. "I heard a sound, and went to investigate. Two men were talking, stowaways, who had come on at the last boarding.

They spoke Greek, but a low class Greek, real slang. It was hard to understand, but slowly I grasped what they were saying. Two others joined them, foreigners who spoke broken Greek. I couldn't place where they were from."

Exhausted from his efforts, he lay back on his pillow and closed his eyes. "That's it. I don't recall anything else."

Zach listened. He tried to imagine Leonidas' last moments before the stabbing.

"They must have said something to alert you to a possible threat, something to do with the Olympics. You didn't just get the idea into your head."

Seeing how fatigued Leonidas was, he stood up. "I've overstayed my visit. Be careful. Rest now, I'll be back tomorrow."

Leonidas opened his eyes. "I'm sorry, I tire easily. Maybe things will come back to me in my sleep."

At the door, Zachary stopped. "You'll remember. You've already made a good start."

He exited the room. Walked briskly toward the elevators, giving the officer on duty a quick glance.

The man was leaning back in his chair with his cap pulled over his eyes. *Is he napping when he should be on duty?* Zach got into the elevator, smoothed his hair back with a nervous gesture.

Wait—that man didn't look familiar. Why the new man? He exited the elevator and saw the officers back at their posts. He grabbed the arm of the nearest man.

"The shift—when does it change?"

The officer checked his watch. "We all switch in another two hours. It's less confusing and safer that way—no new faces."

"So the same police officer should be on duty outside Leonidas' room, right?"

"That's right. Why?"

Zach rushed back to the elevator.

"You two follow me, and you there, cover the stairs. Don't let anybody by you, I mean anybody," he shouted.

On Leonidas' floor, there was no man on duty.

"Hurry!" He raced down the hall and barged into his friend's room just as someone rushed past him, knocking him down.

He saw the intruder flee down the hall and duck into the stairwell.

Zachary rose to his feet and walked toward the bed.

Leonidas lay still. So quiet, Zach was sure the intruder had succeeded in killing him.

The silence unnerved him. He drew closer and felt his friend's hand on his arm.

"Don't worry, I'm still alive. I pretended sleep and watched the guy enter. He pulled a large switchblade out of his uniform."

Disappointment colored his voice, "I would have had him," he scoffed, "if you hadn't barged into the room."

"You were just at death's door, remember? You're still too weak to defend yourself. And don't give me that look, as if I don't know what I'm talking about."

Just then, an officer rushed into the room.

"We got him." He told Zach and Leonidas. "He tried to escape down the stairs. Our man stationed there blocked his way.

Dressed in uniform, the bloke pretended to be on duty, but following your orders, the officer refused to let him pass. The guy pushed him aside. They struggled, but we subdued him. He's in police custody.

"Where's the man who's supposed to be outside the door?" Zachary asked.

"We're looking for him. They're searching all the rooms on this floor."

Zachary glanced at Leonidas, a worried look on his face. "I'm calling Mitch, it's not safe for you here."

A second officer came in. "Our missing man's been strangled. A nurse found him."

Visibly upset, Zach combed his hand through his hair. "He strangled the guard while we were inside talking. And we didn't hear a sound." He shook his head, whirled on Leonidas. "You have to be moved. These people, whoever they are, want you dead." He punched in Mitch's emergency number.

Chapter 28

"What's happened?" Mitch barked into the phone.

"A dead officer happened." Zach pressed the phone close to his ear. "Somebody murdered the man on duty, and tried to get to Leonidas." He stopped talking a moment to catch his breath,

"The guard's body was found in an empty room. We have the attacker in custody."

He cleared his throat. "Leonidas can't stay here. There are too many people around. It's not secure."

"Wait there, I'm coming over," Mitch said. "We'll have Leo moved to my house. It's the safest place.

And I took care of that other matter," he added. "My office is rigged with cameras ready to tape any intruder."

"Good. Let's hope someone tries to steal the file." Zach cast a glance toward Leonidas, then whispered to Mitch. "We'll talk more when you get here."

"Mitch is coming. We're going to move you to a safer place. The doctor can monitor your progress from there. We'll hire a private nurse to take care of you." He squeezed his friend's hand.

"Things will be fine—we'll make them so," he hesitated a moment, "and you're right, you do have an angel looking after you. That's the third time you've escaped an attempt on your life. You're one lucky guy."

"What angel?" Leonidas gave him a curious glance, "you can't mean the one I mentioned. She doesn't exist, it was just a dream. No one was here with me."

"Maybe. Be glad that destiny plays a part in our lives. It wasn't your time."

Zach knitted his brows and went over to pour a glass of water. "The Olympics are only a few months away. Everything's being done to prevent a terrorist attack.

Our critics in Europe are brutal." He moved the chair closer to the bed. "They're predicting that we won't be ready in time, that we won't be able to manage the security for such a large crowd, that we'll botch the Olympics. That's not going to happen."

He eyed him carefully. "You have to recall what you heard."

Leonidas lay back, closed his eyes and focused his thoughts. He felt better, but his mind was still a blank. Opening his eyes, he slowly tried to raise himself.

"The conversation between the two stowaways. They talked about the games. I'm trying to remember what they said, but every time I try, I get nauseous. I break out in a cold sweat just thinking about it."

Zachary leaned forward. "Relax. Try to picture the scene in your mind, play it back like a movie.

Start with before you saw them." Intent on Leonidas, he was startled by Mitch's hand on his shoulder. "Mitch, I didn't hear you come in."

"You two were so busy, you wouldn't hear a bomb go off." He looked from one to the other. "What's going on?"

"Some of Leonidas' memory came back. He heard two foreigners on board the *Deliverance* talking about the Olympics. I'm trying to nudge him to remember more."

Mitch glanced at Leonidas, saw his strained face, his tired eyes. "I think he's had enough. Maybe in different surroundings, he'll remember."

He straightened. "Why don't we stay out of the way, and let my staff do their job. I have an ambulance downstairs with my own driver. Once we leave, no one will find Leonidas. The doctor and nurse are absolutely trustworthy."

Zach stood. "We'll talk again soon, Leonidas. Try to rest."

He left the room with Mitch, just as the nurse and attendants entered.

They moved down the hall, out of earshot.

"What made you come to the hospital this time of night?" Mitch turned toward Zach. "You probably saved Leonidas' life, again. Have you become psychic all of a sudden? You know things are going to happen before they do."

"Maybe I'm developing a sixth sense," Zach fabricated. "I suddenly felt Leonidas was in danger. I brought Alethea to the dock and came straight here."

He pressed the elevator button.

"Do you think there's a plot forming to cause trouble at the Olympics?" Mitch asked.

"Something's going on for sure," Zach confirmed.

Mitch shifted his weight. "We don't need a repeat of Munich in 1972, with bombs exploding in the stadium, killing innocent victims." He rubbed his chin with his fingers. "Greece is taking a lot of criticism from the international community. But we're going to surprise them. The security budget for these games is over one billion euros. It's the most spent on any Olympics, ever."

He folded his arms across his chest. "The first Olympics were held here. Our national pride is at stake. This game must be the finest of all the Olympic Games." Mitch declared.

"No terrorists will spoil it. We'll have seventy thousand police out in force. The Greek police are well trained, well equipped, well disciplined - plus we have support from law enforcement worldwide." His voice filled with passion. "There won't be any trouble at these Olympics."

"I hope you're right." Zach looked up at his friend. "Let's hope we catch the spy in *our* midst before it's too late."

Chapter 29

Alethea sat in her high backed seat aboard the speed ferry, and couldn't keep the secret smile from her face. Every time she thought of Zach, his vehemence against the married state, she wanted to laugh. Men were such fools. Did he actually think he had a choice?

A marriage license, wedded bliss - what did they mean? When two people were meant to be together, they just were, and would be, and nothing else was needed. So why bother to protest and rant against marriage?

She had thought she could control men with sex. How many times did she play with her dates promising them heaven and giving them nothing? But Zach had helped her understand her foolishness. He had showed her that sex wasn't so much about power as about mutual satisfaction. Giving, not taking, with nobody in control of the other.

She snuggled into her seat and closed her eyes, maybe she could get a few winks of sleep. A calm surrounded her as the other people's chattering slowly subsided and they tried to do the same. The boat sped through the night shrouded in darkness.

Alethea was startled awake by agitated voices, exclaiming and cursing. She looked around, and noticed people peering out the windows into a rosy dawning light. Then she heard a grinding, crackling sound. The boat shuddered, shaking from end to end with violent vibrations. Then the engines creaked once more and died. They were adrift in the middle of a choppy sea.

She listened, and could make out different conversations. Most passengers were speaking Greek.

"This is the second time," a fat bald man a few seats down, grumbled, "that I've been on one of these speed ferries where the motor failed. Next time I'm taking the *Mytilene,* it might take twelve hours, but you're bound to get there safely. With these things, you're never sure. If the winds pick up and the waves increase, we might capsize."

"Don't worry," another passenger sitting next to him piped in, "we're not far from Chios, they'll probably send someone to tow us there."

"They don't service these properly. They're always playing catch-up.

In turbulent weather they have to cancel routes and they get behind schedule," added an older woman. "They miss necessary maintenance and have too many breakdowns."

"What's everyone complaining about?" A scholarly looking British man asked Alethea.

"About the high-speed ferries," she answered, "apparently they've had problems before."

"Oh right, I'm sure they'll sort it out. By the way, where are you going- Chios or Lesvos?"

"Lesvos, and you?" She looked down, smoothing her skirt.

"Plan to go bird watching on Lesvos. I'm preparing a book, hope to get splendid pictures. My wife and I, she went to the *loo,* belong to a birders' club. We should get together on the island, maybe have a bite."

"Yes, that would be nice." Suddenly distracted, Alethea couldn't follow the conversation. A deep emotional pain shot through her.

She closed her eyes and tried to concentrate, to understand what was happening. An image of a young woman huddled in a corner crowded her mind. She was afraid, heaving and grasping for breath, her body wracked with silent sobs. Alethea could sense her near, hiding on the boat.

"Excuse me. We'll talk again," Alethea interrupted, "I have to go find somebody." She got out of her seat, and started walking, allowing her intuition to lead her. She found the girl huddled under the stairs to the upper deck, in a small dark space, trying to appear invisible. Alethea bent down and put her hand on the girl's shoulder.

"What's wrong? Tell me." A petite blond stared up at her with sorrowful blue eyes. She wore old jeans, a blue sweater over a white shirt with a pair of tattered sneakers. She looked young.

"Please… little English, so afraid, big trouble," gesturing she tried to explain herself.

"Are you hungry? Come," Alethea raised her gently by the arm.

The girl glanced around wide eyed and tried to push Alethea's hand away. "No papers, no ticket, no money."

The cafeteria had just opened for breakfast. Alethea sat her down at one of the tables, saw the girl's eyes riveted to the cakes and sandwiches on display. At the counter, she ordered coffee for herself, sandwiches and some packaged cookies for the girl. "First eat, then we can talk." Seeing her still fearful, Alethea looked deep into her eyes to calm her. "Don't be afraid. No one will bother you here, I promise."

Famished, if not reassured, the girl ate. She bolted down the sandwiches, nibbled delicately on a piece of cookie, and washed her food down with a glass of water. Finished, she sighed, then cast a fleeting look around before lowering her lashes. She stared at her lap and refused to meet Alethea's eyes.

"Thank you," she whispered.

"What happened to you?" Alethea took her hand and tried to reassure her with her touch.

"What's your name?"

Startled, the girl looked up at her and took a few deep breaths. "Sasha Kosova," she said.

"No papers. Man come to my village in Moldova, he say work here in Greece. He bring us on bus," she motioned with her hands and tried to make herself understood, "say give papers to him, for work permit. Many poor girls leave village, no work, no money, our family hope we work, send money to help." She stopped speaking, her eyes filled with tears.

She covered her face. "So terrible. So bad men, terrible things they do." She pulled at the hem of her shirt, keeping her eyes lowered. "All the time afraid. Bad men slap girls, hurt them." She gulped some air.

"Man on bus, he take us to house, said stay, work here. No papers, afraid, good girl not like house." She stopped overcome by tears.

Alethea moved to her side of the table, tried to reassure her by putting her arm around her. The girl pulled away and stared at her with horror.

206

"What's the matter… why are you afraid of me?"

"Good girl - no sex! Women, or men."

"What?" Startled, she had a vision. *A house with red shutters, she recognized it from her last picturing. She saw men and women leering, a dark room, a bed. She felt raw fear, hopelessness, deep shame.*

She snapped out of it. "No, you misunderstood. My goodness, what kind of place was that?" She shook her head. "No sex, friend," she brought her hand to her heart.

Sasha examined Alethea and relaxed a little.

"Friend in Mytilene, she work there, she from my village, I call, I go to meet her." With pantomime, she showed how she escaped from the house, found her way to Athens. How she swept floors to buy a ticket

"The bus driver didn't check your papers?" Alethea asked, impressed by her fortitude.

"No. Didn't ask papers, just money to buy ticket."

I'll help you. We can stay together until we get to Mytilene. Finish your food," she indicated with her hand, "then we'll find a place for you to sit. I don't think they'll check tickets again.

Anyway, if they can't start the motor they'll have to tow us into the nearest port, which is Chios." She looked at her confused expression. "Sorry, you can't understand me."

"Speak little English." She scanned the area, rubbed her eyes. "No papers, no ticket. Police catch - send back home, no hope, big shame."

"This friend in Mytilene—do you have her address or phone number? When we dock, we'll find her. And I have a friend who can help you get papers."

She gave her a reassuring pat on the arm, "I promise everything will be well. Let's find some seats."

Even though the boat wasn't crowded, Alethea kept an eye out as she mulled over the situation.

This poor child had left her home to come to an unknown place, a place where she hoped to make money to send to her family. Zach was right—these poor souls needed help. Unscrupulous people promised them work, a new life, while selling them into slavery.

She had gotten a glimpse of what she had endured before she escaped.

Moldovia, Alethea recalled, was a former Soviet republic between Romania and the Ukraine. Even though it had rich, fertile land and rolling hills, there was no work to be found. The people led a harsh life, with declining human rights, police corruption and laws that didn't apply equally to all.

Crime, and the rule of the mafia caused the citizens to be wary of each other and to mistrust the government. No wonder Sasha wanted to leave from there. Alethea gave her a sideways glance, and saw her eating part of a sandwich she had hidden away in her pocket.

Shocked, Alethea promised herself, she'd help Sasha with everything in her power. Pity overtook her.

In light of Sasha's misery, her own life seemed charmed, her problems insignificant. Alethea had never been deprived or wanting, always had enough food to eat and clothes to wear, never had to worry about anything. She helped others because she wanted to, and could. But she didn't really take life seriously.

Alethea had left home because she wanted her independence. She hadn't left because she had to survive or to support a family, to start life in a new place, where her poverty stricken family could come and prosper.

She tried to help others, but she felt like a fraud. She could have been that girl, if life had played her a different hand. Her ancestors had emigrated from Greece to America at the turn of the century, looking for a better life. Their determination and hard work, their need to help their families, had made them successful.

What if they had stayed where they were, in a village with no running water, no electricity, and no future, wouldn't she be a different person today?

She would have been poor, deprived of the comforts of life, hungry, maybe even cursed or shunned because of her gifts.

Her parents had overprotected her for good reason. Yet she rebelled, acting reckless, and irresponsible.

Now her problems seemed small compared to this unfortunate woman's.

Her thoughts were interrupted by a loud bang. Out the window, she saw a tugboat pull up to the ferry.

Crewmen scrambled around hooking tow ropes up to the boat. Coast Guard circled, overseeing the operation. The commotion died down; she felt a jolt as the boat started to glide through the waters towards Chios. She noticed Sasha sat with her shoulders slumped forward, as if exhausted from crying.

Alethea pushed back in her seat and gave a sigh of relief—at least they were moving. She watched the boat skim over the choppy aquamarine water. She glimpsed a pod of Dolphins swimming alongside, arcing out of the water. Drawn by their antics, surprised by their size, she watched until they disappeared. They seemed so happy, so care free.

In the distance, she could see white buildings emerge from the fog. They first appeared as tiny spots, and grew larger as the boat approached the port of Chios. Soon, she could see things in detail—people walking around, cars winding through the streets, tourist shops opening in preparation for the day.

She had read somewhere that Chios was noted for its *mastica* (chewing gum), gotten from the mastic tree found only on this island. She'd have to remember to try some.

As they waited to dock, she heard a humming near her; she looked around confused, then realized her cell phone was ringing; the one Zach had given her. She fished it out of her jacket pocket and flipped it open.

"Hello darling—missed me already?"

"And who's your darling?" Zach sounded irritated.

"Why—you are. Who else would call me on this phone?" She teased.

"You're right of course." She heard a smile in his voice, "trying to get a reaction from me, were you?"

"Maybe…do you mind?"

"No, I guess not. I tried to call before, but there was no connection. You must be close to Lesvos now."

"Actually not - we're being towed into Chios. We had motor trouble that couldn't be fixed at sea. They made an announcement. There's going to be a three hour delay."

"They've had this problem before with these high-speed ferries." Zach cleared his throat. "You were right, again, about another attack on Leonidas. I got there just in time, he swears he has an angel looking out for him, and everyone thinks I'm psychic.

We moved him to a safe house. After the ambulance left with Leonidas, I came back home, but couldn't sleep."

"Slow down, I can't catch every word. Of course I was right about the attack, I'm glad you listened to me. I'm sorry about the strangled officer."

"How do you know about the officer? I didn't tell you about him." His deep voice shook her.

"You shouldn't question me—just accept that I know." She sighed. "The assailant must be watched—he's in danger. I hear shots, then death. Listen to what he says."

"Alethea you're doing it again." Zach said in a vexed tone.

"Doing what?"

"You know—giving me bits and pieces of what's to come." He hesitated. "Why don't you fill me in on Leonidas?

Tell me. What's going to happen with him?"

"I'm not sure, yet. I'm never completely sure," she said impatiently, "now stop talking and listen."

Certain that she had his attention, she continued. "I found a young girl on board, a stowaway. She's an illegal who was tricked into leaving her home. Somehow she got involved with a gang of sex slavers," she took a breath, "I promised her you would help. Will you help her? She terrified."

"Alethea. Listen to me. These men are dangerous. They're not going to let one of their birds fly. You can be sure someone is searching for her, right now."

He raised his voice. "I can't believe you got your-self mixed up in this mess. When they find her they'll kill her and you too."

He made an effort to calm down. "I'm sorry I yelled at you, but I hate to think of you in danger. We can help, but we need her cooperation. The big wheels who run this sex trade hide themselves well. She might be the break we need to flush them out."

Alethea cleared her throat. "What's being done to help these women?"

"Immigrant women," Zach explained, "are pro-tected from being arrested, detained, and deported by a law passed in 2002. They're allowed to remain in Greece, with temporary residence permits, until their case against the traffickers is tried in court.

We'll talk more when I see you. I have a call com-ing in. It might be important."

"Wait Zach...."

But he had hung up.

"Mitch what's happening?" Zach asked, as he dis-connected from Alethea. "It's early for you to call. Didn't get much sleep, did you?"

"No, how could I? Leonidas is settled, but I've bad news. A sniper in a passing car shot the assailant while he was being transported to the precinct."

Damn, but she was right on target, again. *How does she do that?* He murmured, then took a deep breath. "What did he say before he died? It's important."

"You don't sound surprised he was shot." Mitch exclaimed. "And how do you know he said anything before he died?"

212

"Don't ask," Zach demanded, "just tell me what he said."

"He said, 'it's the Black Spider and Nick Pappas knows."

"The Black Spider— a code name?" Zach wondered.

"And Nick Pappas—the name you gave me when you came from the States." Mitch gnashed his teeth in irritation, "do you know how many guys named Nick Pappas we have in Greece. It's too common, I checked it out."

Zach walked into his kitchen, and started preparing the coffee. Distracted, only half listening, he didn't hear what Mitch said.

"Are you still there," Mitch grumbled. "Am I having a conversation with myself?"

"I'm sorry, what was that?" He put water into the machine, "I'm making coffee. Nick Pappas, a red herring. I agree there's no such person. We're back where we started, with no clues."

"Not quite." Mitch said.

"You had a good idea. Let's find the ship that dumped those immigrants.

Come to my office. I'll give you a copy of the file to analyze. Maybe you can figure out which ship was involved." Yawning, Mitch added. "It's still early. I'm going to lie down for half an hour. See you about ten-thirty."

Chapter 30

Mr. Oliver leaned his plump self- back into his chair and tried to get comfortable. His corpulent figure was squeezed into an expensive suit, his fat fingers adorned with jewels. He felt a slight foreboding as he waited for the boss in this chic coffee shop.

Located near the yacht club, it sat on the dock at the small port of Piraeus known as *Marina Zeus*. From under the decorative canopy, he watched the luxury yachts that filled the marina; the masts and spars of the sailboats that filled the air, and the flags from different countries that waved in the breeze. He felt envious of the rich who docked their boats here and spent time in the city.

He took another bite, savored the creamy lingering sweetness of the pastry on his tongue. When he looked up, he saw Nick Pappas walking toward his table with decisive strides. He put his spoon down and gulped.

Pappas took a seat, folded his arms and waited for the silence to build.

Mr. Oliver gnawed his lips and glanced at the man sitting across from him.

He was an athletic man in his early sixties with fine lines etched into his face, a face that looked like it had seen much of the world, and had done much in it. A face to incite fear in anyone who crossed him.

"Mr. Oliver, I'm disappointed in you," he finally said, his fluent English tinged with a slight Slavic accent.

"We've lost the dockworker, and I had to eliminate one of my men. That doesn't make me happy.

Nick Pappas fixed him with a stiff-lipped sneer. His deep-set eyes bored into him under his straight brows.

A large man, he was dressed in plain black jeans and a sweater. His hair hung in a ponytail down his back. Pappas pushed wisps of his snowy hair back from around his square face. With a stubborn set to his jaw, he sat brooding a moment then added.

"The games start in a few short months. Any more mistakes and you're done. They won't be tolerated. Do you understand? What a muddle. Our plans are threatened, almost destroyed. Everyone is getting nervous, thanks to you."

Mr. Oliver started to squirm.

"We expect results for the money we pay you." Nick Pappas narrowed his eyes, scanned him, then called the waiter, and ordered a strong Turkish coffee. "I don't like incompetence. The dockworker should be dead, but he's not, I had to kill Bruno, my own man, so he wouldn't talk, and now our contact is afraid to be found out."

"Bruno swore to me that the dockworker was near death when he threw him into the garbage dump, I don't understand how he survived. And at the hospital, there was always someone around to get in his way."

Mr. Oliver wiped the sweat from his brow and licked his lips. He stared at his tempting dessert, and shut his eyes, afraid it might be the last he'd ever enjoy. He remembered only too well what happened to Bruno, when he failed to carry out his mission.

"Don't worry— everything's under control. Zachary Artemidis, the ship owner, is involved, I can sense it. We've got someone tracking what he does, someone in his office is on our payroll." He pulled nervously on his ear lobe.

"I don't know why the dockworker didn't die, but I do know that our secret is safe." Oliver continued. "These Olympics will go down in history as the most explosive of them all." He moved his shoulders around, and raised his eyes.

"A real tribute to the original home of the Olympic games," he smirked, "all will be impressed with the firework display at this year's opening ceremonies, you can be sure of that."

Nick Pappas eyed him. "I hope you're right, but to be sure, you have to find out where they've hidden the dockworker. He has to be eliminated." He paused and stirred his coffee. "Pressure our contact at Central Headquarters. We have to find him."

He tightened his lips. "There's another problem. One of our pigeons has flown from the house in Trikala. That can't be allowed—it sets a bad example. Send a man to pick up her trail.

See what you can find out, and get back to me within the week." He gave him a warning look, "No more mistakes, Oliver."

"No, Mr. Pappas, I'll get right on it." Oliver gave him a cautious look, trying to judge his mood.

He wanted to verify some facts. After all, information was gold and he was a greedy man.

"I've heard rumors. There's another group bringing in *lost sheep*. I heard their boss didn't take crap from anyone. He's called the Black Spider, and people tremble when they say his name."

Mr. Oliver stared at him, to see if he'd hit a nerve, to see if he could make him squirm, so he could flush out the truth. He had never believed this man was the real boss of the operation, knew for a fact that his name was false. But how to make him admit it?

Nick Pappas faced him down, not giving anything away.

"I don't know what you're talking about. It's not safe to ask too many questions Oliver, haven't you found that out?" He finished his coffee and stood up.

"Don't forget what I said. I want results. Things are getting out of control—you'd better straighten them out."

He put on his dark glasses, walked out of the café to the street and waved down a taxi.

He gave an address in the posh area of Piraeus where the shipping offices of Pavlock Shipping did business.

Pappas paid the driver and got out of the taxi at an expensive high-rise building.

Standing a moment, he absorbed the sights and smells of the sea as he looked out across the harbor. Sea gulls flew by, squawking, as the crew of a large fishing boat unloaded its catch. He could hear the men's shouts across the water, yelling orders to the workers.

He strode into the building and up the stairs, preferring them to the elevator, and reached the third floor easily without a catch in his breath.

"I'll be in my office."

"Yes Mr.Pavlock."

Checking his watch, he went through a door into his private office avoiding the commotion of the company's daily activities.

They knew better than to bother Basil Pavlock with mundane things.

Chapter 31

Zachary stood outside Mitch's office, and stared at the open door—a door that should have been closed. He looked in. Officer John Atlantis stood there, putting some folders on the desk. "What are you doing here?" Zach asked, in an accusing tone. "Nobody comes into this office without permission. All paperwork goes next door," he narrowed his eyes. "Where's Captain Petridis?"

"He's down the hall with Detective Stavris. He hurried out just as I arrived." Hesitating, he added, "I heard him tell another officer where he was going, that's how I know." He shifted his weight from foot to foot. "Detective Stavris' secretary Ellen Poulos, told me to drop these off, that's why I'm here," he indicated the folders, "just to drop these off." He turned and started edging toward the door. "I'll tell Captain Petridis you're here."

Strange, Zach thought, he had met this officer before. He always seemed to turn up in unexpected places. A good-looking man, dark complexioned with a scar on his cheek, about his own age, divorced with a small child. He had recently married—a pretty fellow officer, also divorced, with two small children. He remembered seeing her in dispatch.

She was often the voice over the P.A. directing the police to go wherever needed. A petite brunette, with a charming dimple in her right cheek, she had a curvaceous figure that showed even in police uniform.

Hmm, he worked in illegal immigration, she with the phones, they could easily be the informers. What with the new marriage and so many children, they could use extra money.

Leaving that thought, he sat down on a nearby couch and examined Mitch's office. He saw two rooms, side by side, with a connecting door, both had entrances to the hall so anyone could enter and exit without disturbing the other.

Mitch's assistant worked next door, taking care of all necessary details. He kept Mitch's appointments in order, did the paper work and answered the phone. He allowed only the most important matters to filter through.

A seasoned officer, close to retirement, he had wanted a job, had asked Mitch to recommend him for this position, away from the crime on the streets when it became vacant. He was short and stout, with peppered wiry hair that stuck out in spikes if he didn't grease it down. He had a potbelly that jiggled when he laughed, causing a few people to snicker behind his back. Zach had liked him. Now, even he was a suspect.

Mitch's office, larger than his assistant's, was furnished with a comfortable couch and chairs, a cherry wood desk and matching bookcase.

He smiled, seeing his sister's hand in the designer drapes, the matching pillows. Brass frames held pictures of her and the children. A designer pen set sat on his desk alongside a clock radio. A wall clock was behind the desk. Strange. Why two clocks together?

His eyes wandered to the set of prints on the wall of Greek freedom fighters

Mitch came from an old political family famous for its loyalty to Greece. His ancestors had fought against the Turks in the 1800s, and were heroes in Greece's fight for independence. Dressed in white flowing shirts, black vests and white skirts, these heroes were depicted in various battle scenes. Maybe one of those heroes against the Turks was Mitch's ancestor. It would be just like his sister to track one down.

Committed to his job, Mitch didn't always realize others weren't as dedicated. He couldn't understand the need some people had for something his family always had—money.

Zach took a string of amber worry beads or *kouboloi* from his pocket, and started playing with them, running his fingers over the smooth stones while he tried to get his thoughts together.

His life had been going full speed. He'd had more excitement working on this case, in this short time, than he had all year. Now there was murder and mischief, and runaways from a bordello. What else could possibly happen?

And then there was Alethea.

He missed her already, even though she had just left.

Alethea had powers- he could sense them when she was near, when they made love. He readily admitted that their relationship had gone beyond sex, beyond physical satisfaction.

She tempted and excited him beyond reasonable limits. He felt the chemistry, the strong attraction that drew him in, beyond having a casual fling. She didn't want permanence—that's what she said. But she had willingly entered into an agreement with him. Clearly it wasn't just a fling for her, either.

He had a problem though. If he questioned her about these gifts, she would think he wanted her, just, because of them. But it was so much more. Her uniqueness presented a challenge. He wanted to explore, to understand this person known as Alethea. What she saw, what she felt? What made her able to predict what would happen? That's what he wanted to know.

Was she the true psychic his father was looking for? To date, he and the family had only found imposters.

His father's quest had started when he had discovered an old painting in an antique shop in Mytilene, years before Zach's birth. The painting, and the cryptic message on its back, had become the focus of his father's life since. A diary, written by an eighteenth century scholar, had come with it. The scholar specialized in deciphering secret languages.

According to the scholar, the encryption had to do with a race of psychics who had lived centuries ago. The cipher hinted that only a true psychic could solve the mystery of the painting. Now he, like his father, wanted to know its secrets.

Zach was faced with a dilemma.

He knew Alethea was the real thing. She would surely be able to decode the message. His father would be ecstatic, finally realizing his life's dream.

But if he told his father about her, he would lose her, she would never talk to him again.

Absorbed in these thoughts, Zach didn't realize Mitch had come into the room.

"Sorry," Mitch said, "I had a meeting with Detective Stavris, he's head of Europol here in Greece. He wanted to know if I was going to attend the readiness exercises for the Olympics next week. They'll enact various crisis situations, like a dress rehearsal for the real thing."

Zach, startled out of his revelry, dropped his worry beads, "I kept myself busy. What else did you talk about?"

"The Olympic Truce—all countries have been asked to observe it. Peace and understanding through sports—the Olympic ideal." He stared into space.

"Easy to say, much harder to do. Not every country will respect the truce, though we hope they will." Mitch chewed on his lip.

"I wish I knew what Leonidas found on the *Deliverance,* that's really bothering me now." He pointed at Zach.

"Regardless—nothing will mar these games. I won't allow it. Greece's Pride's at stake.

Foreign newspapers have been severe in their criticism, twisting facts to make it seem as if our security is not up to standard. I'm afraid this type of pressure will only increase."

"Did you check the file?" Zach bent down and picked up his worry beads.

"Security has to start here. We know someone turned Leonidas in, someone here at Central Headquarters, someone he trusted. We have to find out *who* before it's too late."

"These clocks by my desk have video cameras in them. I checked both of them and found nothing there," Mitch replied disgustedly.

"If we are being spied on, someone should have tried to steal the file."

"Well, that explains the clocks, anyway." Zach raised his eyebrows.

He got up from the couch, and stood over Mitch's desk. "I'm going to need a copy of that file, so I can study it and look for clues in the report to indicate which ship dumped the immigrants."

He sat on the edge of the desk. "I'm leaving for Lesvos as soon as I can. I have a meeting scheduled to designate assignments. Then I'll be free to concentrate on *other things.*"

"Might these *other things,* concern a certain lady you've been seen with?

Can't say I blame you," he winked, "she's some looker, if I wasn't married…which reminds me. Maro wants you to come to dinner tonight."

"Yes, thanks. I need to talk with Leonidas again." Zach moved around the room. He wanted to confide in Mitch, tell him about Alethea, but knew he couldn't break her trust.

"Alethea's a major part of the reason I'm going to Lesvos," he admitted to Mitch. "She befriended a young girl, an illegal escapee from a bordello. She asked for my help. So you see, I have a legitimate reason for wanting to see her again." He shrugged. "Not that I need one."

This girl might be just what we need. These traffickers have to be stopped. If you need any help, call me." Mitch paused a moment. "You'll be staying with the family, won't you?"

Zach nodded, then swiveled and studied the prints on the wall, curious to see if any of the freedom fighters resembled Mitch.

"I'd come now, but with the Olympics so near," his jaw muscles twitched. "I have to stay to make sure all the security is in place. We have a lot to do yet, before the Big Event." Mitch motioned with his hands.

"We have to coordinate safety measures with the other nations, with *Europol*, with *Interpol. NATO* will help us patrol the seas, and the air. Albania has increased its border police. They will guard our common boundaries." He tilted his chair back.

"Everyone is working hard, so I can't just leave. I'm depending on you to find out what you can."

"When I see Alethea I'll have more information. We didn't have a chance to say much on the phone." Zach rubbed his chin in an abstracted manner. "At this point, I don't even know who the runaway girl is—maybe she'll give us names and places.

I warned her—she's a target along with the girl. But she won't leave it alone. She just jumps right into the middle of things, and never considers the risk."

"Yes," Mitch muttered, "it's a treacherous situation. Do what you can. I'll make a copy of the file, and bring it home tonight. I've been too busy to give it the attention it needs.

These games are the first major international event since 9-11. And I'm worried. Everything, from simple traffic control to major safety measures is on our shoulders. And the pressure…. We have to avoid traffic jams while getting the buildings, the roads, and the transportation system ready in time.

There's pressure about protection for the athletes and dignitaries, and about coordinating all the police. And time is getting short."

He raised his head, "I really don't need this new threat hanging over my head like Damocles' sword, afraid the hair will break and ruin the whole event. I haven't had time to breathe much less to concentrate on this boat tragedy."

"Try not to worry about it. You have enough on your plate." Zach went over to the door. "I'll work on the immigration cases.

One of them is sure to give us the breakthrough we need to find the ring leaders." He halted and looked at Mitch.

"This isn't only our problem. It concerns all of Europe and the United States. There are no borders; they filter from one country into another." As he left the room, he called out, "anyway, I'll see you tonight."

Zach walked through the hall thinking about the current cases. He wondered how they might be related.

When he passed the Europol offices, he peeked inside. A woman, about forty years old, sat at a desk by the open door, working on her computer, she had short, straight red hair, was skinny, almost bony, of medium height. She typed with impressive nervous energy.

She turned her head and looked him in the eye. "What do you want? You'd better move along, this is a busy place. Stop dawdling and go." She shook her head, pursed her lips and started typing again, ignoring him.

Zach stared at her. Who was she? At a guess he

would say she was the secretary Ellen Poulos. She was also, besides being insolent and abrasive, a suspect. She had access to important information and was well placed to know what was happening in the department.

Face it, he said to himself, everyone here is a suspect.

Chapter 32

Later that evening, Zach rang the doorbell at Mitch's house. While he waited, he mulled over his afternoon staff meeting.

He had set up a chain of command for his various enterprises with a director to oversee each department; had set up a system of checks and balances to monitor the operation in his absence.

When he worked he worked hard, he didn't dodge his duty, but this system allowed him some flexibility.

He paid his two directors well for their efficiency, which gave him this personal freedom.

Tom Valakis, was in his late forties, a large man, well built. He'd been a street tough until he met Zach in a bar. Tom had broken the bar up in a fit of anger, had brawled with two others for no apparent reason.

Afterwards, Tom and Zach started talking. Zach hired him. Tom had street smarts and a talent for numbers that was an invaluable aid, just what Zach needed to supervise his captains and to oversee the ships' accounts. It was his job to see that they made money instead of losing it.

Peter Makaris, his other personal assistant, was slight of build, short, and competent. Fluent in five languages, he had left Egypt when the government changed, and relocated in Greece. With his business acumen, he was invaluable to the operation, and was mainly responsible for keeping his directors in check.

Growing impatient, he peered through the stained glass door to see if anyone was coming to let him in.

Suddenly the door opened, and there stood Maro and Zena. They ushered him in, excited, bursting with news.

Zach glanced at Maro. "What's going on? You didn't tell me Zena would be here. You know warn me in advance so I'll be prepared."

Zena, well accustomed to their squabbling, barely lifted an eyebrow. "We'll tell you inside when you're comfortable." They joined Mitch in the living room. Leonidas looked relaxed propped up on the couch.

Zach scrutinized him, "I'm glad to see you're better, it's amazing how fast you've recovered." He sat down across from him, addressed Mitch. "I've settled things at my office, so I should be free to travel at the end of the week."

"It's a good thing you're going to the island," intruded Maro, "Papa called. He swears he found a genuine psychic and wants you there when she examines the painting. I hope she isn't another fake, I don't want him to be disappointed."

Zena leaned closer to them from an adjoining chair. "Do you think we'll finally find out what the secret of the painting is after all these years? It seems all my life, that's the only thing we've ever talked about. Can't say I blame Papa, though. It has fascinated us all—lost worlds, secret writing, hidden clues."

She shook her head. "If this psychic is the real thing, and she discovers the painting's secret," she took a breath," can you imagine the story? I wish I could leave for Lesvos, but I'm knee deep in work. The Olympics is taking up all of my time."

"Thank goodness for that." Zach said. "Since you're going to be so busy, you won't have free time to get into trouble while I'm away."

"Get real. My life's my own—I don't need a keeper," Zena shot back, "I've been married and divorced." She glared at him, "who put you in charge of my life? Even Papa gives me more freedom then you do. Anyway, be sure to call Papa."

"Who's to protect you, if I don't?" He lowered his eyes. "I'll call Papa when I get home."

She got an evil glint in her eye, "Sylvia and Peter will be at their villa when you visit. They're having house guests; I'm sure you'll want to meet them."

"Houseguests? Has Sylvia brought friends from England to tyrannize me with potential brides, again?"

It seemed too much of a coincidence, both he and his father coming across a psychic at the same time. How could that be? Alethea didn't mention anything about going to the island to look at a painting. Was there another psychic, or was she lying to him, covering up her real reason for her visit to *Lesvos*?

Bird watching indeed, research for a story! She must take him for a fool to believe that. But he had.

She had some explaining to do, and so did his father. What was his father up to, what had he set in motion behind his back? He also hadn't mentioned a psychic. This was the first Zach had heard of it.

"Enough!" Maro announced. "Let's go in to dinner." She turned. "I'll bring you a tray, Leo."

Leonidas, feeling the warmth of friends, leaned back into the pillows and closed his eyes.

Zach, Mitch and Leonidas shared a bond formed while working in the Special Services, a bond stronger than friendship.

Orphaned from a young age, Leonidas considered them his family. He had been best man at Mitch's wedding, godfather to his first child.

As an undercover detective, he had worked on Zach's boats to establish himself a cover, then had signed up to work on the *Deliverance*. He had heard rumors of smugglers using this ship to bring human cargo into the country.

Looking for evidence he had seen or heard something, some threat to the upcoming games. After that everything went blank. He wished he could remember.

"Don't think about it," he cautioned himself, "the memory will come. Someone said, if you stop worrying, the memories just suddenly appear." He shook his head, "I hope in this case it's true and I'll miraculously remember."

"Talking to yourself," Zach commented as he came back into the room with a tray.

"I know we're putting a lot of pressure on you, but we can't take a chance on something terrible happening." He placed the tray near Leonidas and sat across from him.

"I want to know if you're sure about what you heard."

"I'm sure the Olympics were mentioned and bombs. That alone made me nervous—why would they say those two words together if not too cause harm?"

"I wish things were clearer. We can't take any action with so little information." Zach gnawed his lip. "Did you hear the word stadium or just the word Olympics?"

"No. I... don't think stadium was mentioned. But I can't be sure. I'm trying to remember. I know it's important but it just isn't happening. The more I push the more frustrated I become."

"I'm sorry I didn't mean to stress you out." Zach got up. "Okay let's leave it for now. If you remember anything, let Mitch know, no matter how trivial. I'm leaving for Lesvos so I'll see you when I get back."

Chapter 33

Basil Pavlock sat behind his streamlined desk and looked out the window at the ships moored in the harbor. The view reminded him of Odessa, a busy port on the Black Sea. It was in his blood, this love of the sea, the sound of the waves lapping against the large freighters, of the horns bellowing as they arrived and departed. He remembered it well as he waited for his special visitor, Alex Vladis.

He leaned back in his chair and thought back to those times when as a small child, he had run free in the streets of Odessa. He and his mother lived alone; his father was a soldier away at the front. He did as he pleased, experienced it all.

The streets were his playground, his joy. He would go from store to store, chattering away at the owners, earning himself a treat or two. With a child's sense of wonder, he watched the big boats, the freighters, the cruise ships, come and go in the harbor.

Until one day he came home and found his mother missing, the house emptied of what little it had held. The next thing he knew he was in an orphanage, his freedom curtailed. Frightened and lost, he was an easy victim to anyone stronger and older.

At the orphanage, Alex had saved him from a beating by one of the teachers. He was an older boy so beautiful, so smart, a natural leader. Smiling, Basil remembered how Alex used his sly wits to keep all in check. He ferreted out secrets, threatened and cajoled until he got what he wanted.

They grew together, Alex the brains, and he, as he grew into his body, the brawn. He grew bigger and stronger than Alex, but not smarter or tougher. Alex knew how to maneuver in the lights and shadows of the new government emerging from the dregs of the old. Alex led and he followed.

Basil pushed back his chair. They were still young children, when gathered up by the rebels in 1948, at the end of World War II, some thousands of them were placed in an orphanage. They made a universal family, learned to work for the good of the state, the hope of the communist future.

Alex was sharper, learned faster how to play the game. He was an excellent student, an excellent pro-spect to advance in the ranks of the communist state. And where Alex went, he followed. He was younger, more easily impressed; Alex was his hero.

Lost in his thoughts, he didn't notice the door opening, but realized he was not alone when the whiff of a fine Cuban cigar and expensive cologne filled his nostrils. He knew that scent. His friend had arrived.

Alex Vladis entered the room, silently, as was his way. He never raised his voice, never gave an order more than once. He didn't have to; there were no sec-ond chances.

Basil turned and looked at his friend. The blue hyp-notic eyes, the sculpted features, straight nose, full lips and head of gray curls—Alex had the classic beauty of a Greek god. He was a handsome man, with a well-pro-portioned body and strong shapely hands. Alex moved with his usual economy of movement as he approached the desk. Basil felt his stomach clench, and the feelings he always had for Alex returned. He loved Alex, always had, always would.

"Basil, you look as fit as ever," Alex greeted him, his vibrant voice mesmerizing. Nodding his head, he went over to the window and looked out.

Watching his friend stare out the window, Alex wondered at his thoughts. They had known each other such a long time, each devoted to the other, each knowing the other's mind as if it was his own.

Alex had married, had children. Basil had chosen to lead a single life.

"How was your trip from London? I was surprised to hear you were coming." Basil rubbed his chin with his fingers and gave him a curious look, "I wasn't expecting you so soon after your last visit."

Alex shrugged. "This trip is pleasure not business. My wife and daughters are at the hotel waiting for me. We're going sightseeing then we're off to Lesvos— some associates from London invited us to stay with them."

He turned from the window and stared at his friend. "What were you thinking about when I came in? You seemed lost."

Basil tightened his lips. "Remember Madam Margo, that mean old skinny teacher, who always picked on me? You intimidated her and she never bothered me again."

Alex listened to his friend, recalled those long ago days, he recalled, too, the weak and helpless little boy who was too scared to fight back.

235

"You exposed her, showed her meanness to the others, and made her life as much a hell as she had made mine." Basil continued. "You understood after the abuse at her hands, and others like her, I had no use for women, no respect for them."

"Women have their uses." Alex interjected with a smirk, blowing a plume of smoke from his cigar.

"I agree." Basil shifted in his chair," These birds are just bodies, as you say, to be used and sold." He twisted his lips in a sneer. "My mother left me for the state to raise. She was a true party member, true public property for whoever wanted her. She's the one who first taught me about women, it was a lesson I learned well."

Basil joined his friend by the window. He hesitated a moment, then turned toward Alex.

"We have a problem. One of our birds has flown the coop. A seamstress from Moldovia. The Bulgarian group picked her up and sold her in Albania, where we bought her for a house in Trikala.

I've put Oliver on it."

Alex pierced him with a contemptuous look. "Someone didn't do their job right. You have to create *fear,* use threats to keep these girls and everyone else under control."

He turned and looked at Basil, chomped down on his cigar and puffed.

"You *shouldn't* feel guilty when you traffic these birds. The new states are too crooked to govern themselves. Corruption is the norm rather than the exception. We take advantage of poverty they've created to further our own good. Nothing wrong with that. Hope is what we give them. And despair is what they get. Little do they suspect what awaits them.

"You're right," Basil nodded, "I have no heart— feel no guilt. It's not our fault the Soviet Union disbanded and threw Eastern Europe into sheer chaos, with abject poverty the result. Why shouldn't we reward ourselves? We had no party loyalties."

"The leftist rebels who abducted me from my parents, from my village, expected me to serve the state." Alex sank into a chair opposite the desk.

"I had no loyalty for them. The good of the state became goods for my pockets." He pulled an ash tray closer.

"An uprooted flower doesn't easily root in foreign soil. So I waited and grew and learned to work the system and became rich.

Now we have enough money, you and I, to control the government and head our own organization. Right?" He smashed the cigar in the ashtray.

Chapter 34

Alex gazed around the room, and noticed its stark-ness. Done in black, white and shades of gray, by the best interior designer money could buy, it was com-pletely impersonal—no color, no personal touches, nothing to reveal whatsoever the person who worked there.

His friend didn't believe in the pleasures of life, he lived a utilitarian existence, and ran his life along Spar-tan lines. His office was rich in cost, but poor in com-fort. Alex was just the opposite—he enjoyed living and indulged himself to the fullest.

"With your charisma you could have become an elected official. But you said you'd rather be in the shadows controlling the politicians than in the limelight giving speeches. Remember?"

Basil walked from the window, and sat behind his desk, facing Alex. "And, of course you were right. The true power lay in having enough money to buy the poli-ticians, not become one of them. So we bought ships and became rich."

"Of course I was right. These ships made us a for-tune—but not by shipping cargo world-wide. The money's in the trafficking of illegals, and of course, our dear little pigeons."

Alex leaned back in his chair, crossed one leg over the other, and took out another cigar.

"Power, fear that's what makes it work. Some call me evil, some bad for society. But who cares. I make my profit and to hell with the others." He blew out some smoke.

"I know." Basil replied. "Threaten their families, take pictures of them in incriminating situations. Shame them, and they'll work and pay. Each girl brings us big money." He clasped his hands together, pushed forward on his desk.

He noted the casual elegance of his friend's silk suit and tie. Alex was intimidating in his good looks, a true fallen angel.

Alex raised his eyebrows. "That's for sure. Two hundred thousand off each girl."

"What about the Bulgarian and the Albanian? Their mobs are trying to take over our territory. I've got them under control—for now. We don't mess with their baby business and they leave us alone."

Basil scratched his head. "There's so much chaos in the Balkans. Police, doctors, lawyers—they're all on the take, all lining their pockets. And they answer to know one." He scowled, "I won't deal with children or babies. Let the Bulgarians have that business. I want no part of it."

"I agree—babies and drugs, let them keep that business. The birds are where the money is. The men sample the goods and turn a blind eye." Alex took a puff of his cigar then waved it in the air.

"My cruise ship company gives me a chance to mingle with big money, helps me gather information. We were smart to keep the two companies separate."

"You married a shipping heiress, the cruise ships are a good front. No one will ever suspect you're not legitimate."

He stared at Alex, biting his lip—*you left Russia in a hurry, got your money out and left me to face the music. They weren't happy. You'll never know how much I had to pay to keep them from going after you - and me.* Basil's dark eyes settled on him. "You always were able to make me do whatever you wanted," *I had no choice but to fix things, or they would fix me.*

Alex gave him a shrewd look. "If I could do that to one I love, then you can imagine what I can do to one I hate. And I do love you, Basil. But the opportunity was too good to turn down. She fell head over heels in love. Who was I to resist fate? Especially with so much money attached."

"Now you have your posh London offices and run Vladmire Lines from there. Your daughters are invited everywhere the rich and famous go. Anna is how old? Twenty-five? And Patricia, about twenty-three. Your wife must be looking to marry them to rich high-society husbands, maybe even snag a title"

"Actually we're going to Lesvos at the invitation of a ship owner friend. His family has a summer house there. Do you know Zachary Artemidis, the cruise ship owner? They're trying to introduce him to one of my daughters." He looked pleased with himself. "I purposely cultivated his sister Sylvia and brother-in law Peter's favor. I like to know who my enemies are."

"Artemidis' name has been coming up lately," Basil nodded, "in the hospital he prevented Bruno's attack on the dockworker."

"Yes. His sister Maro's married to Mitch Petridis, of Greek Interpol. Zach amuses himself by playing amateur detective. He's made a special effort to be involved in this case."

Basil snickered softly. "That would be something, if he married one of your daughters without knowing who you are, or what you're involved with." He tapped his fingers on the desk. "My money is on Anna, she's the most like you."

Alex gave him a derisive look. "Maybe, we'll see. Daughters," shaking his head, "they're good for only one thing—to marry well. Sons carry on the family name. They count. They create a dynasty." He blew out a breath. "Well, we'll see what happens. At least he's rich." He sat back in his chair, and stared at Basil.

"So what are you doing about the dockworker? The group put ten million euros into my account; another ten million will be added when the job is done," Alex dipped his head, "that's incentive for making sure nothing stands in the way of the big blast at the Olympics."

"I gave Oliver his orders," Basil narrowed his eyes, "he has to find this dockworker and snuff him. Then we get rid of Oliver. He's starting to ask too many questions. He asked me about the Black Spider."

Alex twisted his lips. "What does he know? It can't be much. But I see your point—he's fishing." Alex gestured, vaguely.

"The black spider lures the fly, then traps it. And like the spider we tempt and trap those we ensnare. Yes, I found enough of the greedy, the evil, to make my web. I found their weakness and used it. And nobody knows who I am.

The dockworker's snooping interfered with my plans, but only briefly." Alex went on. "Nothing was found on the ship—I had the explosives moved to a warehouse away from the dock. All's ready for the big bang at the opening ceremonies—the fireworks, the bombs! Our machine is ready to wreak havoc in the European states, to make a mockery of the games—this symbol of world peace."

Alex sat back in his chair. "When I was approached, not me but my contact, to make this deal, I was pleased. People aren't good. They're willing to do anything for money. This contract is paying big. Why shouldn't I collect it?" Alex squashed his cigar in the ashtray.

"If the dockworker regains his memory, we might have a problem" Basil stared him in the eye.

"The dockworker saw the crates with the explosives, he heard the men talking. I've learned he's actually an undercover detective, friends with Mitch Petridis.

Oliver bungled it, and he's becoming too nosy. I'll take care of him."

"Good." Alex stood up, brushed some ash from his pants.

"I'm bringing in Peterson," Basil looked up. "Oliver doesn't know him. Peterson will take care of the girl, and Oliver, once the dockworker's dead."

"Any news about our contact at Central Headquarter?"

"I got a call about Zachary Artemidis. He's got quite a reputation as a problem solver. He and his brother-in law, Mitch are do-gooders, incorruptible,"

Basil smirked, "they still believe in saving the world from evil."

"There's no evil, just a difference in point of view," Alex said. "Some men call those evil who take advantage of another's misfortune. Others say one man's bad luck is another's good fortune."

"Another thing," Basil said, "Artemidis set a trap for the mole in their midst." He stood and joined his friend. "Mitch Petridis wants him to find who was responsible for the death ship, the one in the news. He thinks that incident and the dockworker's stabbing are connected, that our spy would hear about it and try to steal the file.

Since we weren't involved—the file stayed exactly where they put it. None of our captains would do anything so stupid." They walked together to the door. "Now they're confused—just the way I want them."

"You're right; our ship captains don't panic if something goes wrong." Alex nodded.

"The captain who dumped all those people overboard certainly drew worldwide attention—all those bodies drifting toward the coast. We weren't involved, but it serves our purpose. They're going after a false trail. I think that Bolshivik group did it."

"Those idiots—ships are being watched more closely, there are more inspections of cargo, and papers are examined more carefully." Basil scowled, "it's cost me twice as much in pay- offs."

Don't worry we'll make it back." He put a hand on the door knob.

"I'll be in touch from Lesvos—don't try to contact me. Once the explosion occurs, an Arab group will be blamed, their name will be broadcast around the world. There's a lot of money involved. Don't let me down."

Basil stilled a moment, put his hand on Alex's shoulder. "These games will be remembered like the

243

Munich Olympics for the death and destruction they'll cause. Many are criticizing Greece's security for the games, so none will be surprised by the big bang." Basil gave him a farewell pat, and watched while he walked to the elevators.

Alex paused before the doors and lit another cigar. "My stay in Lesvos should be informative. Zachary Artemidis is a paradox, worth observing. I'm curious about him." He pressed the button, and waited, shifting his weight from one leg to another. "Sylvia and Peter have a house on her father's property. We'll be seeing a lot of Zach and his family. His father, Ari, is a self-made man, about our own age, who's quite an art collector. It should be an interesting visit." With that, he got into the elevator, leaving his friend staring at the closed door.

You built this web of intrigue, thought Basil, *that's why they call you the Black Spider.*

Chapter 35

"Women," Ari Artemidis murmured under his breath. "All they seem to do is collect, dissect, and then distribute the gossip of the day."

Reading his book, he tried to block out the chattering of his family while comfortably ensconced in his favorite armchair. He took a breath, ran his hand through his snow-white hair, and thought himself both cursed and blessed.

He loved his women, all six of them, counting his wife, but just didn't understand them. They were a breed apart.

Thank goodness for my son. He mused. *What can I say? Women just don't understand the ways of men. But a son, well—he's been my universe from the day of his birth.* "Not that I neglected my daughters," he reflected out loud. "Didn't I spoil and pamper them, give them everything they wanted? But with Zach I shared my heart, my interests—only he understands me. Only he can take my place and carry on my name."

"Oh Papa—why are you sitting alone?" His daughter Stella, bright eyes sparkling, stood by the doors. "Come be with your grandchildren, Papa. They love to talk with you. And Sylvia's brought company, they'll think you rude if you don't join us."

"I'll be there in a moment, daughter." Out the glass doors of his study, he could see them gathered by the swimming pool—his oldest daughters and their families.

Antigonie, his beautiful wife, left the group and came to the door. Not showing her sixty odd years, slim even after so many children, she was tall and elegant with short silver blond hair framing a finely sculpted face.

Sylvia, his eldest daughter, waved. She was the mirror image of her mother, and dear to his heart. Shortly after his own son had been born, she had given him his first grandson.

Now Sylvia, almost fifty, had grown sons of her own. He waved back at her, took off his wire-rimmed glasses, put his book aside, and briefly closed his eyes.

It felt nice to be retired, with nothing to worry about but his own interests. Not that he'd a choice. He had a weak heart. The doctors insisted that if he wanted to live, he must step down from his seat of command.

"Ari. We're waiting for you." Antigonie said. "Come join us."

"Yes," he motioned to her. "Come sit with me a moment."

Antigonie entered. "What's the matter, Ari?"

"Nothing. I was just thinking. How much I accomplished—me, a poor boy with no father. I dowered my sisters and my daughters, and left my son a million dollar business."

"Yes, you've done well, my Ari." She leaned forward, and saw a man whose will and need were too strong not to have succeeded. In his early seventies he was not short, but not tall either. His sparkling golden yes hid a ruthlessness, which made him the success he was.

"We've done well with our son." Ari sat back. "He

has taken on the responsibilities of business and family, and lifted the burden from my shoulders. I'm proud of him."

"He loves you. He wouldn't have allowed your company to suffer. Your heart, your health are important to all of us." She took his hand, stroked it. "But Ari, isn't it wonderful? Now that you've retired, you can indulge your passion."

Ari looked at his wife, and squeezed her hand. "You're right, I can finally pamper myself." He pulled on the ends of his white moustache, and gazed around the room. A collection of old manuscripts, behind a glass-fronted bookcase, caught his eye. He gave a satisfied smile. He had accumulated artifacts, paintings, sculptures, and archaeological pieces that many museums envied.

Sylvia looking in on them, cried out. "Why are you two sitting there? Come join us."

Ari and Antigonie smiled at her. "One moment, Sylvia, we're talking."

"The girls are getting impatient—we'd better go out." Ari grasped his chair arm ready to rise.

"Wait, first tell me what you're thinking."

"You know I never had a formal education," Ari moved his hand. "I educated myself. Books were my means of escape from the mundane. After the war I succeeded in making money through stubbornness and hard work."

He drummed on his chair. "It wasn't easy. War-torn Greece left many starving people, many dying from hunger. I had to be ruthless, to be stronger, meaner than others, and I was."

"I know this, Ari," Antigonie said with an impatient wave of her hand.

He looked at his wife, and continued. "But when the day was done my home was my sanctuary, my family my succor, and my studies my solace." He leaned forward, put his elbows on his knees.

"I found my two treasures in an old antique shop." He looked down at his book, and put his hand lovingly on its protective cover.

"This old book and the painting have provided me with hours of close study. The diary hints at a lost civilization of psychics, but where? The translation's unclear in its meaning."

Antigonie listened in silence. She had heard this before. Ari often rehashed this story.

Ari folded his arms across his chest. "The cipher is a riddle. It hints at a people with special abilities, living thousands of years ago.

The author claims the original frame fell apart, eaten away by time, but the painting survived miraculously intact. The writer rolled the painting into a tube, and stored it in a leather case, thus protecting it for future generations."

He glanced up at the canvas. "I hung the painting, framed in elaborate gold leaf, so I could study it and try to fathom its mysteries." He motioned with his gloved hands.

"In his diary, the scholar claimed the painting held the secret to an ancient world. One only a true psychic could glean, a psychic who was descended from this race. Protected through the ages to appear only when the time was right."

He sat forward and looked at his wife. "I'd hoped to find a true psychic to reveal the painting's mystery. But," he shook his head, "all I've found are frauds."

"Don't I know this, Ari? You talk about it all the time. Your children grew up as anxious as you to find this psychic and put your mind to rest." She took his hand.

"We all want the secret in the painting revealed. Didn't Stella just find a psychic for you?"

"Yes, she did."

Stella had seen an article in a New York paper about a woman who had used her powers to help find a child. Knowing Ari's fascination with this subject, she had called him.

Ari hired a private detective to track her down, hoping she wasn't another hoax, as many had been before.

"Her name is Alethea Karras, she's of Greek descent, from a small town in upstate New York. Rumors abound about her abilities, but no one will come out and say what they are."

Ari turned to his wife. "She works for a detective agency that specializes in insurance claims." He took a deep breath. "The detective's report convinced me she's the real thing. But how to get her here to see the painting?

Stella and John helped me devise an elaborate plan to bring her to the island. I didn't tell you about it so you wouldn't be angry." He smiled sheepishly.

"John reported the painting missing from our New York City apartment. He then contacted the detective agency where she works, reporting the painting stolen from his collection. He claimed to have received an anonymous tip that it had been taken to Lesvos. He explained that he needed a psychic to find the painting, and had asked for her by name."

Ari brought the tips of his fingers together. "Alethea means truth in Greek, which fits the message on the painting.

Truth will come to find the way. Don't you see Antigonie, it's all falling into place."

"Ari, please don't get your hopes up. She may be a fraud like all the others. I wish you had told me what you did."

"Alethea is coming, soon. In fact," Ari nodded and rose from his seat, "she should've arrived by now. I'm so sure about this, I called Zachary to be here for the unveiling." He turned to his wife, eyes aglow. "He has helped me with research and translations; he understands my passion better than the girls do."

He took a deep breath, and tried to calm himself. He didn't want his heart to fail, now, that he was so close. "I worked all my life for profit, for others to have a better life—you, my sisters and my children. This I do for myself. I'm not seeking riches, but answers. I need to satisfy my curiosity. A world ruled by psychics— think of the possibilities."

"Ari I'm just as fascinated by this as you are." She looked up at him. "This isn't about gaining fame or increasing your fortune. You just want knowledge. I understand this."

"Yes, you always understand me." A few more days, and this secret would be revealed. He must remember to call the hotel to see if Alethea had checked in.

Chapter 36

Alethea had indeed arrived. After a five-hour delay in Chios, she found herself on a regular ferry, not the original high-speed kind with which she had started her trip.

As they moved through the breakwater into the harbor, she gasped at the glorious sights. Mytilene's Statue of Liberty was outlined against a mountain of pine trees with a Venetian castle at its crest. Large freighters were moored in the deep waters. New villas and historical mansions lined the shore.

Trying to absorb it, she barely noticed Sasha Kosarvo, the stowaway, clinging to her side.

"Please, don't worry. You're not alone. We have people to help you. I talked to Zach. And we spoke with Luda. She'll be at the dock. You'll be safe with her.

Look, there are *tavernas* on the edge of the water with colorful fishing boats tied in front. See the waves coming in. There're slapping at their sides causing the boats to bob in and out of the water.

And over there the sun's reflecting off the golden dome of a church." She pointed out these sights along the shore, and tried to distract her from her turbulent thoughts. She could sense them, and felt sorry Sasha had undergone such an ordeal.

Lines of people on shore watched as the boat backed into port and dropped anchor. Taxis, cars, and loaded trucks parked, and waited for the passengers to disembark.

Sasha brightened. "There is Luda. I see her. She came as she promised." They stepped on the dock; Luda hurried to meet them.

Luda, a plain girl with dark brown hair in a knot on top of her head, hugged her friend. "Sasha what happened?" Briskly she took charge. "Come tell me. Your call worried me."

Sasha grabbed Luda's hands. "Oh Luda, I'm in so much trouble. I'm so afraid." Close to tears, she rubbed her eyes. "I'm so ashamed."

Alethea stood aside and watched the two women.

She breathed a sigh of relief, touched Luda's arm. "Sasha's in danger. She'll explain when you're alone. You should know—she's gotten involved with bad people. Let's exchange phone numbers. When my friend comes - I'll call. We'll meet then."

She spotted her hotel, the *Blue Sea,* on the corner across from the harbor, and turned to leave. Luda grabbed her suitcases, surprising her. Together they avoided the many cars and trucks going by, and safely crossed to the other side of the street.

Lesvos was a working town, one that depended mainly on commerce, not tourism. Large trucks loaded with produce drove off the ferry, while others waited, loaded to the brim, to make the return trip to Piraeus.

In front of the hotel, Alethea parted from them and entered, confident Luda would take care of Sasha.

She checked in at the *Blue Sea*, and found several notes waiting.

In her room, she put down her messages and her suitcases and went to open the balcony doors. A warm breeze ruffled her hair, blowing her scarf into her face when she leaned on the balcony railing.

A small port shaped like a Greek amphitheater spread out before her. Luxury yachts and fishing boats of all sizes, moored along its three sides. Across the harbor, she saw again the dome of the church. It towered over the other buildings.

Houses were scattered in layers, covering the hills, surrounding the port. They stood out clearly, their pastel walls, red tiled roofs, shuttered windows outlined starkly by a ribbon of green trees at their crest.

Closing the curtains, she went into the bathroom for a quick shower.

Wrapped in the plush hotel robe, she lay down on one of the beds and closed her eyes, trying to relax, to sleep.

Sasha's emotional turmoil had drained her. Having to screen out, to empty her mind so she didn't perceive others feelings, sapped her strength. She had tried to shield herself, but she still felt people's intense emotions. Supersensitive to stimuli—smells, sights, and sounds bombarded her, sometimes to the point of madness.

She had learned to block these intense feelings, from a young age, but the techniques required her to be constantly aware, which caused her to be constantly on edge, exhausting her.

Only in her room, in soothing solitary seclusion, could she truly relax, truly retreat from the world.

She took advantage of this time alone, and practiced exercises she had been taught to take the edge off her nerves, to calm herself. She opened her mind, let it drift, all controls removed. Centering on an internal point, she blocked out everything else and concentrated, until her mind escaped its tight rein, and she drifted into a dreamlike state.

Finally she slept.

Zach dominated her dreams. Her attraction for him was so strong, it blurred her mind and threw her thoughts into disorder. She was distracted, disoriented, and finally at the mercy of her emotions.

In her sleep, erotic images appeared. Out of her control they bombarded her senses. She could hear her heart beating; her breath quickening. She felt his body cool to her touch, then gradually heating.

Her tactile senses feasted as she ran her hands over firm skin encasing sinewy muscle. She absorbed his strength as he held her. Licking and biting, they grasped each other as their emotions intensified. She shuddered to feel him throbbing against her.

She felt his leg on top of hers, weighing it down, a hardness piercing her, strong hands cupping her warm sex, then holding her breasts gently then ever more firmly as he squeezed and pinched them. They fed on each other escalating their tempo, finally joining, in perfect harmony. His hips rocked, her muscles tight-ened, a rhythm started slowly, gradually built, pushing, pulling- then chaos.

Chapter 37

The ground shook; the wind blew the curtains wildly, as the balcony doors crashed open filling the room with rain. She was there seeing it, feeling it as if on a movie screen.

A woman and man lay on the bed naked, entwined. Startled they gasped, sat up—a blond woman with amethyst colored eyes, voluptuous like Alethea, but not her; the man, golden eyed with rich brown gilded hair, muscular like Zach, but not Zach. Hugging, clutching each other, they stared at the glasslike particles shattered over the floor.

They were in an extraordinary room, a room that belonged in a different time. Strange plants, knocked over by the wind, lay on their sides, spilling onto the floor. A large crystal hanging from the ceiling glowed, shedding a bright light over the room.

A tapestry on the wall stirred with the wind's movement, its colors dancing with the lights and shadows that passed over it. Intricately carved creatures on the bed's headboard and bedposts seemed to come alive as they held up its canopy of red and gold silk.

Two chairs stood before a table, a peculiar game on its surface. A flat screen hung on the opposite wall, showing a picture of a solar system, like ours but different. Next to it, a computer system more complicated than any she'd ever seen. What could it all mean?

The man rose from the bed and hurried to the window, stepping carefully across the rain soaked floor

After gazing outside a moment, he pulled the outside shutters closed, preventing more rain from coming into the room. He turned to the woman on the bed.

"Tatanya—it has begun. You were right in your prediction," he crossed the room, and started dressing, "hurry- the storm's getting worse, it has already knocked down several trees. Can't you feel the house shaking? We must leave before we're trapped."

She stared at him from the bed. "It won't do any good Zeph, these winds won't stop - the earth will crack open. Everything will fall into it. The ocean will swell, washing away what's left."

"Come, dress," insisted Zeph, "we must meet the others, the starship is ready. We must leave. Those who are away will survive, their descendants will start again. Our daughter will start a new line."

She hugged herself, rocking back and forth. Just then a wave of water knocked the walls down and pounded into the room, washing out all in its path.

Alethea flinched. She could feel their surprise, their attempt to reach each other as the water flooded the chamber.

She woke in a sweat shaken by all she had seen, all she was feeling. She remembered her dream, the drowning one she had had at the start of this adventure. Before she could analyze what this meant, before she could get her equilibrium back, she heard her cell phone ringing.

Dazed she picked it up from the night table. "Oh…Zach," relieved, with a tremor in her voice, she gasped, "it *so* good to hear from you."

"You sound upset. What's wrong?"

"Bad dream," she pushed her hair from her face, "I'll be alright in a moment."

"I've been calling you for hours. You weren't picking up."

"My phone battery died," she sat up and leaned against the headboard, "I didn't think to charge it until I got to the hotel."

"You had me worried. What happened with the girl you found? You could both be in real danger if somebody followed her. These mobs play rough."

"I'm sorry. I had to help her. Her name is Sasha," she replied, "in case you're interested. She's staying with a friend from her village. She's safe there for now."

"I'm not criticizing, you did the right thing. But there's a problem. And, you need to know about it." Zach sounded knowledgeable, his voice ringing with authority.

"These women fear the police with good reason. They're here illegally, they don't know the language or who to trust—not all officials are honest. So it's difficult to break-up these gangs."

He softened his tone. "I'll meet with her when I come. We'll put her in a witness protection program. The crooks won't be able to get to her then."

"Zach," she whispered into the phone, "when are you coming? I miss you. Your serious side hides a real lion underneath." She lowered her voice.

"You've changed me. Before we met I didn't know what I was missing. Now you've become as important to me as breathing."

"Alethea," he countered, his voice hoarse. "This lion is anxious and more than able to please. My yacht is almost ready.

Meanwhile, we've had some excitement. A bomb went off at a police station in Kallithea. Everybody's been running around like bees protecting their hive, Mitch hasn't had a night's sleep in days. This is the second bombing this year. He's worried about the Games."

"That's too bad." She ran her fingers through her hair, "but it might be a blessing in disguise."

"There you go again, making those cryptic remarks." He admonished. "What do you mean?"

"You'll see. Tell Leonidas about the bombing, you might be surprised by the results."

"You really like to confuse me, don't you?" Exasperated, he released his breath. "We're going to have a long talk when I get there.

By the way, don't forget to rent a car. We'll need it for sightseeing, and for your assignment. You can't look for birds without transportation. Didn't you say you came here to do research for a magazine article?"

"Yes, your right, the bird watching. I almost forgot about it." She tapped the phone with her finger, ignoring his mocking tone. "Well, I have to hang up. Call me when you're coming."

"Bird watching indeed, what a little liar she is." Zach disconnected. He twisted his lips and ruminated out loud, "she still won't admit the truth."

Zach went into the kitchen for a snack. "Tell Leonidas about the bombing. What did she mean by that? Whatever does she expect will happen if he learns about it?" Mulling over their conversation, he scratched his head, as he took out bread, feta cheese and olives. "I'd better call Mitch."

"What am I going to do about Zach?" She thought, unpacking her suitcase. *Just hearing his voice stirs me.* He draws me toward him like metal to a magnet. And he's one hunk of a man.

Always, before," she murmured out loud, "I was in charge. With Zach it's different—he makes *me* want to lose control. His smell, his voice, his touch Wow- they make me tingle." She took a deep breath.

Jeez! I could eat him alive. I want to devour him with my kisses, to run my hands over his naked skin. She sat to put her shoes on and sighed. With him she knew she would experience the ultimate thrill. And she wanted it, again and again. What had he done to her?

She grabbed her purse. The island appealed to her, something about it, drew her. As she readied to leave the room, she couldn't help commenting aloud. "Bird watching indeed… what am I supposed to do about that lie? Admit the truth?" …hmm, "I don't think so."

Chapter 38

Zachary Artemidis finished his supper, then looked over the bow of his 157' motor yacht, *Utopia,* and watched a school of dolphins. Sleek bodies with beak-like snouts hurled themselves into the air then plunged back down into the water, dancing to their own rhythm, like synchronized swimmers in a show. Perfectly attuned to each other, they followed alongside the yacht as it cut through the deep Aegean.

He took one last look, then walked below to the main deck, to the owner's suite. In the wood paneled room, he sat on the bed, undressed and recalled his last hours ashore.

After Alethea's cryptic message, he had gone straight to Mitch's house to talk with Leonidas. He had told him about the bombing. Leonidas had listened, asked for details, but had no other response.

Zachary didn't know what to think. He had anticipated a revelation, some instant flashback to explain what had happened. He had left disappointed. Alethea had made a mistake this time. The police station's bombing meant nothing to Leonidas. Shaking his head, he walked into the bathroom.

Alethea. Thoughts of her made his heart pump faster. He wanted to possess her, to own her. Anxious to be with her, he had hurried through last minute preparations, consulted with Mitch and avoided both his sisters. Finally ready, he had driven to the small port at *Marina Zeus* in Piraeus, where his yacht anchored.

The yacht was for his use first. When he didn't need it, he chartered it out. He hoped to make good use of it touring the Greek Isles with Alethea. Time would tell if that was still possible. Right now, she had some explaining to do.

Zachary put on a pair of casual pants, strolled into his office and opened the file Mitch had given him. He wanted answers. He spread a map of Greece on the desk and started pinpointing the locations of the dead bodies. He used his computer to research weather conditions, ocean currents, and wind velocity at the approximate time of the mishap. Gradually a pattern emerged.

A major storm had covered the area. Any craft caught in open waters would have had trouble navigating. A rickety boat loaded with people would have had no chance at all. These conditions had meant certain death to those pitched overboard. Those bodies which hadn't become fish fodder had eventually drifted toward shore.

But which ship was it? His shipping records indicated a North Korean flagged freighter, the *Korean Rose,* with a Georgian captain and a Ukrainian crew, had sailed through the Southern Peloponnese at about the time of this storm. Its destination was Piraeus. Near the same time, a ship from Odessa had sailed through the Dardanelles into the Aegean, heading south to unload its freight, also at Piraeus. Of the two, after studying his notes, diagrams, and charts he would put his money on the *Korean Rose*.

He stretched out his arms, to take the kinks out, then pushed up from his chair. He shook his legs to get some circulation back and walked into his stateroom. It would be tough to prove which ship had committed the crime. The Greek seas, busy with commerce, teemed with vessels from all over the world, and the port of Piraeus catered to them all.

Gangs operated from the East as well as the West. Freighters as often as not carried contraband, as well as illegal immigrants.

The Merchant Marine Ministry kept a close eye on the ports, trying to make sure they kept unlawful activity to a minimum.

The Coast Guard monitored the shores, but the sheer volume of Greece's involvement in shipping made it difficult to catch all the illegal action. And now fear of possible terrorist attacks coming from the sea concerned them more than catching crooks smuggling goods into the country.

Pressure built as the date for the Olympics approached and tourists, reporters, dignitaries, and athletes started arriving in Athens. Stress increased as critics bombarded Greece, claiming their transportation system couldn't handle the crowds, that their sports facilities wouldn't be ready in time, that they didn't have proper measures to prevent attacks. Mitch couldn't sleep, worrying.

No matter how many precautions they took, that unknown factor that possibility of surprise which could cause an auspicious event to turn into a disaster, hovered over their heads. To top that, bombs had exploded around Athens. A warning or a coincidence? And Leonidas, with important information, had lost his memory.

Alethea had helped save Leonidas, had warned about possible danger at the Olympics. How she did it was a mystery, an enigma he wanted to solve. What an amazing person, but, he admitted, not an honest one. "She didn't tell me the truth about why she came to Greece," he murmured to no one in particular before drifting into sleep.

Alethea sat at a trendy coffee shop near the hotel, and thought of Zach. She savored the enticing cinnamon aroma wafting from the chocolate pastry she'd ordered. He'd called, just before, assuring her he would arrive in the morning.

What a dilemma— she should have told him about her job, about why she had come to Greece. She tried to be honest, most of the time. But sometimes she had to bend the truth, to protect herself. Bird watching indeed—what had made her tell such a lie?

"Oh well." She shrugged her shoulders, "I'll have to find a way to deal with it." She thought about her last uneventful days.

Following her guide book, she had gone to the art museum, viewed Theophilos' paintings; she had seen the ancient theater above Mytilene, toured the museums, and strolled through the Venetian castle just above the hotel.

The small, gold Nissan Micra she had rented proved the perfect car for her.

Alethea finished her pastry, licking the last crumbs from her lips, and got ready to leave, when suddenly she felt a wave of malice wash toward her.

Evil surrounded her—she could sense it. Her skin crawled and chills streaked up her spine, but where was it coming from, and why? She looked around and saw an idyllic scene - couples, friends and families out for the evening, seeing and being seen.

She shook her head, disturbed by this feeling. She trusted her instincts. Someone here was plotting evil. Everything appeared tranquil, on the surface but she sensed strong undercurrents, pulling at her, telling her to beware.

She scanned the crowd, checking each table. A man, a woman and two children sat at the next table, eating ice cream.

Beyond that, she saw a group of four men drinking *ouzo*. A few tables back, she spotted the British couple from the high-speed ferry, drinking coffee.

Nothing here to indicate danger, but she felt it just the same.

She settled her bill and walked to the Blue Sea. She looked nervously over her shoulder several times, hoping she wasn't being followed.

In the lobby, she stopped at the desk to pick up her mail and messages. There was a letter from her mother, and a message to call her office.

Stillness greeted her when she opened the door to her room. She went out to the balcony, moved the sheer curtains aside, and looked down into the street, into the harbor. She saw nothing suspicious. She breathed in the sharp smell of the sea air drifting into her room, listened to the sound of the sea lapping at the shore, the boats at anchor, drifting, rocking. The ship lights, the street lights, the light from the cafes—all brightened the night, making everything stand out clearly.

So clearly that she noticed a man standing in the shadows, looking up at her. Startled, she retreated into the room's darkness and hid behind the drapes near the glass doors.

She looked again, but whoever had been there was gone. Had her mind been playing tricks on her? She shook her head and walked to the bathroom and filled the bath tub.

Relaxing in hot water scented with sea salts, she wondered about the man she had seen, about the evil she had sensed. It was probably nothing. She closed her eyes and breathed deeply.

The room had steamed up, fogging the mirror and dampening the porcelain surfaces. She wrapped her hair in a towel, put on her nightgown and lay down with her mother's letter in hand.

Curious to see what was happening at home, she read.

Dear Alethea,

By now you should be in Lesvos so I've mailed your letter to the Blue Sea, you did tell me that you would be staying there. I haven't had a good feeling about this trip, so please be careful.

The police caught the kidnappers of that young child you found. Apparently, Jennie Ward, the owner of the Seagull's Nest—I believe she was a schoolmate of yours- contacted the police once the story got into the newspapers. She had overheard two men talking about a house on Sea Gull Lane; catching bits and pieces of their conversation, she guessed they were responsible for the child's kidnapping. The police showed her mug shots and she picked them out. It seems they had a criminal record. The mother recognized their pictures, too. They had posed as telephone repair men, and had

*entered the house supposedly to check the layout. What
an awful thing to do! I'm so glad you helped them.
We're all proud of you, and Captain Duffy thanks you
again*

*I know sometimes it's hard, being you, but it's all
worth it when you help others, sometimes even saving
lives. It is our legacy, passed on from mother to daughter, like our names, like the diaries we each keep.
Alethea and Sophia, truth and wisdom, go from mother
to daughter, and the name Atalanta joins with our married name so the line won't be lost. Never forget that
the diaries help us to understand what each of us endured, what each of us has conquered with this talent.*

Alethea got up, shook out her hair. She took a bottle of water from her bag and walked to the balcony. All
was quiet. She took a sip and sat in the chair, with her
Mom's letter—thinking. She opened the letter and read
on.

*Talking of diaries, I went through my mother's
trunk the other day. I knew our family came from
Greece, but wasn't sure exactly where, since we seem
to have been in America forever.*

*Anyway, I opened the trunk and found the books
lined up in chronological order. Your grandmother was
a meticulous person, thank goodness, so I found the
first book easily. It was dated 1850.I started reading
them. You're not going to believe this, but our ancestor,
this one named Alethea Atalanta Andries, came from
Lesvos. Where they originated from it's hard to tell, but
they lived there on a farm until a great calamity struck.*

*She writes there were forty days of rain and warm
southerly winds followed by a great frost. Spring had*

arrived, so the olive trees believed, until the tempera-
ture dropped suddenly on January 10, 1850. The olives'
warm damp skin froze and burst, the trees died. So did
the domestic animals. Everything froze, there was noth-
ing left. It was total destruction.

Alethea and her husband and daughter Sophia left
the island and came to America. Many others also left,
because to stay meant certain starvation.

But a few did remain to rebuild, among them
Alethea's mother and her sister Athena. That branch of
the family is still probably there in the ancestral home.
Alethea writes in her diary that she had letters from
them—they made the frozen wood into charcoal, and
sold it. They brought soil up to the mountains on their
backs, built stone terraces to keep it in place, and
brought new trees to plant better than the old ones. The
island became green and prosperous again.

"Way to go, girls. Who would have thought we'd
have ties to this island?" Alethea muttered. "Maybe
that's why it attracts me." She went in to lie on the bed.

Lesvos went into a golden age - shipping olives, ol-
ive oil, ouzo, sardines and other products all over the
world.

The family became rich, bought more land, and
built on to the original house. According to the diary
it's located above Perama, and looks out over the gulf
of Yera.

Try to find it, to learn more of our family history.
Check the phone book for either Alethea or Sophia Ata-
lanta. You know about Atalanta, don't you? She was a
princess warrior, an archer—she sailed on the Argos
with Jason... so the legend says. Your father sends his

*love and says to stay out of trouble. He's grumbling
that I'm not paying him enough attention, so I'm closing for now. Please be careful and as your father says-
Stay Out Of Trouble.*

Love,
Mom

Who would have thought we had roots on this island? She would try to find these relatives, but doubted
they existed, here, after all these years. She turned off
the light and drifted off into sleep, unsuspecting and serene.

Outside her window, looking up, a man waited in
the shadows.

Smoke curled into the air from the cigarette between his lips. Thin browed, thin-lipped with an ordinary nose and weather-beaten face, he blended into the
scenery. Nothing exceptional in his appearance to draw
attention. Tossing his cigarette, he found his car and
drove away.

He would follow her tomorrow. He had seen them
together on the boat, saw her befriend the girl, quiet
her. He thought--*a hunter waits, watches, then moves in
for the kill. When calm and unaware, the hunted becomes an easy target.*

They would meet again, and he would do his job,
one he was well paid to do, one he enjoyed. Slowly, ag-
onizingly, savagely Sasha Kosarvo would die, and he
would watch, feeding the ruthless craving he had to in-
flict pain. The bird should never have flown the coop,
now she was his.

The black spider's moves its skinny legs, gangly but deadly. Its beady eyes scan and search. It glides, spinning its web, enlarging it with sticky strands.

Each strand carefully placed to connect with the next—reaching, covering surfaces, ready to trap the innocent, the unsuspecting.

The prey is caught, ensnared, entangled. The spider descends—weaving more and more strands, encapsulating its victim in a shroud– suffocating it in sticky mesh.

The spider feasts, sips from it, sucks the life from its victim, until only an empty shell remains.

Chapter 39

Sasha Kosarvo sat with her friend Luda Pavlov, drinking tea in Luda's small kitchen. Disgusted with herself, she rubbed her hand over her chin, her forehead.

"Madam Rena Popavitch introduced me to this man. We've known her all our lives. Why would I suspect her?" She stared dejectedly at Luda. "She plotted against me while smiling and assuring me that this was a chance of a lifetime, that I would have a job as a seamstress in an important clothing shop.

She convinced me I would help my family." She sobbed into her hands, and moaned. "What a fool I was." *How could I have allowed myself to be so deceived?"*

"Please don't talk about it, if it upsets you." Luda said softly, "here, drink your chamomile tea, it will calm you."

"No, I want to tell you, I don't want others to go through what I did." She sipped her tea, and exhaled slowly. "Madame Rena said this man was head of a large employment agency and needed seamstresses, nannies, cleaning women, and receptionists."

Putting down her cup, she looked out the window. "It's hard to believe that someone talking to you with such sincerity, promising you everything is really a *Judas* - selling you out. All of us innocent as sheep so easily fooled into believing all we were promised, all that was said. On the bus we chattered, so happy, excited looking forward to a new life, expecting new jobs, hoping that with hard work we would be able to better our lives and those of our families.

Luda, it was terrible. They locked us in a room—we saw neither night nor day. They named me Delilah, made me strip naked then took pictures of me, making me pose in disgusting ways. A man came to check if I was a virgin.

After that, a man took a video of me. They auctioned me off like a slave. One man paid a lot of money to be the first. After that— many men had me. They blackmailed us with these sex pictures and films, threatened to send them to our families if we didn't do as they said.

We had a room in a house. The police turned a blind eye. They were corrupt, and for a few euros and use of the girls, they pretended ignorance. We serviced…too many." She started to cry again, then wiped the tears from her eyes. "I couldn't take it anymore. I felt so dirty.

These men sticking their ugly tongues into my mouth like snakes, it disgusted me. The smell of stale booze, the stink of sweat, it made me gag. Rough hands tearing at me, pinching me, hurting me. I still have marks all over my body." Closing her eyes, she shuddered.

"We were sold like meat from one butcher to another—some as exotic dancers, some as bar maids, some for prostitution. They shipped us from Turkey, to Albania, to Greece, then from Larissa to Trikala. Then something—terrible happened." She broke down, sobbing, and closed her eyes. "Don't ask me what. After that I escaped. I don't know how I managed it, but I did. Lucky for me Alethea found me and promised to help," she looked at her friend, "She'll get me papers. I'll stay and work." She squeezed her hands together.

"Sasha, these men sound dangerous." Luda warned. "We'd better be careful. Are you sure you weren't followed? I hope they can't trace you to here." She got up to clear the table, then started moving things around in her small kitchen. She tried to stay calm, but she couldn't get her hands to stop shaking.

Sasha sensed her friend's distress, and tightened her fingers around the table's edges. "I shouldn't have come, I shouldn't have involved you. Now you're in danger."

"Nonsense, where else would you have gone?" Luda took her friend's hands and sat. "Try to think. Did you tell anyone about having a friend in Lesvos? If we know what we're up against, we can better protect ourselves."

"No, I'm sure I didn't." Sasha mulled it over. "I'm sure. We had no time to talk with each other." She lifted her chin and gazed at her friend. "We lived a nightmare. They said we had to do this to pay off our debt. The one we owed them for bringing us into the country. But we never could work it off and got in deeper and deeper. We were their slaves." She broke down and started sobbing again.

"Stop crying Sasha. Alethea will help you." Luda rubbed her friend's hands trying to calm her. "Her friend will help. He works for the police. Trust me."

Sasha pulled herself together, and wiped her tears. "Yes, you're right. Alethea is good.

Alethea, at that moment, opened her hotel door to Zach's persistent knocking. "What are you doing here? You're going to give me a bad name."

"No one knows I'm here. They told me your room number when I called yesterday." He pushed into the room and looked around. "Anyway—why do you care?"

"I just do." She pulled her robe tighter around her, and sat in the armchair near the bed.

"You look luscious in that robe, good enough to eat." He lifted her from the chair and sat back down, with her in his lap. "You're a nice handful." He bit her ear lobe, and whispered,

"I missed you."

She snuggled down into his arms, and felt so right there, so safe and secure. Strange she should feel this way, she who had never been afraid of anything, had always dashed into danger without a thought to her safety. But something about Zach made her feel protected. And lately, she was feeling the need for his strong presence.

"I missed you too."

She put her arms around him, and gave him a warm kiss.

"I'm glad you're here. I've this nagging fear that something bad is going to happen. It makes me feel threatened and helpless."

"Maybe it's this helplessness in you I find so appealing." He hugged her a little closer, then started stroking her shoulders, her back, soothing her. "You're not wearing much under your robe, are you? Just the way I like my women, helpless and nude."

273

"Your male chauvinism is showing." She raised an eyebrow. "Is that all I am to you? A body for your pleasure?"

"And I'm a body for *your* pleasure—remember, this thing goes both ways. We're in this together. No one's taking advantage. We agreed—an honest relationship with no strings attached."

"A few strings attached. Remember our contract?" She combed her hand through his hair, and looked him in the eye. "As long as we're in this relationship, we stay faithful."

Zach preoccupied, opened her lavender robe. His determined gaze roamed over her as he peeled it from her shoulders. Her floral smell surrounded him and swamped his senses. He licked her skin.

"Zach you're not paying attention." She pushed his head. "Stop, I'm getting chills."

"I'm paying attention." He looked her over. "Beautiful—so beautiful you're a feast for my eyes." He pushed the robe off, leaving her naked in his lap. He shifted her to a more comfortable position, "and I agree. As long as we're together, we stay faithful to each other."

"Not fair. I like to look too." Pulling his shirt over his head, she tossed it to the floor. "You've got too many clothes on." She ran her hands over his chest, and felt her excitement building as his taut muscles rippled under her touch. "You're impressive—those arms, so hard." She pulled his head toward her and gave him a deep kiss, teasing his lips with her tongue.

Zach caressed her back, pressing her into his chest. He felt smooth skin. Curves accentuated by a small waist pushed against him. Her nipples, aroused and pointed, grazed his flesh.

When he touched her bare skin and felt the sudden heating of it, a shudder ran through him. He stroked her, appreciating the fine tone of her muscles, firm but soft in all the right places.

She caught her breath. "You're giving me goose bumps."

"You fascinate me. Everything about you fascinates me. You're special, a real diamond." He played with her ass, massaging it, savoring its texture.

"You're smart pretending to be stupid, strong wanting to seem weak—a real contradiction."

"And that's what attracts you?"

"That—and your body," he moved his hands over her, "and what a body."

She opened the snaps on his white linen pants and pushed them open. "I want to look too.

Wow, you're just the right size for maximum pleasure." Taking hold, she started stroking him. "It's a formidable weapon and you certainly know how to wield it. In fact you're an expert."

Watching her, he couldn't help his body's reaction

"Very impressive indeed," she wet her lips and stared down at him.

He lifted her to face him.

Kneeling, she straddled him, holding on to his shoulders, she let herself slowly glide down.

"Hmm, so good. Makes me greedy—so habit forming." She kissed him as she felt him stretching her.

Zach pressed into her, and quickened his rhythm. Absorbed in his pleasure, he became insensible to their surroundings, unaware of the morning traffic that clamored past their window. He became oblivious to everything but the sensations coursing through him.

Alethea became even more excited as she absorbed his passion. Moaning, her appetite building, she became insatiable. Increasing her tempo, undulating her hips, she moved over him savagely, seductively—her breasts bouncing, her arms clinging, her body slipping, sliding as she caressed him with it. Alethea hugged him tightly, then gasped as she exploded in his arms.

Zach, overcome with his need, grabbed her ass and thrust deeply into her one last time, bringing on his own pleasure.

She fell on top of him, too overwhelmed to move.

Satisfied, they rested a moment, catching their breaths.

He nuzzled her neck. "I hope this isn't some trick, this making me hot for you."

"Don't. Don't spoil it." She gazed into his eyes. "I don't use psychic tricks. I'm not a magician, or a witch. I don't manipulate emotions. What we have is *real*."

"It's overpowering." He narrowed his eyes. "You make me lose control. And I hate to lose control."

"But it's mutual, isn't it? With you, I want to have sex all the time." Alethea caressed his cheek. "You've turned me into an addict."

"Hmm," he kissed her. "That's a very good thing—for me."

"You bet it is." Alethea gave him a saucy glance, and went into the bathroom.

"Hot," he whispered. "You're one hot babe." He watched her saunter away.

He picked up his clothes, then got up and moved around the room. Her emptied suitcases lay next to the wall, her clothes hung in the closet. She had stacked her undergarments in neat columns in the drawer. In that respect they were similar. They both liked things neat and tidy.

But in other ways, they didn't match. Honesty was not one of her strong points. An enigma, that's what she was. He had every intention of learning her secrets. Before the day was over, she was going to tell him all about herself.

With a determined expression on his face, he watched her come from the bathroom. She flaunted her body shamelessly. Watching her, he felt his ardor rising again but brought it under control.

"We're going out. It's a beautiful island, lush and green." He shifted his feet. "Bring a bathing suit, it would be a shame not to swim in the clear Aegean."

She straightened her lilac top and smiled, while she gathered her swimsuit. "You're getting bossy- tone it down."

"Your fault, you bring it out in me." He grabbed a towel and stuffed it into a tote bag. "Where are your car keys?"

Alethea searched her purse. Flustered, she grabbed her jeans and started going through the pockets. "I can't seem to find…." She scratched her head, and tried to remember.

"Lost your keys? Why don't you use your talent to find them?"

"You're crazy. I told you I don't do parlor tricks. This gift—you can't press a button and it's there. I can't control it. The damn thing controls me." She bit her lip and shook her head. "I never know when I'll have a vision or when I'll sense someone's fear, or when someone's anger will overcome me." She raised her hands. "You find them."

"O.K. I'd better help or we'll never leave." He spotted them on the floor next to the bed and picked them up. "Here they are."

"Good, you can go down first. I'll meet you outside." She raised her eyebrows, "a girl has to think of her reputation."

"Bullshit!" He twisted his lips into a smirk. "We're going to play this game - really?" He shook his head. "Who cares what people think? We're both adults."

"I guess it's my small town mentality, where everybody wants to know everybody else's business." She stopped with her hand on the doorknob, "actually that's their number one recreation - spying out secrets and sharing them with other snoopers."

"You don't have any secrets, do you?" He asked, giving her an impish smile. "Did you manage to do any bird watching for that article you're writing?"

"Some." She gave him a questioning look as she opened the door.

"You'll get a chance today." They left the room together. "Scala Kalloni has plenty of them. On the salt flats you'll see flamingos walking and flying around, it's a stunning view."

He scanned the hall. "I'll take the stairs down and you can take the elevator."

"Thanks. I know you think this is silly, but humor me." She grimaced.

"I just have this feeling we shouldn't be seen together."

"You're the lady with the psychic flair. I bow to your judgment. And you know we're going to have a long talk about that." He pressed the button for the elevator.

"What do you mean?" Surprised, she stopped a moment.

Zach pressed the button, and didn't answer right away. "I'd like to know about this thing of yours. You keep surprising me."

"I don't like to talk about it." she emphasized as she turned toward him.

"But I want to hear about it," he added, giving her a steady look.

Flustered, she waited, letting the subject drop.

They stood there in silence until she passed into the elevator.

Zach took the stairs at a run, went down into the street and waited for her to join him.

Alethea walked with steady steps through the lobby. She gazed left and right, but didn't spot the man who stood at the bar, checking her progress. She didn't see him take his cell out of his pocket or punch in a number. She didn't hear him say. "She's leaving the hotel, bring the car around. We'll follow her." She didn't see him glance in her direction or see him observe her enter a vehicle driven by an unknown man.

Zach gave Alethea a mocking glance. "Satisfied?"

"Yes, I am." Shrugging her shoulders, she bit her lip, "it's a girl thing—I doubt you'd understand, but I like to keep my private life private."

Chapter 40

While Zach drove around the horseshoe shaped harbor, he pointed out his yacht. "You see that beauty? Next time we'll tour the island on it."

Alethea leaned to get a better view of the sleek boat moored near the dock.

He shifted gears, then made a right hand turn at the intersection to take them out of town and onto the major road to Kalloni. He chugged up the steep hill and muttered.

"Couldn't you have gotten a car with a little more power? We're just creeping along."

"It's great on gas mileage and easy to manage through narrow streets, so stop complaining."

"You know I like speed in my cars and in my women." He pushed his sunglasses more firmly on his face, then executed a sharp turn as he crested the hill.

"Oh, is that right? And what kind of speed are we talking about?"

"The kind that puts a woman in my bed as quickly as possible." He nodded his head. "Saves me time. Dating is a wasted effort."

"You're so full of it." She closed her eyes a moment. Then turned and glanced at him. "In other words, you're not interested in getting to know her as a person."

The road sloped downward in a zigzag pattern. He concentrated on driving and didn't answer until it leveled off. "Let me think about that, it sounds like a loaded question." *What a stupid thing to say, especially to her. What was I thinking?*

Alethea decided not to get into any heated discussions with Zach.

"Never mind it's such a wonderful day for a drive," she snuggled into her seat, and watched the scenery.

"Look Zach, on your left, all those acres of olive trees, the mountain side's filled with them. They go right down to the water's edge."

She put her hand on the arm rest and leaned slightly forward.

"What a contrast - the silver green olive leaves against the aqua water."

"Yes, it's a verdant island due to natural water under the ground. They even have hot springs in Thermi and Polichnitos."

Zach turned the wheel slightly to avoid a branch in the road.

The sweet smelling air inundated her senses when they passed a grove of lemon trees. Interspersed between them, she saw pomegranate trees, also in full bloom.

"I love it. So beautiful—those deep orange flowers bordered by the white ones. Who would have thought such sweet smelling blossoms would have such a sour fruit."

"About the question you asked." He stopped at the light. "I'm interested in a woman as a person. Women are important to me. I just don't like the game playing. I don't have time for it."

She licked her lips. "Yes I can sense that you care for women, they're not objects to you. When I'm with you I feel cherished, protected, and treasured. But when we first met you were rude, preoccupied and uninterested."

"I guess I was. I had things on my mind, but you certainly got my attention,"

"Yeh, sorry." She looked down at her lap. "You intrigued me. I liked the way you carried yourself, and there was this sense that you would be important in my life." She lifted her head and stared at him. "I had this compulsion to meet you, and you just—ignored me."

"Well not for long. That cold water you spilled made me notice. You did spill it on purpose, didn't you?"

"Busted. You got it." She gave him a sheepish look.

"As regards this psychic sense of yours," Zach bent toward her, "I want to know about it."

"You mentioned that before. In fact several times." She took a breath.

"To know about it," she leaned her elbow on the window's ledge, and played with her hair. "How to explain it? Waves of emotion bombard me. People's thoughts, their pain, their sorrow, I can feel their deep emotions."

Distracted, Zach forgot to move when the light changed. The cars behind him honked their horns and got his attention. Zach drove on, while he listened attentively to Alethea.

"Sometimes I can manipulate energy. I helped Leonidas heal, but I don't know how, and wasn't even sure I could. It's unpredictable, this talent. And, it doesn't always work, it doesn't always help me to solve problems, but it does *always* get me in trouble. People don't understand when I warn them about a coming disaster, a coming crisis. They look at me as if I'm crazy."

She touched his hand as he shifted gears. "

You didn't question me, accepted what I said and acted on it immediately. That saved your friend's life."

"Yes," he nodded, "I trusted your instincts."

Alethea widened her eyes. "You have no idea how unusual it is to have someone trust me so completely," she prodded him. "But why?"

"You were very convincing." He deliberated, "what you had endured couldn't be faked."

Still suspicious, she raised an eyebrow. "You didn't think I was a lunatic? You accepted it as if it was an everyday occurrence." She blinked her eyes, then shook her head. "You're a man in a million. Anyone else would be running scared by now or laughing his head off." It satisfied her that she didn't have to pretend around him, and could openly use her powers. But why should he be so accepting—what did he want from her?

"Don't forget I'm a scholar, life's puzzles intrigue me, and you're one of life's puzzles. There's so much we don't know, so much that has been lost to us. You're something unusual, something unexplained."

"Jeez. Just as I thought—you think I'm a freak." She closed her eyes and rubbed her forehead.

"No," he put his hand over her mouth, "don't say that."

"Alethea took his hand in hers. "Warning them of danger doesn't do any good. Most people don't listen when I talk, they hear whatever they want to hear."

"That must be frustrating—knowing that something bad is going to happen and have people not believe you." They were passing the salt flats where water birds waded and flew.

"Look over there, Alethea—the flamingoes. See how they strut around, one right next to the other, making a pale pink blanket. Flamingoes cluster here, but other types of birds are attracted to the area, too. You'll have plenty of material for an article."

"Yes, I should have brought my camera." She rolled her eyes. *I should tell him why I'm really here, he keeps picking at me about this bird watching, making me feel like a fraud.*

"Let's go swimming and have lunch. You can tell me more about your powers." Maybe *you'll tell me why you're really here before my father's unveiling.*

"My powers, again," she raised her chin. "You seem more interested in them than in me."

"I'm interested in all of you." He gave her a curious look. "Does that bother you?"

"I guess it does. The last time someone was interested in my talent, he betrayed me and exposed me." Tilting her head, she watched him, trying to sense his motives.

"When we first met, in all honesty, that did set you apart. It surrounded you with an air of oddity. I'm drawn to the rare and unusual. But it's your own fault you exposed yourself on the plane with your card reading. It definitely hinted at psychic talents."

She tried to probe his psyche while he was talking, but got nothing. His thoughts were blocked, his expression one of searching inquiry and mild speculation. "So

284

you weren't just interested in my body," she turned her mouth down at the corners, "how disappointing."

"Honey all I think about when I look at you is your body, and what to do with it."

"I don't mind, I like it." She took a long, look at him as he turned the car toward the beach, placed her hand on his arm and caressed it. She gave him a slow smile. "It's a mutual attraction—sparks seem to fly between us. Besides, you make me feel normal. With you—I can be myself. You accepted my psychic vision; you didn't ridicule me."

"Talk about strange," he turned toward her, "what happened to that girl, the one you found on the boat? You called asking my help, yet," he raised his eyebrows, "you haven't said anything more about her." He parked the car and turned off the ignition. "You know I'm helping Mitch with this immigration problem. Part of it entails the trafficking in women and young girls smuggled in for illicit purposes."

"She's good for now. I'll call and set up a meeting, but she has to be protected. Danger surrounds her, I can sense it." Alethea opened the door and glanced back. "I don't want anything to happen to her."

"She'll be safe, I promise." Zach paused a moment with the keys in his hand. "In exchange for her help, I'll arrange for her to get her working papers. I know she's in danger—I'm not going to pretend she's not. We've been trying to catch the top men in this operation for years. They're as slippery as eels." Zach twisted his mouth. "But we'll find them, I guarantee it.

Chapter 41

Alethea sat with Zach, at a sidewalk table outside a *taverna*, and absorbed the sights and sounds bombarding her senses. The olive trees' silver green leaves shimmered, stirred by a light breeze. Red, pink and white geraniums gleamed through the branches.

Enthralled, she listened to the squawking of sea gulls sailing overhead, heard the water's beating rhythm slapping the shore. And always there was the reminder, by the whooshing of cars, the chatter of people, the urban smells, that nature was no longer unspoiled. Humans had arrived, to appreciate and in some cases, destroy it.

She had enjoyed their afternoon. They had frolicked in the water and sunned themselves stretched out side by side.

Now they ate fresh fish and enjoyed a fine *ouzo,* distilled locally.

Zach cast her a glance, and admitted to himself it was more than her beauty, more than the sexual attraction that drew him. After all, he had had all that before. Alethea simply captivated him.

Alethea, dressed in a lilac flowered bathing-top, shook out her hair, then ran her hands through it, taking out the snarls. She gave him a beguiling smile when she caught him looking.

Mesmerized by her movements, Zach watched her twist and turn, adjusting her matching wrap-around skirt to cover her bikini bottom. He gulped water from his glass. Who was he kidding? She had become his number one obsession.

Her beauty, a number one factor in his initial attraction, was now, not enough. He wanted more. He wanted to learn about her, what was inside of her.

He held up a bottle. "Here, have some more *ouzo*, it's the specialty of Lesvos," he poured, giving her a thoughtful glance, "try these sardines, Kalloni is famous for them." Squeezing lemon juice on them, he pushed the dish toward her.

"I'll pass on the sardines," she made a face, "I don't like raw fish."

"They're not raw," he smiled, "they're cured with salt."

"No," she wrinkled her nose, "I've had enough."

"Suit yourself." He put a sardine in his mouth and drew it through his teeth, separating the flesh from the bones.

Alethea picked up her glass, and watched, as the iced *ouzo* turned the water a milky white.

Zach wiped his mouth with a napkin. "How did you find this girl? The one you want me to help." He narrowed his eyes for a moment. "I mean, how did you know she was in trouble?"

"I sensed this great wave of pain, it hurt so much. I had to find the source. I left my seat and walked around. The signals grew stronger as I got closer. I found her huddled under the stairs."

"You said *it hurt so* – did you feel actual pain?"

"The pain of her sorrow, that's what I absorbed." She closed her eyes, rubbing at her temples. "I feel fear, sometimes physical pain, sometimes grief… it can be draining, barraged by these emotions. I have premonitions about events just before they happen. Remember I told you about a woman's voice crying for help, well she was that woman." She put her hands on the table, "my powers are erratic. I'm never sure when they'll come or what they'll mean."

She took another sip of her ouzo. "Did you know we only use a small portion of our brain?

We live in a mental rut, traveling the same road daily with few changes, just so we don't have to do any extra thinking.

From a young age I was trained to concentrate and focus, trained to rest my brain from all these waves attacking it, by putting up barriers. Ordinary people do this naturally.

They filter out unwanted noises, unwanted sights and smells. In other words—they only see, hear and smell a fraction of the world around them.

My brain is not normal." Alethea put down her glass, and stared at him.

"It's energy moving through me, then out. I manipulate it with the force of my mind. Stillness helps me to receive energy from around me.

It's like what happens when you use a lens to pinpoint sunlight and the object you focus on bursts into flame."

She played with her fork. "Most people just copy what they see, never leaving the recognizable realm. I have no such limits. Those with imagination have no such limits.

They free themselves from the known and fly into the unknown. They can accept the new, the foreign, and the strange because their mind, like mine, is open to possibilities." Pausing, she gave Zach a serious look. "The human body is a well-run machine. My body is a more streamlined model." Stopping a moment, she took a sip of her drink. "But I only use my powers if there's a real need. And I sense there are powers I haven't even tried yet." She took a deep breath. "Please, let's talk about something else."

Zach cleared his throat. "But where do these powers come from? What's the cause? Haven't you wondered?"

"All the women of my mother's family had special abilities going back generations. They kept journals," she shrugged, "most of them have been lost."

She wrapped her hands around her glass, and bowed her head. "Please, let's change the subject, I don't like talking about this."

Not leaving it alone, Zach continued, "I've seen some of your powers at work, but what about the rest? Couldn't you do more to help mankind?"

"Please, I'm a freak as it is." She smirked at a thought she had. "Can you picture me flying over New York City in a Superwoman costume?"

She picked up her fork. "I can't be everywhere. I do what I can."

"By writing articles on birds. That's not using your talents."

My goodness how am I going to admit the truth after lying all this time? She stabbed an olive with her fork and kept silent.

"I know you helped Leonidas and I'm grateful to you for it. I just feel you could be doing more. I mean with your talent you could do so much to help humanity."

She ate the olive and waved the fork in his face. "Stop picking at me about this. I saved your friend's life, right, so don't tell me I'm not using my gifts for mankind." She poked him, "and don't get me any angrier, you won't like the result."

"Calm down. Here comes the waiter with the fruit, let's finish up and leave."

Neither spoke as the watermelon was placed before them.

"Let's do that." Alethea riled, started eating her fruit.

Silence, Zach decided, was called for, and said nothing more.

Alethea, fork in hand, suddenly felt a malevolent presence, one she had sensed before. She looked around.

The restaurant was filled with people; nothing unusual caught her eye. Seated near them was the couple from the high-speed ferry, the bird watchers.

"What a coincidence! We met on the boat, you remember? I'm Birdie Falcon and this is my wife, Trudie. You left before she came back from the *loo*. We lost track of you after Chios but I see you got to Mytilene." The man stared at Zach expectantly.

"Yes, I did." Noticing where his attention was directed, she said. "This is Zachary Artemidis, a friend of mine. We've been sightseeing."

"Have you been bird watching?" He looked eagerly at Alethea, and waited for her answer

"No," she looked sideways at Zach, "I plan to do that in the next few days."

"We just visited the salt flats." A blissful expression came over his face. "We actually saw a red footed-falcon, grey heron, and of course the great flamingoes. Exciting.

Tomorrow we plan to drive by the Gulf of Yera. They've significant wetlands, kept for the birds by the government. No one is allowed to build there."

"How interesting. I'll be sure to go there, the more birds the better for my article."

"Well, hope to see you again." He took his wife's arm, and directed her out to the curb.

"They're certainly the most ordinary looking people," commented Zach.

"He said he was a devoted bird watcher. Now, I don't know." She tried to fathom this feeling she had. "Sorry if I'm imagining things, but they seem *too* ordinary.

When they reached the hotel, Alethea got out of the car and stopped Zach from following her. "I have to get some work done. Give me a few days. I'll call you."

She started to leave, then turned back. "I almost forgot. We'll have to meet with Sasha, but the longer we delay the safer she is.

No one knows she's here, but if anyone saw us together, they might be waiting for me to contact her. So I won't. At least for a while."

Zach nodded. "I'll give you a few days, but after that, *your time is mine.*

We'll arrange to meet with this girl, and hear what she has to say. I'll contact Mitch about her. Once we get her in protective custody, she'll be someone else's responsibility, and we can tour the Islands."

"I like the sound of that. Once my assignment's done, I can take a vacation." She waved to him as he went to park the car.

"Drop the car keys at the desk, please." Alethea called out as he drove away

Chapter 42

"Jeez, where has my mind been?" Alethea berated herself as she entered the hotel. "I came her on a mission, not to get involved with a man. Zach has made me lose my focus." She realized she had forgotten to get in touch with her office. What had she been thinking? All their messages sat next to her bed.

Back in New York, Anthony Petros paced back and forth in front of his desk. He turned to his secretary. "How many messages have we sent?"

"Four to the Blue Sea hotel in Mytilene," Sandra replied. "She did call from Athens, and talk with Lucretia. Everything was on schedule. Since she got to Lesvos we haven't heard from her."

"She has to get in touch. I got a call; they're waiting for her to see the painting."

"All right, but why so anxious?" Sandra asked, with a curious expression. "All she has to do is verify that it's the stolen painting. Nothing too complicated there. She'll see it, call us, and we'll contact the owners to see if it's theirs or not. Wasn't that the deal?"

"It's not as simple as that." He leaned back against his desk, crossing his arms.

"I suspect the painting was never stolen. They never reported the theft to the police. I did some investigating—contacted my underworld friends. They knew nothing about a stolen painting or about a robbery. I'm sure it's a trick to get Alethea to the island to examine the painting."

"You knew this and didn't say anything?" She narrowed her eyes. "That's terrible!"

"I guess the money blinded me," he tightened his lips.

"Besides, I didn't know it was a hoax when I sent her on this case. Now it makes sense. They asked for her specifically, said they had read an article about her. They were adamant she could help them, with her psychic abilities."

He lifted a hand and smoothed the twitch starting to throb under his eye.

"You can't give them reassurances about her psychic talents. You might suspect she's psychic, but you don't know for sure."

"You're right, I don't, but they seemed sure she was a gifted psychic. It was a simple assignment. All she had to do was find the painting and report to us. We would contact the client and they would do the rest." He pursed his lips.

"Alethea didn't like this deal from the beginning, but I bribed her with a trip to a Greek island in the spring." He folded his hands across his chest, pleased with himself.

"I told her to think of it as a paid vacation. That did the trick."

She gave him a glacial glance, and enunciated, "You always were an unctuous, uncommon, uncommunicative man who defied society's conventions and made your own rules."

With hostility in her eyes, she stood up.

Stunned by her vehemence, he couldn't help asking. "What exactly does *unctuous* mean?"

"*Look it up!*" With a disgusted look, she put her hands on her hips.

"When Alethea learns that she was sent on a wild goose chase that the painting was never stolen, she's going to be one pissed off lady. I wouldn't want to be in your shoes."

Alethea checked at the desk for messages and found two more from her boss. "My head has really been in the clouds," she murmured to herself as she hurried to her room.

Checking her watch, she saw it was the right time to call the States, with a seven hour time difference, everyone should be at work. She dialed overseas. Waiting, she sat on the bed contemplating what excuse she would give for not contacting them sooner.

"Hi Lucretia, how are you?"

"Alethea, about time you got in touch. We've all been anxious. The boss keeps asking if you've called. He's become a real pain."

"I know I should have," she hesitated, "but I've been busy."

"Busy as in good busy—like finding a man?" Lucretia teased.

"Something like that." Alethea mumbled.

"That's great. When do I get the details?"

"Another time." She changed the subject. "Which reminds me—how's your cards?"

"I've been practicing, but I'm afraid they're not working. Nothing's happened."

"Well, keep at it; you'll get the hang of it."

"If you say so, but I think I'm missing something." Remembering that she was there to do a job, she said quickly. "Here, let me put you through." She buzzed his office. "Mr. Petros, Alethea's on the phone."

"Why haven't you called sooner, Alethea? We keep leaving messages, but you're never there. I know I said to think of it as a holiday, but I meant after you got the job done." He paused letting the momentum build. "You're there for a reason—to find the painting." He took a breath to calm himself. "My client keeps calling here, complaining. They've arranged for you to get into the suspect's house this weekend."

"Well, I'm here in Mytilene, Mr. Petros," Alethea replied calmly, unperturbed by his ranting. "Just give me their number, and I'll contact them." She wrote the number down and asked, "What are their names?"

"John and Stella Mensis."

"I'll phone them right away. Do you have anything else for me?"

"No, just keep in touch."

"Check - I'll call as soon as I have news. See yuh."

She dialed the number. While she waited she twirled strands of hair around her finger and tucked her legs under her.

"Hello, I'm Alethea Karras. I believe you're expecting my call."

"Yes, Ms. Karras, we are. I'm Stella Mensis." She sounded annoyed. "You took your time calling. There's to be a gala at the suspect's house and we've arranged an invitation for you. The party is Saturday, and we feared you would miss it when we didn't hear from you."

"Sorry, I got sidetracked. How will I know where to go?"

"We'll come and pick you up. It's this Saturday at seven." She paused a moment. "We have your picture, we'll recognize you. There's a couch and two chairs in the lobby right by the large windows. They look out onto the street. You can sit and wait for us there."

Chapter 43

The mansion stood boldly on the crest of a winding road. The ride from Mytilene had been long but comfortable, her hosts a surprise. She didn't know what she had expected, but it wasn't the distinguished couple, in their late forties who picked her up.

John and Stella Metsis were both friendly and warm. After the abrupt phone call, she had expected a more hostile meeting.

She gazed out the car window, and marveled at the panoramic view of this beautiful island. The shores of Turkey, sharp and clear, shone over the Aegean, and the village of Petra, built at the foot of the mountain, embraced the shore. The main road passed in front of tourist shops and restaurants, and separated them from the long, sandy beach.

Peering over the mountain's side, she noticed they were on a motorway that ran parallel to an imposing rock near the seashore. This rock had a small church on it.

John used a remote control to open the decorative wrought iron gate. The house was three stories high and towered over its surroundings. A brick and stone neo-classic mansion, it had marble stairs leading up to stained glass doors abutted by white Grecian columns. Contorted olive trees, hundreds of years old, made curious designs in the yard.

They circled the horseshoe driveway, then stopped at the front door.

Stella looked at her and put her hand on her arm. "You'll fit right in. You look beautiful; that color becomes you."

"Thank you." Alethea, pleased, bent her head. She wore a silk salmon dress that left one shoulder bare, her blond hair secured on top of her head with tendrils caressing her face.

John, too, cast an appreciative glance in Alethea's direction.

Stella rang the decorative bell. They could hear the melodious chimes echoing throughout the house. A maid opened the door and ushered them into the foyer.

Stella took her aside. "We hired you to find a stolen painting. We believe it's somewhere in the house. Your psychic talents should lead you to it."

"These talents are highly over rated. Anyway, how do you know the stolen painting is here?"

"A friend of ours saw it and called us. We're sure you can find it."

Alethea half heard her as she looked around. Money, she smelled money and lots of it. A gold-leafed floor length mirror filled one wall and two matching antique chairs stood at either side. Painted cherubs and angels looked down at them from the ceiling, and a huge crystal chandelier sparkled with light.

She shook her head. With all this wealth why would they need to steal a painting?

This assignment, Alethea thought, had to be the strangest she'd ever had. And why a psychic to find a stolen painting? Conscious of her high heels tapping a staccato rhythm across the black and white marble floor, she tried to lighten her steps. Her silk skirts made a loud swishing, sliding sound as she moved toward the door at the end of the room.

She was nervous, overcome by strange feelings, and felt as if she stood at the threshold of a new life. She took several deep breaths; a familiar light headedness assailed her. Things were not as they seemed.

Alethea paused in the doorway. She felt like a bug under a microscope ready to be examined and dissected. People turned toward her. Their curiosity hit her like a tidal wave rising by degrees, getting higher and higher, swelling with each motion until it peaked and crashed.

But she sensed something else, too. An underlying excitement radiated from them as well as an expectation. That she couldn't understand. What did they want from her?

Stella led her into the room, to a small group standing by a set of French doors draped in blue and gold. She touched Alethea's arm.

"Alethea, this is my sister Sylvia, and her husband Peter. These are their guests, Alex Vladis and his wife Alice and their daughters, Anna, and Patricia. They've just come from London. Alex and Peter are both in the shipping business."

Alex Vladis extended his hand in greeting.

Alethea avoided shaking it by reaching for a wine glass offered by a passing waiter. She hoped she had covered her rudeness. She hadn't wanted to insult him, but as a rule, she didn't touch strangers.

She looked at him over the rim of her glass. She had to admit he was a handsome older man. His wife, in comparison, was plump and plain. The oldest daughter

Anna, a mirror image of her father, was a beauty. She had his high cheekbones, deep green eyes, and a finely sculpted face.

Vladis strutted around like a preening peacock making small talk with the other guests. He must be used to women falling at his feet, she mused. She would make a point of avoiding him. It wouldn't be hard, because frankly, she didn't like him or his daughter Anna. Something didn't seem right with them—they both put her sixth sense on alert.

"Vladis come with me, you must see this." Peter insisted, interrupting them, "There's a painting I'd like to show you. My father-in-law picked it up at an auction. Knowing your passion for art, I'm sure you'll like it." Alex, along with his wife and youngest daughter followed him.

Alethea noticed Anna had stayed close to Stella and John, ignoring her sister's signal to come.

"Have you been in Greece long, Alethea? You're American aren't you?" Sylvia asked."

"I've only been here a few days, but I'm captivated by its beauty. And yes I'm American, but my roots are Greek." She answered absently and returned her gaze to Stella and Anna.

"Zach," Sylvia spotted him coming in from the adjoining study, and waved him over. "Why don't you take Anna to the terrace and show her Mother's garden."

Chapter 44

What is going on? Why was Zach here? Who are these people? Did he know them? Confused, she stared at Zach. *Sylvia told him to show Anna - Mother's garden* so Zach must be Sylvia's brother and Stella's too, since they were siblings. What the ....

Alethea saw Sylvia wink at her sister Stella and twist toward her. She heard her whisper. "They've spent the past few days together, enjoying each other's company. Anna is perfect for him, rich, beautiful with all the right connections. And she seems interested."

"Zach where have you been? I've missed you." Anna's husky voice could be heard.

Zach, distracted hadn't noticed Alethea, didn't see the startled look on her face.

Alethea watched Zach come toward them. She saw Anna, dark haired and with a ballerina's poise, grab his arm, waylaying him before he could say two words. She saw her hang on to him, determined to show ownership, and saw her give him a pouting look.

She should have told him the truth about why she had come to Greece, but once caught in a lie it was hard to get out of it. Besides, she hadn't believed their paths would cross again.

Anna tugged on Zach's arm and pulled him away. "It's so hot in here. Let's go to the terrace?"

Zach nodded his agreement and said nothing. He followed her to the other side of the room and out the French doors. Anna, was a pest, but right now, he needed her to distract his sisters. He didn't want them to know he had feelings for Alethea, to sense the waves of emotion between them.

He had spotted Alethea in the group, but wasn't ready to confront her. So he ignored her, for now.

First, he needed a private conversation with his family. One look at Alethea's face told him the game had gone on long enough. His family had to be honest with her.

What had his father been thinking when he had arranged this whole farce? A robbery of all things. They should have consulted him before this started.

Alethea could feel her temper rising. She stood there, and glared at his retreating back. How dare he pretend he didn't know her? And why was that woman all over him?

"Didn't I tell you that Anna would be perfect for Zach." Sylvia sounded ecstatic as she turned to her sister, "they seem to have hit it off from the beginning. It's about time our brother found a wife and settled down."

"Well, she's certainly a beauty, he could do worse," commented Stella.

"Her father has cruise ships, so they certainly have a lot in common, but I wouldn't count my chickens just yet; our brother is very good at avoiding the marriage trap."

Alethea, all but forgotten, listened attentively to their conversation.

Seeing Zach manipulated by that woman was bad, but hearing him talked about in this way was worse. She understood that these were the much talked about sisters who kept interfering in his life. Her temper ready to explode, she tried to soothe her frayed nerves by silently counting to ten. Control of her reckless streak was definitely in order here. He had his nerve. He just walked away, without a greeting, pretending she didn't exist. Something certainly smelt foul in Lesvos.

"Stella, I'm sorry, but this is a family gathering. I'm confused—who invited me and why?" Alethea looked around and tightened her lips as realization dawned.

"This isn't a suspect's house, is it? What is going on and what exactly am I doing here?" She held up her hand, "and don't tell me it's to find stolen art work."

"I'm sorry," Stella took a breath and decided to be honest with her.

"When we were in New York, John came across a news article that discussed your psychic talents. He knew my father had been trying to solve the mystery of an old painting he uncovered in an antique store years ago. But in order to do this a true psychic had to be found. My father found many fakes but no real one, even after years of searching. This is his house and he's waiting for you."

"How can you be sure I'm a true psychic? I could be a fraud, too."

"We had you investigated," Stella admitted, "and from the stories we gathered, decided you were the real thing." She looked Alethea over to see how her words affected her.

"If the painting was never stolen then why these lies?" Alethea folded her arms across her chest and scowled. "And who gave you the right to investigate me? That took a lot of nerve."

Stella bit the inside of her lip. "I'm sorry, Alethea, but we had to make sure you were the real thing. This meant too much to my father to foist another fake on him. He's a sick man and this is his life's dream."

"And what's so special about this... thing?" She raised her eyes in an incredulous expression. "You created this whole farce to bring me from New York for some picture on canvas?"

"It's you and this canvas together that's what's special." Stella took her arm and led her toward the door. "Come, let me introduce you to our father."

Alethea wanted to bolt, but her curiosity, damn it, wouldn't let her. Why had they devised this elaborate charade? And Zach, had he known who she was from the beginning?

Had he known his father had engineered her trip to Greece? Frowning, she shook her head. Here she thought she had lured him, and all along he was leading her on. That's why he kept asking her about her bird watching. He knew that wasn't why she was here. What a bastard!

Lies. Everyone was telling lies.

Chapter 45

Alethea walked rigidly next to Stella as they entered the study. Her eyes scanned the room and passed over an elaborate desk. Lighted cubicles at its back showcased various ancient relics.

As she stepped further into the room, she saw a carved fireplace. Hanging above it she recognized the supposedly stolen painting. She stopped to get a better look.

It was a large painting surrounded by an elaborate gold frame. Up close the colors caught the eye in an impressive montage. She twisted around toward the room.

An older couple, in their late sixties, sat on a beige leather seat facing the painting. Stella introduced them as her parents Ari and Antigonie Artemidis.

Next to them, in a matching armchair, was a handsome man with olive skin, dark curly hair and dark soulful eyes. Seated on the arm of his chair sat a blond woman with her arm around his shoulder. Stella presented them as her sister Stephanie and her brother-in-law- Mohammed.

I'm Alethea, I believe you were expecting me." She went over to a matching sofa.

Ari Artemidis seemed lost in a trance. Not answering, he stared at the oil. He turned his eyes to her at the sound of her voice. "Finally, you've come. I must apologize for the deception in getting you here, but I'm afraid it was the only way," he paused. "You wouldn't have come otherwise."

"You couldn't be sure of that."

"Yes," he nodded, "I could. I studied you once you were found, knew you wouldn't want to expose yourself for something like this." He gave her an apologetic shrug, then smiled at her in an endearing way.

"I hope you'll forgive the ruse, but you're the key to my life's quest."

She found it difficult to stay angry so she smiled back. He was a charming man, with a bewitching grin and the same sparkling golden eyes as his son.

"This life's quest," Alethea queried, "has something to do with this oil, I presume?" She lifted an eyebrow. "But what does it have to do with me?"

"It has to do with your special talent as a *psychic*," Ari explained.

"What possible connection could my talent have to this painting?" Alethea cried out.

"With the painting, came a diary. An eighteenth century scholar had translated, as best he could, the cryptic words on the canvas' back. In this translation, it's clear, that only a *true psychic* can decipher the mystery of a long dead civilization of these gifted people."

He shifted fretfully in his seat. "I've searched everywhere for a true talent, but in vain. I found only charlatans. My children also searched. After all these years, with their help, I found you."

Alethea blinked her eyes and caught everyone staring at her. She raised her hands as if to block them off. "Whoa, I'm not a magician, I can't pull rabbits out of a hat. You're expecting too much." She glanced pointedly around, "and I don't like to be on display. I really don't appreciate this. I'm not a damn side show"

Her little speech finished she turned her back to them and glanced up at the painting. What she saw and felt, took her breath away. Light and shadow, joy and sorrow emanated from it— enveloping her, enticing her, bombarding her with emotion.

Done in muted colors, an olive grove with twisted trunks, surrounded a woman. She leaned against an old gnarled tree and looked down at a man. From their dress she would place them at the time of the crusades. His head lay in her lap, her hand rested on his wounded scalp. Light radiated from her hand as she covered the wound, a serene smile on her face.

Above the woman's head, carved into the wood, she saw symbols, translated, they meant *the mind rules*. How she knew that? She couldn't say.

In the background, a city filled with tall buildings floated in the air, with flying objects above it and ramps in the sky around it.

She saw colors. The muted pinks of the buildings, the silver white of the flying objects and ramps showed through the aqua mist.

She experienced exhilaration, anticipation-a home-coming, while looking at it. But again, she couldn't say why.

She snapped out of her reverie and scanned the room. The family had gathered all with expectant looks on their faces. Stella leaned forward anxiously; Sylvia pushed nervously back into the cushions. Ari and Antigonie sat holding hands, with Stephanie and her husband Mohammad nearby. A weird situation, to say the least, and just when she thought it couldn't get weirder, Zach came into the room, and sat down beside her.

Chapter 46

Ari turned to her, breaking the silence. "Do you know what your name means in Greek?" Not waiting for an answer, he continued. "It means *truth*."

"Yes I've taken Greek lessons," Alethea responded sharply, "that would be the translation." She gave him a quizzical look. "What does that have to do with why I'm here?

I'd like an explanation." She wasn't ready to admit how deeply the painting had touched her.

One of its verses translates, *Truth, come find the way*." He leaned toward her. "Ever since reading the verses, I've been obsessed—I've wanted to solve this mystery. When I heard your name, I knew you were the one."

He handed her a piece of notepaper. "I've written down the verses from the back of the painting." Alethea took it, then leaned back in her seat and started reading out loud. Her voice filled the room, creating an atmosphere of discovery, of expectation, of exploration. An atmosphere that promised an examination of unknown enigmas ready to be solved.

Of a sudden, she felt a sense of peace as she realized—*this is about me.* But how could that be? She passed a hand over her face. *What does my family have to do with this?* She shook her head. *This is so unbelievable. The painting belongs to me, to my family. A race of people, my people, had psychic gifts and they existed,* according to this translation, *many years ago. They lived and breathed on this earth, but when and where?*

Alethea kept reading—the hair on her arm rising, her scalp tingling. Unprepared for what she heard, she took a nervous breath. She absorbed the words into herself, feeling the torment, the trauma of the people who had left this cryptic puzzle. She thought again about her dream and knew it had to do with these people and the catastrophe that they had endured.

Daughter of time
Daughter of mine
Lost but alive
You will survive
Powers of yours
Against the boors
Nature too strong
Wreckage so wrong

Wind, rain, and fire ravaged
Great civilizations savaged
Master minds once cherished
Great cities now perished
Psychics and protectors in turn
Our race to space returns
Seventh daughter of seventh daughter
Through time and through slaughter

She who traveled will discover
Remains buried to be uncovered
Polished and varnished they will shine
Knowledge and gifts of a great line

Decipher the message hidden
You are finally bidden

To sense, to bring to light
The roots to human might
Daughter of time
Daughter of mine
Our secrets you will find
Near stone forests they bind

Clues only for you remain
Meant to see and to claim
Truth, *come find the way*
Read, then lead this day
Our powers in you reside
Fear not, accept and decide

Control the mind we can
Gifts to you we plan
Revelation *falls in your hands*
Only you will understand
Seventh daughter of seventh daughter
Through time and through slaughter

I'm the seventh daughter. This painting is mine.
This message is meant for me. Aletha realized this,
then looked towards Ari. "I can understand your obsession," she admitted. "But, how did you get this painting? I'm sure it belongs to my family—my
mother, in her last letter, wrote that our roots are from
this island, that I might even have relatives here. The
painting must have come from them."

"At the foot of the castle in Mytilene, there are many antique stores. I found it in one of them." Ari rubbed his hand over his chin, a thoughtful expression on his face. "That makes sense. Since you're the only psychic we've found who isn't a fraud, it must have a connection to you."

"The translated verses reveal a psychic world that existed a long time ago on the verge of disaster. It hints at things but never comes out to say them plainly. When I first looked at the painting, I felt a lot of emotion coming at me. Nothing else." She leaned back in her chair, opened her hands and shrugged. "But now, I see a city in the sky. It's in the background, and the writing on the tree reads—*the mind rules.*"

Ari blurted out. "Where? I see only mountains in the background," he shook his head," and there's a bole in the tree - no writing." He ran a hand through his white hair. "You're seeing things we can't see."

Antigonie took his hand. "Ari, how can we believe she's seeing these things?"

"How can we believe she's not? She's got to be the one." Ari dazed, sat back in his chair. "Now what? I never believed this would happen. I'm not prepared. I don't know what to do."

"Ari, this quest has a real chance. I'm sure, now, we'll find some answers." Antigonie squeezed his arm. "I'm excited for you."

Zach ran his hand through his hair. "We have to investigate, to find these *things hidden.* The verse means something, or it wouldn't be on the painting's back. "

Alethea, startled at his words, turned to him. "How

do you propose we do this? They haven't exactly left a map." *Or have they*, she mused. She peered again at the painting.

"History is like a jigsaw puzzle," Ari interjected, "bits and pieces are found throughout time. It's up to us to piece them together, to find the greater picture."

He raised his hands, excitement in his voice. "What do we really know about the past? The winners of every war write their own history, distorting what isn't to their advantage." He took a deep breath.

"Floods and fires destroyed countless ancient texts. How many civilizations became lost, buried under dirt and debris accumulated through the centuries? Neglected - unknown, unfound, unsought they vanished from mind and sight, waiting to be uncovered."

"Please Ari try not to get too excited," Antigonie warned. "It's not good for your heart." She laid her hand on his arm, and gently caressed it.

Ari ignored her. "Think what this could mean, if a great race of psychics actually existed somewhere on this planet."

He nodded his head. "It could have happened. If you go back and re-read history with that in mind, it makes sense. The gods of mythology, of Olympus could have been from there."

He contemplated a moment, "if you read the bible as an historical book and not as a religious one you would get a whole different picture of history.

In Genesis it says that *man was created in God's image*, and later it says *there were giants in the earth in those days, and also afterwards, when the sons of God came into the daughters of men and they bore them*

313

children. Those were the mighty men who were of old, men of renown.

Since it happened so long ago, we can only speculate about what actually happened," Ari explained. "Missing pieces are still being uncovered today. The *Dead Sea Scrolls* came to light in 1947 and their meaning is still unclear." He shrugged. "Who knows what else might be recovered from the earth? A big clue to our origins might be lost in a cave, covered by lava, or found in the ocean's depths."

Alethea's rapt expression caught Ari's eye. He leaned forward. "You do understand. That pleases me. So you will help me to find these clues?" He gestured to his children. "My family will help you as best they can. They know how much this means to me."

Aware of Zach seated next to her, she wondered at his silence, and at his coolness to her. He acted as if they had never met. Confused by his attitude, angered by his deceit, and surprised by her jealousy, she kept her body rigid. She avoided eye contact, her face averted from his, and did not touch him.

Zach cast her a look under his lashes.

"I'll try to do what I can, but I'm not sure, Mr. Artemidis, if anything will come of it. But I'm fascinated. If an ancient world of gifted people existed," she stared again at the painting, "it would be a great discovery, especially if we could learn about their culture, and about what destroyed them."

She stood up and gave her full attention to Ari, turning her back on Zach. "I'd like to leave now. This has been—a *revealing* visit, to say the least.

By the way," she added, "I have a friend who's an

314

archaeologist. I'd like to call and tell her about this. She's busy - I'm not sure she'll come, but her help could be vital in verifying the authenticity of anything we find."

Antigonie held out her hand. "Your friend would be more than welcome. And please call us."

"Yes, I will," Alethea looked back at the painting. "I'd like to come when there aren't so many people. I'd want to study the painting while I'm alone. I need to see the actual writing on the back to see if the translation is correct. I'll see the truth if I look closely enough."

Stella stood up. "I'll get John and we'll drive you back."

Zach, also standing, decided to take this opportunity to talk to Alethea. "I'm leaving anyway," he looked at Stella, "I'll drive Alethea. Stay and enjoy the party. If you don't mind I'll borrow the Mercedes. You can pick it up down in the village where my boat is docked."

Alethea looked sharply at him, but didn't protest. The time had come for a confrontation. She couldn't wait to get him away from his family. She so wanted to give him a piece of her mind.

She could feel quizzical eyes staring at them as they walked together across the room. She cast a sideways glance at Zach, then quickly made her way out of the study and away from the probing eyes.

The guests in the living room paid them no attention.

Zach took her elbow. Together they went through the foyer, out the decoratively carved front door, down the front stairs and to the waiting car.

Chapter 47

In the car, she let out the breath she hadn't realized she had been holding.

Zach gave her a quick glance but said nothing. He put the key in the ignition and started the car. Turning to her, he held up his hand. "Save it. I can't deal with your temper right now."

"You tricked me." she sputtered and looked daggers at him.

He ignored her and concentrated on his driving. The beams' light brightened the area, as he sped down the curving road, heading for the small village of Petra.

Alethea faced him, raised her voice. "You are a snake, you slithered into my life just to use me." She tightened her hands into fist. "Ugh, I hate this. What was I—some scientific experiment?"
He reached the dock in the small village, stopped the car and turned to her. "Stop yelling at me. Let me explain. What makes you think I wanted to use you?"

"Why? You kept asking me questions about my talents. You picked and probed to find out about my gifts and capabilities. And all to make your father happy." Sniffling, she held back her tears, then wailed. "You weren't even interested in me until you knew I was a psychic, I had to spill water on you to get your attention."

Zach gaped at her, dumbfounded. "How could you think that?" He looked at her. "I noticed you all right. I just didn't want it to be obvious." He placed his arm around her. "I honestly didn't know what my father was up to, he planned this with my sister Stella's help, not mine. I found out recently, when he invited me to this revelation." He drew her closer.

"Believe me—please," he touched his head to hers, "you mean more to me than any scientific experiment. I want us to be together, to have a life together."

"Are you proposing to me?" She looked intently at him and raised an eyebrow.

"Not exactly, I just want us to stick to our agreement." Zach rubbed the back of his neck. "We don't need a legal piece of paper to bind us. We're fine the way we started."

She smiled at him through her tears, "I agree. But no flirting with others, like this Anna." She pointed a warning finger at him. "That's part of the agreement."

"Are you jealous?"

"Stop changing the subject. I trusted you with my secrets, with my soul. You betrayed me."

"No, you're wrong. I had nothing to do with it. My father doesn't know we met before today." He took her into his arms and caressed her back. "Would my sisters be playing matchmaker if they knew we were together? I purposely shunned you so they wouldn't be suspicious." He nuzzled her ear, and gave her a squeeze.

"Let's go on board my yacht. We can talk there." He threw the keys under the seat, and opened her door. Together they crossed the dock and boarded the yacht.

Zach seated her in a red and white cushioned chair and went to talk to the captain. He planned to put out to sea tonight, destination Mytilene's port. When he came back, he took a seat next to her.

"My father has been looking for a true psychic for years. I just wasn't in on his latest effort. He started this on his own, I don't know the details but I'll find out, be sure of that."

"Wait!" Alethea turned to him. "So no one stole the painting? My boss had to have known or suspected something and sent me anyway." She narrowed her eyes. "When I get my hands on him, I'll wring his deceiving neck." Her fisted hand banged down on the arm of her chair. "He knows I hate to be used, he held out the carrot of a great vacation in Greece, and I, like a dumb bunny, nibbled. How could I resist?" She shook her head in disappointment. "I hate people who lie to me. This is the end. I'm going to quit my job."

Zach raised his eyebrows. "Talking about honesty and people who lie—you said you were here to write an article on birds for a magazine. You lied to me, didn't you?"

"Oh that." She scowled at him. "What was I supposed to say?" She waved her hand. "I came to find a stolen painting and might have to use my psychic talents to find it. You would have laughed in my face."

Zach's cell phone rang. "Mitch," he answered, "what's going on?" His expression changed to shock as he listened. He took it all in, then said." Right. Call me again with more info."

"What was that about?" Alethea asked.
"A big explosion near the docks. They caught two men. They have them in custody."

"That's wonderful," exclaimed Alethea.

"That's not all. Leonidas saw the arrest on the evening news and all of a sudden he recalled every thing. The two men were the ones he saw on the *Deliverance.* He remembered the two foreigners and everything else that happened—even whom he called at Headquarters."

Alethea leaned forward eagerly. "Don't keep me in suspense. Who was it?"

Zach stared at her, drawing out the moment. "Ellen Poulos, she's the Europol chief's secretary."

"Ellen Poulos? I haven't met her." She leaned back and crossed her legs. "What's she like?"

"I just saw her briefly. She has short red hair that sticks up in peaks and a bony figure. She seems efficient, but nervous and harsh. I wonder why she did it. She doesn't look the type."

"What's the type?" She propped her chin on her hand and tried to picture what a spy should look like. She smiled.

"Sorry, it's hard, from your description, to picture her as an informer. I thought it would be someone more glamorous, more *a femme fatale.*"

"You've been reading too many spy novels." He tapped his fingers, "Mitch isn't going to confront her. She's only a small fish. We hope, through her, to catch the bigger fish."

He pulled on his ear. "You were right, again, Leonidas did get his memory back after a bomb explosion. This last explosion jarred it.

Leonidas heard the men on the Deliverance planning to use the explosives at the Olympics, became upset and rushed to call Mitch on his private line. He got no connection, so he called Central Headquarters. There he found Ellen Poulos. He confided in her, stressed she should try to find Mitch, told her, he needed a squad sent to the pier where the *Deliverance* docked. That was as far as the message went." He gazed at Alethea, sighed, and squeezed his lips together into a grimace. "The next thing he knew somebody tried to kill him."

Zach leaned forward. "Mitch is going to have her line tapped. He also plans to have her tailed and to keep a close watch so she doesn't have a sudden accident. Maybe, just maybe, we'll get lucky and she'll lead us to the evasive big guy. This might be our first major lead." Zachary's eyes roved, scrutinizing her.

She licked her lips. "What about the drowned im-migrants, did you get a lead on them? Maybe it was the same ship."

"No, the *Deliverance* had nothing to do with them. Its itinerary didn't fit, plus it's a sturdy ship. The one involved had to be a rickety old boat." He shook his head. "I narrowed it down to two possibilities. A North Korean freighter called the *Korean Rose* is the most likely, but there's no proof against it, and since it's long gone, there isn't much we can do. Too many mobs work this area, it's hard to pinpoint which one did it."

Alethea sensing his frustration, took his fingers and pressed them. "It isn't your fault—don't take the weight of their deaths on your shoulders."

He squeezed back, felt waves of sympathy. A soothing quietness calmed his agitation. Her violet eyes, as bright as amethysts, sparkled with reflected light. "Anyway, that threat to the Games is gone. With the explosion, everything went up in smoke, including their plans to cause chaos at the Olympics. Those were the bombs from the *Deliverance*. It's too late to bring in more.

Athens has tightened its security. Nothing, but I mean nothing, will get through. Patrols police the sky, the streets and the water, and the borders are secured." He shifted in his seat. "Mitch is relieved and Leonidas is back at his own house. He starts work tomorrow fully recovered."

"You must be thankful. That's one less problem for you."

"Yes I am. We're one step ahead of where we were—thanks to your help."

"Don't let it go to your head, I'm not always right." She gave a wink, "only most of the time."

Alethea stretched her arms over her head, fell back in her chair and let herself relax—left her senses free. She smelled the sea air wafting by, heard the motor humming, and felt the soft breeze caress her hair.

Tilting her head up, she saw sparkling points of light, scattered in patterns across the sky. They mesmerized her and made her wonder. Did people live on other planets, people much like her?

Zach watched her, letting his eyes roam. She was truly lovely sitting there absorbed in her own world. He fell silent, sensing she needed the solitude, the silence to recharge. She wasn't like any woman he knew. Today must have been draining on her. He pulled her from the chair and into his arms. Cradling her face in his right hand, he traced her eyes, her mouth with his left, outlining her lips before kissing her.

"You look tired honey, let's go inside… it's time for bed." He put his arms around her waist, hugged her then walked with her through the sliding glass doors into the cabin.

Chapter 48

Back at the Petra complex the next day, Alex Vladis sipped iced tea, on the patio of Sylvia's house. Set on the mountain's side just below her father's, it overlooked both mountain and ocean. He enjoyed the view and mulled over last night's party.

Things weren't as they seemed. His dealings in all sorts of illegal ventures, made him instantly aware of undercurrents of secrecy, of an underlying excitement.

He had listened carefully to bits and pieces of conversation—something about a lost civilization of psychics, a painting with a hidden secret, a message meant for only a true psychic to unravel.

What a find it would be if this lost civilization had actually existed.

A huge and lucrative market existed in the trafficking of stolen artifacts—fanatic collectors would pay any price for what they wanted.

He could just imagine what these artifacts would be worth on the black market. He puffed his Cuban cigar. Maybe the Black Spider should look into the possibilities.

His cell phone rang, interrupting his train of thought.

"I told you not to call me here, Basil." Alex admonished his caller.

"I had to—didn't you see last night's news?"

"No, what's happened?" He set down his drink, and bent forward.

"The warehouse, where we moved the explosives, went up in flames. Nobody knows why." Basil enunciated each word, "it's- a- nightmare. The whole place is swarming with cops."

"Idiots! Can't they do anything right?" Alex smashed his cigar into the ash tray.

"That's not all. They have two of our men. They found them lurking around the warehouse." He cleared his throat, "we can't get to them. They're in a high security prison."

"How much do they know?" Alex took out another cigar, clipped the tip and lit up. He inhaled and waited for an answer.

"We're safe," Basil assured him, "they've only had contact with Oliver."

"Then leave them. Do you have any more—good news?" Alex asked sarcastically

"The dockworker, the one who got stabbed, Leonidas. He recognized the captured men. All of a sudden his memory came back." He sat silent a moment. "He's the one who identified them from the *Deliverance.* He told the police what he overheard on the ship—about the explosives and about their plan to bomb the Olympics."

"What did you expect? It's your fault. He should have been dead." Alex said coldly. Disgusted, he played with his cigar. "At least we moved them from the *Deliverance.* If they hadn't exploded they wouldn't have been found." He raised his eyebrows, "don't do anything, I mean anything to expose us. No more killing—for now. What a mess! Our plans are ruined. We can't get any more explosives past the security they have in place for the Olympics." He muttered under his breath.

"If we give up the plan, they're going to want their money back." He sifted things through his mind, and shook his head, "I can't see how we can make it work." Agitated, Alex could feel the blood rushing to his head. Things had gone from bad to impossible. "Are you still there?"

"Yeah, Sorry. It's a disaster." He heard the snap of a pencil breaking in two while Basil whispered gruffly under his breath. "I've lost control. I swore this wouldn't happen again. Now what?"

"Never mind," Alex chewed on his cigar, "let's cut our losses." He took a quick puff and blew out a cloud of smoke.

"What about the runaway? We don't want that business ruined too. We're going to take a loss with the damn bombing fiasco, but I won't accept another disaster." Throwing down his cigar, he stomped it with his foot. "What of our contact in Central Headquarters? Did the dockworker remember who he talked to?"

"I'm not sure."

"What do you mean, you're not sure?" Alex roared. "Find out! We might have to eliminate her if she's been exposed."

"About the *pigeon*, the runaway, she's been located on Lesvos. Apparently a woman, Alethea Karras, befriended her on the ferry.

My man is on her, she'll lead us to the girl. He's been ordered to kill her when she's found," he paused a moment, "accidentally, of course."

"Make sure they don't mess this up." He hung up

the phone and sat thinking. *Alethea Karras and Zach Artemidis— they're starting to be a problem. And with what I learned at the party, they're going to be more trouble than I thought.*

Alethea stood on the saloon deck and breathed a sigh of relief. Barefoot, hair disheveled, she surveyed her surroundings. They had traveled from Petra and docked at the port of Mytilene not far from the Blue Sea hotel.

Thankfully, she could soon change into something more suitable. She liked to be as inconspicuous as possible, to blend into the background. Walking around in the morning dressed in evening clothes would definitely draw unwanted attention.

Zach, coming out from the saloon just then, gazed at her from afar. He admitted he was smitten. He wanted her in his life, might even consider marrying her. What they had together was deep and meaningful, much more than sex. He sauntered up behind her and placed his hands on her shoulders.

"It's a beautiful day. Almost as beautiful as you."

"You're amorous this morning. Didn't you get enough loving last night?" He was dressed in a casual short-sleeved shirt and white linen pants.

"I'm not complaining." He nuzzled her neck and blew softly in her ear, "though I'll never get enough."

Moving her head to one side, she smiled. "That's nice to hear."

"I've ordered breakfast. Then we can do whatever you want." He gave her a final hug, walked over to the table and sat down.

"First, I'd like to go to my hotel room and change. We should also, call Luda. The sooner we get protection for Sasha the better." She joined him at the table, took out her cell phone, and dialed Luda's number.

"Luda, I have my friend here, he'll make sure that Sasha's put under police protection. As it is, you're both in danger." She took a quick look around, scanning the walkway. "Where are you? Wait a minute, you can give Zach the directions, he knows the island better than I do." She passed the phone to Zach.

Zach listened to Luda, pulled a pen from his shirt pocket, and started writing on a napkin. He folded the napkin and looked up. "I'll call Mitch. He'll find a safe house for her. And I'll arrange a plane to take her to Athens today." He swiveled and caught sight of one of his crew.

"Here comes Dino with breakfast, let's eat. Then I'll get the car while you change."

Back in Athens, Maro and Zena made their way to Mitch's office at Central Headquarters.

"I can't wait to tell Mitch, he's going to be surprised." Maro shook her head and looked at Zena, "she had us fooled, I mean she acted so, so …dumb. Who would have thought she was the psychic papa was searching for."

"Dumb and blond," Zena nodded. "Stephanie called this morning and told me about last night's party," she stopped and looked down the hall. "When she mentioned the psychic by name, I remembered her. That's the woman Zach brought to the hospital, the same one I saw at his apartment."

"Too bad we missed the party." Barely whispering, Maro pointed to the room they were passing. "There's where Ellen Poulos works. The door's open. See if you can get a peek. You know who she is—Leonidas told you. Shush!" Putting her finger to her lip, "don't make any noise."

"Shush yourself," warned Zena, "you're making enough noise to wake the dead."

Once past Ellen's door, Maro said loudly. "You're just going to love the way I've decorated Mitch's office."

Zena looked back and asked. "Oh? What color did you do it in?"

Opening his door, they went in.

Ellen Poulos noticed the two women as they went by her office, and wondered at the odd looks they gave her. She had had a phone call. An anxious boss wanted to know if they were suspicious of her. She had told him *no.* She explained that when they asked about the phone call she told them she had passed it on to John Atlantis. It was out of her hands.

It was an answer, not a good answer, but an answer. It would be her word against his. She pursed her lips. Too nervous to sit, she started pacing and pacing and pacing. She clasped and unclasped her hands, and tried to think. She should never have taken the money. What to do? Her terminally ill mother needed expensive care. They had found out about it, and tempted her. Her life wasn't worth a shiny euro. The boss would kill her.

Chapter 49

Zach watched Alethea stroll toward him outside the Blue Sea hotel. She wore a light blouse over a form fitting lilac top. A striking look—especially with the matching lilac shorts that left a lot of limb bare. The Grecian style sandals that covered most of her calf with bands, accentuated her curvy legs.

"You look stunning. How am I going to keep my eyes on the road with you next to me?"

"You're sweet." She put her sun glasses on. "But you'd better concentrate on your driving or we'll never get there."

Checking the directions one last time, he folded the map, then handed it to Alethea. He proceeded north, took a road that ran parallel to the sea and drove for about an hour until he came to a crossroads. When he took the road toward Kalloni, he saw a sign for the small village Luda had mentioned.

They turned onto a mountain road, paved but narrow, which cut through a forest. The earthy smell of pine filled her nostrils and the sudden darkness gave her chills. Huge trees blocked the sun. Only occasional rays of light dappled through, making it hard to see ahead as the road curved upward. She sensed his growing fatigue as he took one sharp turn after the other.

Finally they emerged into full sunlight. They had reached the village at the mountaintop where Luda lived. Zach drove over stone paved streets, and passed horse drawn wagons and cars parked on either side. The street ran along the edge of a valley. Below them, sheep grazed, chickens scattered and bulls bellowed. They maneuvered through the narrow street at a crawl, backing up to let other cars pass.

The road stopped at a town square surrounded by buildings. Straight ahead stood a large church—restaurants and cafes bordered on either side. On the other end were tables and chairs shaded by eucalyptus and centurion plane trees.

"Luda and Sasha said they would meet us here." Zach explained.

"She mentioned there was a big celebration so no one would notice them. It looks like the whole village is here. It's a catered affair. A local man migrated to the Congo, made his money selling bread there, retired and came back to his village to live among family and friends. His son is now running the bread factory. His grandson is being christened today."

Alethea spotted Luda and Sasha at a table under a huge tree. She grabbed Zach's arm, and led him across the courtyard.

"Luda, Sasha—this is Zachary Artemidis. I told you about him, his brother- in- law works for Interpol. You can trust him. He'll make sure you're protected."

Luda gave him a firm handshake.

Sasha, coloring, couldn't look him in the eye. She gazed down at her hands tightly held in her lap and shuffled her foot through the pebbles.

Alethea, sensing Sasha's unease, touched her arm. "I described your ordeal to Zach. You don't have to say anything about it. Later maybe, but not now. Zach wants to keep you safe."

"You don't waste any words." Zach quirked his eyebrow.

"Don't interrupt me," she scolded. She looked back at Sasha. "And even with police protection, you might not be safe, that's why I involved him. He'll look after you—he's a good man."

Zach, taken aback by her compliment, didn't know what to say.

Luda did. "When will you start? I have fear for my friend. She has no papers. If the dreadful men come, we are not strong. Police can't help. We can't ask anybody for help."

Zach looked at Sasha. "I've arranged a private plane for you. It will take you to Athens where you'll be put under police protection.

Mitch, my brother-in-law, will meet you and escort you to a safe house." He stared directly into Sasha's eyes.

"I'm afraid you're going to have to tell your story. I'll make sure a female officer records it.

Try to think of as many details as you can. Anything, no matter how insignificant, is important."

He checked his watch. "We need to go. Sasha has to be on the plane by eight."

Alethea looked around. She felt that wave of evil pulsing towards her again. Someone was watching them. But who?

"Look, Zach. It's that bird-watching couple from England. What an odd coincidence. This is the third time in a few days that I've seen them."

"Don't let your imagination run away with itself." Zach interjected. "There aren't many tourist now, so of course you'll see the same people. Bird watchers especially. They come to see rare breeds of birds that migrate through here this time of year."

"You're probably right. They're probably harmless." She turned and headed for the car.

But the man hidden in the trees, the man who had followed them from Mytilene—Alethea didn't see him. Was he also harmless?

"Do you need a ride home, Luda?" Zach asked.

"No, I live nearby. Please keep my childhood friend safe. She has been through so much." She picked up a small satchel and handed it to Sasha. "Here are a few items for you—a change of clothes, some underwear, soap, a toothbrush, and a comb and brush."

Sasha hugged Luda, and took the satchel. She whispered, "Thank you," and rushed after Zach and Alethea, tears streaming down her face.

Chapter 50

Zach held the door while Sasha got into the Micra's back seat and Alethea slid into the front. He backed up onto a narrow street, swiveled, then started back down the road out of the village.

He passed simple houses, centuries old, marked by wooden balconies filled with potted red and white geraniums. As he inched through the cobbled street, he felt as if he was in another era.

"It should be easier going downhill," Alethea noted as they exited the small village and started down the paved road that connected with the highway.

"It's going to take us forever to get to the airport." He looked disgusted. "Couldn't you have rented a bigger, more powerful car? This one just creeps."

"Sorry, I didn't think of you, and your needs." She shook her head. "We've had this conversation before, get over it already. I told you, it's great on gas mileage."

"God save us from frugal women." Zach scoffed, as he drove downhill on the darkening road, bumping over several potholes. He shifted gears, concentrating on the road as it worsened. He finally sped up when the forest ended.

Alethea let her mind wander. *This adventure is over, I did what I was hired to do. I found the painting that wasn't really stolen. I'm not happy about being used, but I'll live with it.* Looking over at Zach, she watched him make a difficult turn. *I've met the love of my life. He's fighting it, but he'll come around.*

Sunlight suddenly illuminated them, snapping her out of her reverie.

Her skin prickled and the hair stood up at the nape of her neck. Death lurked somewhere near. Zach had proved a competent driver, and she trusted him but— her instincts never lied.

Groves of silver leafed trees filled the mountain-side. Shelves of rock sectioned off each grove, and kept the soil from sliding.

Widening her eyes, she saw a sheer drop on the road's one side, and a wall of mountain on the other.

On either side, at regular intervals Alethea noticed memorial shrines—some simple, some more elaborate. They all indicated the same thing—a loved one's death.

Zach, used to driving on mountain roads, kept a cool head as he executed a sharp turn. He checked his rearview mirror, and noticed a Jeep Cherokee speeding toward them. The road's tightness made it impossible to pass.

And the Jeep kept coming. Zach sped up. So did the other car. At this rate if the other driver didn't slow down, they would collide.

Alethea turned and looked back at the car.

"Zach I've seen that man before, at my hotel.

Oh!" She grabbed a hold of the handle to keep from being knocked around. "Be careful he's coming fast."

Zach raced down the highway swerving left and right to keep the car on the curving road. He tried to slow down, but the tailgater started bumping him.

He accelerated to put some space between them, only to have the Jeep bump him again.

Zach tightened his hands on the wheel, preventing the car from going over the side.

The road was too narrow for much maneuvering. He held on as he swung into a tight curve. Keeping a steady hand on the wheel, he brought the car around the bend carefully, purposely, determinedly.

The Jeep, trying to drive them off the road, temporarily lost the game.

"Damn that car." He tried to out distance the Jeep, but couldn't. The next thing he knew, it hit them harder than ever.

"Hold on,"

Zach yelled as the Jeep sent them over the side. They plunged over the road's edge toward the ravine. Ploughing through the dirt, he tried to stop, but the tires slipped over the ground. Rocks flew up at them and branches knocked at the windows.

Miraculously, they halted just short of crashing into a gnarled olive tree. With the sudden stop, Zach banged his head against the windshield. Stunned, he had one thought—that Jeep had almost killed them.

Clutching the steering wheel, he took a moment to get his bearings. Half scared out of his wits, not for himself, but for Alethea and Sasha—he looked around. Silence greeted him. He had promised to keep them safe, had almost failed. What kind of protector was he?

Sasha was slumped on the side of her seat, with her hands covering her head. She looked frightened but intact. Alethea seemed unhurt.

Zach pushed his door open and staggered out. He

leaned on the car for support and slowly tried to recover from the shock. A severe gash on his head bled steadily, blinding him.

Alethea joined Zach by the car. *Deciding drastic situations need drastic measures*, she took a handkerchief from her pocket and wiped his eyes. She concentrated with her other hand to her forehead and a beam of light formed. She directed this energy, laid her hand on his head, and closed the wound.

He glanced at her, but made no comment. Zach put his hand over Alethea's.

"Oh Zach, we could have been killed." She hugged him tightly glad for his strength, glad that she had the ability to close his wound.

Zach turned his head left and right—the jeep was gone. "That was a close call," he took a deep breath to steady his nerves.

"What a lunatic! Where did he go? He tried to push us off the road into the ravine. That's a very long drop. If that had happened, we would be dead, for sure."

He squeezed Alethea tighter, then checked her over to make sure she wasn't hurt. "We just barely missed hitting that tree."

"He stopped, but when a car honked to pass, he took off. I recognized him. He was watching my balcony one night. It was creepy. When I went to look again, he had disappeared." Alethea's hands trembled.

"Look, there's a police car coming. That other car must have called them. Thank goodness. Now maybe we'll get out of here. We've got to get Sasha on that plane." Shaken by their close call with death, Alethea clutched Zach.

"This is all my fault," she cried. "For the past few days I felt somebody watching me. I knew something was wrong, and ignored it." She opened her eyes wide, and put a hand over her mouth.

"I led them right to her. They must have seen me with Sasha on the boat, watched and waited for me to get in touch." Hugging her waist, she bent her head. "Jeez, they tried to kill us."

Zach wrapped his arms around her, pressing her close again.

"This isn't fair. She's a victim. Damn it! What's wrong with the world?" Alethea pushed the hair away from her face as she distanced herself from Zach.

"Sasha has gone through too much. Slavery is an open sore worldwide. We have to stop it." She swiveled and looked at Sasha, "I'm sorry, but you have to help. We have to save others from falling victim to these animals."

Sasha, regaining her wits, straightened in her seat. "I afraid," she gulped. "But I help."

Chapter 51

A few hours later two relieved people sat on the deck of Zach's yacht, *Utopia*, relaxing with drinks. Zach turned toward Alethea.

"I'm glad we managed to get Sasha on the plane. By the time they realize she isn't dead, she'll be tucked away under Mitch's protection."

Alethea pensive, played with her wine glass. "Are you sure Mitch will meet her at the airport? He will protect her—right?"

"Don't worry. Mitch is good at his job, it's in his hands. She's an important witness. You bet he'll be there." He tightened his lips. "I'm afraid Maro and Zena will be with him. They found out what happened. Zena, when she smells a story - she's impossible. But at least they'll help Sasha feel comfortable. She needs women around her."

"She seems so meek." Alethea sipped her white wine, "but she must have an inner strength to have escaped and survived. She'll help the police, but she has to have her papers if she's to stay here legally."

"Of course—without question. Believe me this is the first big break we've had." He put his glass down, then leaned toward her.

"Money is power - it makes crooks out of honest men. This human slavery is a lucrative business. That's why it's so hard to dissolve. But with her aid, we might manage to break this ring up, maybe even find the Black Spider."

"Well I guess that's that." Alethea holding her glass up, caught the reflected candle light. "Why did you have me check out? Wouldn't it have looked better if I'd kept my room?"

"To whom? You don't know anybody here. I mean, who cares. Your boss? You'd told me you quit. Besides - he fed you to the lions. Let him worry about finding you. I'm possessive, protective and primitive when it comes to you. I'm not letting you out of my sight."

"Oh no! I don't like the sound of that."

Zach watched her, "You healed me. Thank you, I didn't say anything before, because of Sasha." He took her hand.

"I know what you're capable of. You might think you can take care of yourself, but no one is invincible." He leaned closer. "I want to take care of you."

"Only if you don't interfere." She raised an eyebrow. "Are you O.K. with that?"

"As long as you don't put yourself in danger, we won't have a problem."

They sat in silence, could hear the sounds of oars moving in and out of the water, the splashing of waves against rocks and the whisper of far off music.

"You know I read the inscription your father gave me. I do want to help him. When I realized I had been duped, I became angry. But he had such a hopeful expression on his face, I couldn't say no."

She looked down at her glass. "He's sick, isn't he?"

"He has a heart condition and can't deal with stress. That's why I took over the business."

338

"As I told him, I have to look at the painting alone, really study it. I'm sure there's a map hidden in it or something that will point us in the right direction." She stared at her glass turning it left and right.

The painting is for me. I could sense it. I don't know its history or how it was lost, but I'm going to start asking questions. Maybe my grandmother's diaries will help.

"Stella will pick us up at the dock at Petra in the morning." He squeezed her hand looking steadily at her. "It's no use pretending we're not a couple, Stephanie talked with Maro."

"It doesn't matter, I'm not hiding anything. We're adults, we can do as we please."

She finished her drink.

"By the way, I tried to call Camila from the hotel phone. She's the archaeologist I mentioned, one of my closest friends. But she wasn't available. She left for Brazil the same day I left for Athens. She gave me a number, but she won't be there until school starts. It's hard to communicate with her now."

Tenting her hands together, she brought them to her chin. "Camila said that Brazilian archaeologists found ancient structures in a remote corner of the Amazon that may cast a light on the past. They think the artifacts are over two thousand years old. She went there to join them.

The point is—when new things are discovered it puts a new light on history. Something as astonishing as what your father found, could be possible." Alethea stared at Zach. "I feel connected to this, as if it will help solve a part of my family's history."

"Well that's intriguing," Zach exclaimed. "I'm game. Let's do it. Let's find this place."

"Yes, the message on the painting was written for me. I'm sure if I can spend some time examining it, being with it, the painting will lead me to its secrets."

She turned to Zach and took his hand. "It's an amazing story, worth looking into. Maybe it'll explain these dreams I've been having lately."

"What dreams? You haven't mentioned them."

Alethea stood, went over to the side and gazed down at the waves splashing against the hull. She looked uncertain. Tightening her hands on the rail, she bowed her head a moment, before she turned and spoke.

"A man and a woman are in a strange room. There's a storm that frightens them with its intensity. They have to escape, to leave this place. There's a ship waiting for them. I can feel the woman's pain, her sorrow, and her fear that they won't make it in time. Then I wake up." She scrutinized Zach's face, and wondered if he understood the connection.

Zach turned toward her. "You think this dream has to do with this lost race of psychics?"

"Yes, I do. The man in the dream said something about the woman's predictions of disaster. So she was a psychic." She inhaled deeply, then closed her eyes. "In the dream they left behind a daughter, sure she would survive and continue the line."

Zach stood and came over to Alethea. "I want to be with you." He hugged her and they looked out to the sea. "We'll find this truth, whatever it is, together. The Greek Isles are enchanting and well worth seeing. And

340

in August we'll go to the Olympics in Athens." Zach nuzzled her neck and whispered.

"Remember when we first met? I promised you we would be here for this event, and we would be to-gether."

"Yes, I remember." She snuggled into him. "I thought I didn't like controlling men, but that was until I met you."

"And I didn't like controlling women," he squeezed her tighter, "but you can go ahead and control me any time you want."

Word from the author

If you enjoyed Reckless Revelation please spread the word. Tell your friends and book club. Write a review on Amazon or Good read. Please check my web site NinalekKa.com and email me at Ninalekka@ymail.com when you write a review so I can thank you personally in an email. Look for my next book in the *Reluctant Virgin Series*—**Miserable Mishap** featuring our ice maiden Blossom White and millionaire playboy Michael James. If you'd like to tell the cards like Alethea check out my **Psychic Cards to a Psychic Self** coming soon.

Thank You for choosing my book.

Nina